MW01139718

## *Books by the author*

### The Captive Series

Captured (Book 1)

Renegade (Book2)

Refugee (Book 3)

### The Kindred Series

Kindred (Book 1)

Ashes (Book 2)

Kindled (Book 3)

Inferno (Book 4)

### The Ravening Series

Ravenous (Book 1)

Taken Over (Book 2)

Special thanks to my husband for always believing in me,
my parents for always being there for me,
and Leslie from G2 Freelance Editing for helping to make
this book even better.

# **<u>PROLOGUE</u>**

The figure slipped silently into the room. The deep gray cloak it wore covered most of its body; the hood shielded its features as it moved with inhuman silence. But it was not inhuman; Gideon was reminded of that fact by the solid beat of its heart, and the alluring scent that pricked his appetite. But this human, *especially* this one, was completely off limits if he was to keep his life. Although he couldn't see the features, he knew that it was female, knew who it was by the sweet aroma she emitted.

No, no matter how hungry he may be at the moment, he would not touch this one. He valued his life far too much to do such a thing. He'd eat rats first.

She stopped before his desk, her head bowed as she inhaled a small breath. Slowly, ever so slowly, she lifted her head and drew back the hood. Her dark auburn hair was the color of blood in the candlelight that flickered over it. Her features, though pretty, were not stunning, especially not under the pallor that now marked her normally healthy hue. Her hand trembled, but there was a steely resolve about her that Gideon couldn't help but admire.

"I spoke with Jack and Ashby."

Gideon froze for a moment, his hand tightened around the pen he was holding. "I see."

Her mouth was pinched, her eyes steady despite the tumultuous fear and anguish he sensed rolling just beneath her seemingly calm exterior. "I understand what needs to be done."

Gideon let go of the pen before he snapped it in half. He didn't care about the instrument, but he was far too meticulous to have ink coating him. "You do?"

For a brief moment tears shimmered in her eyes before she blinked them back, thrust out her chin and nodded firmly. "I do."

"He cannot know about this."

"He won't."

Gideon was silent for a long moment. "The bond cannot be completed."

She winced as a flash of grief struck her like lightening. For just a moment her composure seemed to crumple. "It won't," she whispered.

Gideon didn't know what to say, he hadn't known what to expect from her or how she would react to what Jack and Ashby had to say to her. He realized now that he should have known this was the path she would take, that she would not shy away from this. She turned away from him, but her step wasn't so sure, or as silent, as she made her way to the door.

"You know what this may mean for you?" he inquired before she could escape.

She stopped in the doorway, her head turned back to him as she studied him over her shoulder. She swallowed heavily as she managed another stiff nod. "If we are unable to dilute his blood in me my death may be the only solution to separating us for good."

He was immobile, struck by the fact that this young girl was able to see what the others refused to. "And you accept this?"

"It's what I came to you for," she breathed.

That answer didn't surprise him either, he was the only one she could turn to in order to ensure such a thing was carried out. "No one else can know about this."

"They won't," she vowed. He realized he'd just made a deal with the devil as she slid the hood back over her head and slipped from the room.

# CHAPTER 1

The Barrens. The place where horror stories were born, cautionary tales were exchanged and people were frightened by the mere thought of entering them. They were desolate, somehow cold, even with the sun relentlessly pounding the earth around them. There were few people that had entered The Barrens and ever come back. The ones that did often ranted of strange creatures, monsters that hunted within the sand, appeared out of nowhere, and were even more vicious than the vampires. Few believed the extent of the stories, but even fewer wandered into The Barrens after hearing them.

And now they were here, preparing to jump head first, straight into hell. They had traveled hundreds of miles through *her* forest to this godforsaken land of sun and sand. The supposed new home of the vampires that had at one time been some of the most spoiled aristocrats. They were the aristocrats that had stood against the king during the war, and fled the palace when it became clear that they were not going to win and their lives would be forfeit.

Aristocrats that Braith now sought to gain support from for this upcoming battle. That was, if they could ever find these mysterious vampires amongst the vast expanse of emptiness that unraveled beyond this last border town. The town was frightening enough, the lands beyond were overwhelming. Aria wasn't used to such emptiness, not after being surrounded by trees and caves for most of her life.

Anxiety twisted within her belly. Sweat trickled down her back as she kept her head bowed and the hood pulled low over her brow. She could feel the curious stares burning through the dull gray cloak of the servant's class covering her. Braith was stiff beside her, his shoulders squared as his body thrummed with tension. She didn't know what to do with her hands as they walked silently down the street. She ached to reach out and touch him, to somehow connect with him but it was a move she knew she couldn't make.

She had to fight against the urge to look up. She itched to see the town they had entered, to take in the details of it, but she had been told repeatedly not to make eye contact. No matter how badly she wanted to look, she wasn't about to endanger the men surrounding her by disobeying.

She started as Braith suddenly grasped her upper arm, swallowing it within his massive hand. Immediately her skin heated to his touch, and though they were in this awful place a low sigh of pleasure escaped her. Her heart leapt in her chest, longing spread through her as her toes curled in her battered shoes.

"Keep your head down." Braith seemed to have sensed her wish to look around.

Her shoulders slumped, her gaze focused on the dusty, pitted road. Beside her, she could feel William's growing resentment at being ordered around and having to maintain a subservient demeanor. From the corner of her eye she could see more people moving to the side of the road. Well, at least some of them were people. The others, they were something else entirely and not at all who Braith and Ashby were looking for. These were the more lawless vampires, and therefore more unpredictable than those living within and around the palace, even though these vampires still lived under the king's laws here.

She had seen far too many of these beaten and broken towns with their battered and starving occupants lately. Sometimes she feared that they would never find what Braith and Ashby sought, and that perhaps the legends and rumors of the surviving aristocrats were just that, legends and rumors. Though it felt like they'd walked forever, it had in fact only been two days since they had turned the horses loose at the edge of The Barren's. Aria refused to bring the animals with them if there was no guarantee they could feed or water them, so after riding for two weeks, they had been forced to walk.

If she was honest with herself, two weeks wasn't that much time, she had spent far more time away from home than this. It only seemed so awful because she was never given a moment alone with Braith, they were never allowed to be on their own as either William was standing protectively close, or Ashby was quick to intervene.

Aria understood her brother, it annoyed her, but she understood his determination to stubbornly try and protect her virtue. It was actually a little amusing coming from William, the man that had left broken hearts in every corner of the forest. However, Ashby's interference was beginning to grate on her last nerve. It was most certainly annoying Braith as he'd completely lost his temper with Ashby when he had unapologetically followed them into the woods yesterday. It had only been Aria's interference that had kept Braith from completely losing control.

He hadn't even had a chance to feed from her since they'd left Ashby's rambling tree house. Aria ached for the renewal of the bond, ached to establish that connection with Braith again. She hoped that once they arrived at their destination they would finally be rewarded with some time alone again, but until then she was well aware that her two guard dogs, as she now thought of them, were not going to be shaken.

Oh well, there were many things she wished were different right now. She missed her father; she'd barely had time to speak with him before they had been separated again. He had been uneasy and somewhat uncertain as to what was going on between her and Braith. Her father seemed to want to believe that she really did love Braith, and that Braith did in fact return that love. However, she worried that a part of him still believed that the bond they had forged was only due to her time spent as Braith's blood slave.

She may be almost eighteen, but her father had still been wary of letting her go with Ashby and Braith, had absolutely refused to let it happen until Braith had finally relented and agreed to let William come along with them. Even then, her father was still hesitant to let them go. However, this mission was necessary to try and gain some much needed vampire support for a war against the king, and there was absolutely no way that Braith was going to leave without her.

The whole situation nearly turned into a debacle that had threatened to unravel the tentative plans they had formed to overthrow Braith's father. Cooler heads had finally prevailed, mainly Jack's and surprisingly, William's. Her father had wanted Jack with them on this journey, he trusted Jack, but so did many of her father's followers in the rebellion. If any of the people in the rebellion were going to believe that the vampires were willing to ally themselves with humans, then her father would require Jack's help to convince them. Jack would also be essential to help convince the young vampire girl's village, and other vampire villages, to possibly aid them in their quest.

Her brother Daniel, as their father's second in command, had also been needed to help gather human forces. And Max, poor Max, well he hadn't been able to get away from her fast enough. Tears clogged her eyes and throat. Max had sacrificed himself to try and save her when she had been taken as a blood slave, and now he hated her. So much, in fact, that Aria was terrified he would never forgive her. That he would despise her and everything she was, for the rest of her life.

She loved Max and this whole situation broke her heart. He had been her first crush, her first kiss, her best friend and confidante when she'd been so alone and broken by the revelation of Braith's engagement to another vampire. Max had understood what she had endured as a blood slave, even if it was nowhere near as hideous as the torture and abuse he had suffered. And now he didn't understand or even tolerate her existence at all. He saw her love for Braith as a betrayal, one that she didn't think he'd ever forgive.

Braith's sister, and Ashby's bloodlink Melinda, had reluctantly agreed to return to the palace to be their inner eyes and ears. Aria had understood Melinda's pain as she and Ashby embraced and touched and cried with each other. She knew how they felt; she couldn't bear the thought of being apart from Braith for so long, even if it was for a good cause. Ashby had agreed to come with them knowing that if they succeeded in their goal, he and Melinda would never have to be separated again, or risk their lives in order to see one another. Ashby was almost as determined as Braith to overthrow the regime.

That was *if* their plan succeeded. *If* they could somehow convince these possibly half crazed, half starved aristocratic vamps to aide them in their quest. She hoped they weren't crazed, hoped that a hundred years in this land of sweltering heat hadn't fried their brains. More so, she hoped that the four of them weren't walking right into a death trap.

She didn't mean to do it, but without thinking her head rose to Braith. She needed to see him, needed the reassurance of his presence. Even though his eyes were shaded by his dark glasses, she knew the moment when they latched onto hers. Her heart lurched; she could barely breathe beneath the weight of that stare. He was magnificent, and he was hers.

She knew he wanted to tell her to look away, to look down. She saw it in the tight pinch of his mouth, in the muscle that jumped in his cheek. He remained silent though, his eyes locked onto hers and for a single moment it was just the two of them. His hand stroked her arm as he pulled her a step closer.

"We're almost there," he murmured so quietly that she barely heard him. "Please Aria, look down."

Ashby quirked an eyebrow but refrained from saying anything. It was strange to hear the prince say please to anyone, let alone her, a human, a blood slave, a rebel. She was still surprised to hear him call her Aria, as he had always used her full name, but being around people that didn't use it had finally started to rub off on him.

She sighed and reluctantly did as he asked. The tension in his body notched up a level; she knew he was struggling not to grab hold of her and run out of this town. To run would only attract more attention though, and possibly entice the thrill of the hunt. And there would be no more running, not anymore.

Aria shifted uncomfortably. She hated the coarse wool and dull color of the servant's class cloak she wore; she despised even more what it represented. She had resented the golden chain that bound a blood slave to their master but this cloak was worse. At least the chain had marked her as a fighter, someone not to be trusted, someone that had rebelled and been made to pay for that rebellion. As far as she was concerned, the cloak signified a coward and a traitor that had bowed to the vampire race.

More legs gathered by the side of the road and whispers began to spread through the crowd. These outer vamps weren't used to strangers and they were wary and distrustful of them. Though they had not encountered any problems so far, Aria doubted they would be so lucky all the time. The vampire's that lived here were hungry, and so were the people. They were poor, and strangers offered them a new opportunity for fresh blood, perhaps even money. If Braith didn't emanate such an aura of power and dominance, she was sure they would have been jumped before this town, even with Ashby at their side.

The whispers grew louder; they grated against her skin as harshly as the coarse cloth covering her head. Dust drifted up around them, it stuck in her nose and throat. It was cloying, awful. The town smelled of blood, body odor and death. The woods weren't like this. Though they held the smell of decay, it was the earthy decay of leaves and dirt. Fresh air was what she required, freedom, and Braith.

Braith suddenly grasped hold of her hood and jerked it forward. Aria had been so entrenched in her thoughts that she hadn't realized it had slipped back to reveal her hairline, and some of her features. It wasn't that anyone would recognize her, they were far more likely to recognize him, but Braith was adamant that she stay as covered as possible.

He thought her blood was too big of a lure, Aria felt it was only a lure to him, but she wasn't going to argue just in case he happened to be right. She wasn't in the mood to be a snack for a pack of blood thirsty vampires, none of them were. She moved to adjust the hood but he grasped hold of the hand exposed by the movement and pulled it smoothly down to her side. "Remain covered Aria."

This time it wasn't the touch of him that caused her heart to leap and her chest to constrict, but the tone in his voice. She was frightened by what might be unleashed if she looked up. A tremor worked through her. Braith was strong and powerful, but the circumstances of the past two weeks had forced him to feed from animals instead of her. And though animals sustained him, human blood was better, and *her* blood strengthened him even more. She had a strange effect on him, she empowered him in ways that neither of them had ever imagined possible.

And now, when he needed that strength most, he was being denied it. And they may all be about to pay for that if the increasing crush of bodies around them was any indication. "Are you willing to sell one?" a loud voice inquired.

Braith raised his arm, pushing it against her chest as he halted her beside him. It went against everything she was, but somehow she managed to keep her head bent and her appearance demure. William took two more steps forward before Ashby, in a far less graceful manner than Braith, jerked him to a stop by the collar of his robe. Though Ashby remained expressionless, his bright green eyes twinkled with amusement as William grunted slightly. The two of them had gotten along well enough, but they tended to pick at each other, sometimes to the point that Aria became exasperated with their delight in tormenting each other. William bristled against the highhanded treatment, but thankfully her hot-tempered twin managed to keep his calm.

There was a moment of silence as the town became hushed in expectancy of Braith's answer. He didn't know these lands, didn't know the people or the etiquette that prevailed here. In their land servants were not sold, they were not owned and traded like the blood slaves. That may not be the case here.

"They are not for sale," Braith finally answered.

A pair of legs stepped forward, separating themselves from the crowd. The clothing on these legs was of much higher quality than the ones surrounding it. Even with the sand swirling around them the shoes somehow remained black and shiny. "You look hungry," the legs stated. "I will make a trade. Two for one."

Her heart was in her throat, goose bumps tickled her skin. "Why would you make such a trade?" Braith demanded.

Though she couldn't see it, she could almost feel the man's casual shrug. "I have grown tired of them. You know how that is, I'm sure."

Sorrow stabbed her as she realized Braith knew exactly how *that* was. She tried not to think of his past, tried not to think of the blood slaves he had gone through when she had escaped the palace, but every once in awhile she would be slapped in the face with a stark reminder. She may have been his first blood slave, but she had not been his last, and he had not treated the others anywhere near as kindly as he had treated her.

Braith's arm pressed closer to her, he was trying to offer her some sort of comfort, but she found none. Her face was on fire; William was as still as stone before her, his breath seemed to have frozen in his chest.

"I do, and I have not yet grown bored with mine."

Aria's breath sucked in, her stomach cramped. No matter how much time she spent amongst them, she would never become accustomed to the cruelty and open brutality of some within the vampire race. She was not naïve enough to think that all humans were good either, after all, the only real abuse she had suffered as a blood slave was at the hands of a human, but it never seemed as overt amongst the humans as it was with the vampires.

She wasn't a possession though, she never truly had been, and she bristled against being thought of as such. Braith must have sensed something in her pulse or a shift in her demeanor, as right at that moment he pushed her back another step. It took everything she had to appear outwardly tranquil while inside she was seething. She was tempted to pull out the hidden bow on her back but she wasn't sure who she wanted to shoot more…Braith or the man trying to bargain for her.

"Let me at least get a look at her," the man prodded.

"I think not."

His answer was accompanied by a collective inhalation from the crowd. Aria's annoyance vanished as apprehension surged to the forefront. They were in danger here if Braith didn't tread the right path, and judging by the crowd's reaction, he had just made a serious misstep by disobeying the request.

"No?" Though he tried to hide it, Aria detected disbelief in the man's voice.

"No."

She cringed. Braith wasn't used to being ordered about nor was he used to anyone questioning him, except for maybe her, and he certainly didn't react well to it. He was not versed in diplomacy like her father, Daniel, Jack, and Ashby. Braith was used to giving the order and having that order obeyed. As prince, he'd never had to learn anything different, and he wasn't willing to tolerate insolence now.

Aria wished she could talk to him, reason with him, but if she opened her mouth and exposed any sort of feeling between them, then they would be in even more peril then they were now, if that was even possible.

"I'm sure you understand that sometimes, when your toys are shiny and new, you tend to like to keep them to yourself," Ashby interjected smoothly. Aria took no offense to being called a shiny toy. She felt only relief at Ashby's light tone and thankfully easygoing demeanor.

"She is new then?" the vampire inquired.

"Oh not brand new," Ashby replied flippantly. "Are any of them anymore? It's hard to find something that hasn't been battered and tossed aside now." His comments were met with snickers and muttered agreements from the crowd. "But she is new to my friend here, and as I'm sure you're beginning to realize he's none too bright, and he really hates to share."

Braith stiffened, irritated by Ashby's words. Aria held her breath, hoping Braith would keep his composure as the muscles in his arm rippled against her. The man, who had inquired to buy her, pondered Ashby's words. "No, none of them are untouched anymore." He made a regretful sound. "Damn shame too. What about yours?"

Ashby jerked the hood back from William. "It's a boy, and a redhead to boot."

The hideous vampire chuckled. "Ah, neither of those attributes appeal to me."

Aria held her breath, praying that William wouldn't explode, that he would hold his tongue despite his pride and arrogance. Ashby jerked the hood back over his head. "Not my preference either, but I don't have to look at him to enjoy him."

There were a few titters from the audience. The tension in the air eased. "Ah well, perhaps if you pass through again..."

"I'm sure my friend will be far more willing to discuss a deal then."

Some of the crowd began to disperse as it became apparent no blood would be shed today. Ashby and the man exchanged a few more words before they finally said their goodbyes. Braith was so rigid she was frightened he might break his teeth if he didn't unclench his jaw. The buildings fell away as they slipped free of the confines of the town. The bleak landscape enveloped them, as they were encompassed by The Barrens.

Aria barely had time to take her first easy breath before Braith's arm wrapped around her waist. He pulled her firmly against him and kissed her with an intensity that left her breathless and limp. His fangs pressed against her bottom lip, nicking it enough to draw a drop of blood. A small groan escaped him as he nibbled lightly before his tongue swept in to claim possession of her mouth. Pulling her hood back, he burrowed his hand into her hair and tenderly cradled her head. She was enveloped by love, aflame with need as she clung to him in a desperate attempt to stay grounded despite the rising desire threatening to engulf her. She forgot about everything that had just transpired in her desperation to get even closer to him, to feel even more of him.

William coughed faintly and then more loudly as neither of them acknowledged his existence. He cleared his throat before grunting his displeasure. Braith was the first to pull away, his lips were still wet as he buried his face in the hollow of her neck and pressed them against her skin. Aria brushed his dark hair back with her fingers, relishing in the softness of it as she sought to ease the tension clinging to him.

"I never should have brought you with me." Panic tore through her as her hands stilled in his hair. "It was selfish." He shook his head, his fangs pressed briefly against her oversensitive, heated skin.

"There were no other options," she assured him when he pulled away.

His moment of weakness had vanished and she found herself faced with the inflexible, seasoned vampire she knew so well. A vampire she could sense trying to distance himself from her, trying to formulate a new plan. Aria braced herself for the battle she knew was about to ensue.

"I should have left you at the tree house."

She snorted. "Like I would have stayed."

"Arianna." It was a low growl of warning, one she was sure would have sent many a man and vampire running, but it only served to infuriate her further.

"You're not going to figure out some way to keep me out of this Braith. I've been fighting my whole life for this war, this chance at freedom, and I've made it this far…"

"You're seventeen!" he snapped.

Her eyes narrowed as she slammed her fists on her hips. "That's old enough for you!"

Ashby and William inhaled sharply as they took a big step away. Aria didn't blame them, Braith was wound taut as a bowstring about ready to snap. He loomed over her, bending low so that his face was just inches above hers. "If I decide that you are to stay somewhere safe, then you *will* stay there."

Aria wanted to scream in frustration, she wanted to punch him in the gut or kick him in the shins. Instead, she simply glared back at him as she tilted her chin defiantly. "You just try it Braith and see what happens."

"What? *What* will you do?"

"If you try to abandon me somewhere, I will *not* stay there. I'll find some other way to help in this cause, something else to do. I will not be pushed aside."

Their noses were almost touching now. "Don't threaten me Aria."

"Don't threaten me, Braith!"

He cursed vehemently as he spun away from her. Aria jumped in surprise, wincing as he smashed a fist into the side of an abandoned brick building. The wall shook, for a moment she was terrified it was going to tumble down on him as dust cascaded around him. He stood, his hands fisted, his shoulders heaving as he tried to regain control of himself. Ashby and William were staring at her as if she had sprouted two heads, she stared insolently back at them, refusing to back down no matter how infuriated Braith became with her. He wouldn't hurt her, she was certain of it, those two may be intimidated by him, may even have something to fear from him, but she didn't.

Not unless he really did try to leave her somewhere.

"There is nowhere safe Braith. There never has been, not for me, not for William," she continued more reasonably. He was frightened for her, and that made him volatile, she understood that, but she wasn't willing to be shut out of this fight. He turned back toward her. Frustration filled her, she wished she could see his eyes, she hated those glasses. "We're human Braith, we were born into the rebellion; this is our life, it always has been. We'll be ok, *I'll* be fine. We knew when this started that it wasn't going to be easy. Braith…"

He was back before her; she'd hardly seen him move before he was standing there. She didn't think she would ever get used to how fast and powerful he was. It was as thrilling as it was frightening. He bent over her but this time it wasn't in anger, he was going to kiss her again. Her toes curled and her lips tingled with anticipation.

"We should get going," Ashby interjected loudly. Aria blinked, startled out of the reverie that had enveloped her. Braith's hands tensed on her shoulders, she could feel his frustration, his aggravation as he focused on Ashby. Ashby gulped but forced a smile. It was nowhere near as cocky as normal though. "Don't you think?"

Braith squeezed her shoulders before slipping her hood back into place. Disappointment filled her. She never thought she'd miss her captivity in the palace, but she found herself missing the time when they had spent hours together, uninterrupted as they shut out the rest of the world. No matter what happened, she was certain this wasn't going to end well for them. She needed as much time as she could get with him before that time came, but it wasn't going to happen now.

"Stay covered," he whispered. She nodded as she slid her hand into his.

# CHAPTER 2

"What is a chev…ro…let?"

"Excuse me?" Braith inquired in response to Aria's halting question.

Braith turned away from Ashby, his attention brought back to the twins as they studied something that he couldn't see. It was a little disconcerting how similar the scowls on their faces were. Aria turned to him, her gaze inquisitive while William simply continued to look aggravated. She had slipped the hood from her head again, as had William. Their dark auburn hair, dampened by sweat, gleamed in the bright light of the wastelands. It was an annoyingly bright homing beacon in this washed out land of little color. Frustration filled him as he stalked back to them; it was bad enough she didn't listen to him, but neither did her damn brother.

"That." Aria thrust her hand out to point at something hidden by a dilapidated building. What was left of the roof was sagging; the walls were leaning toward whatever Aria was pointing at. He stepped around the corner of the building, focusing upon the rusted out hunk of metal housed in what he now recognized as a garage. Years of bad weather and bright sun had stripped the vehicle of any semblance of its former glory except for the back end. The roof of the garage had held up over the ass end, and though it was rusted and falling apart, it was not in as bad of condition as the rest of the car. "What is that?"

"A Chevrolet," Braith informed her.

She blinked in surprise; her blue eyes were bright even though she squinted from the bright sun. "What?"

"It was an automobile."

"A what?" the twins asked simultaneously.

Ashby stopped whistling as he walked over to join them, he was grinning as he leaned back on his heels and folded his arms over his chest. Braith would like to punch him, not just for that smug look, but also for all the interference he'd been running between him and Aria for the past two weeks. He tried to tell himself that Ashby was simply missing Melinda and that was why he kept interfering, but Braith was growing tired of it all.

"An automobile," Braith explained. "At one time humans used them to get around."

Aria frowned at him; she looked completely confused as she glanced back at the hulking bucket of rust. "Why didn't they just walk?"

In her world he could understand that question, but a hundred years ago... Well, it had simply been different. "I don't know," he admitted. "They were fun though. I had one of these, and a Mustang."

"So, I had a mustang once too," William informed him.

Ashby guffawed loudly and even Braith nearly burst out laughing. He managed to keep it contained as both Aria and William shot Ashby disgruntled looks. "A Mustang was a different kind of automobile."

Aria's attention returned to the car, her head tilted to the side as she studied it inquisitively. "It doesn't look like it would get far, walking would be a lot quicker."

Ashby spun away and walked briskly to the corner of the building. Aria and William couldn't see him anymore but Braith clearly could. Ashby's shoulders shook with laughter as he covered his mouth in order to stifle the noise. "It didn't always look like this," Braith assured her.

"What did it look like?" William wondered.

"It was pretty, and it was fast. Very fast."

"Faster than a real mustang?" William inquired.

Ashby was laughing harder now and Braith wanted to throttle him. "Yes," Braith answered.

They both looked even more confused. Aria shook her head; her hair tumbled around her shoulders and down her back. For a moment he was captivated by the dark red color that flashed with strands of brilliant gold in the bright sun. "Weird," she muttered.

He didn't know how to explain to her that it hadn't been weird at the time. That he had, in fact, actually enjoyed his cars. "Why did they stop making them?" William asked.

Ashby had stopped laughing, he had turned back to them but there was no merriment left on his face. "There was no one to make them after the war was over. They required upkeep and without someone to do that…" Braith shrugged as he ran a hand through his hair. "After a time they became obsolete. Vampires don't need them to get around so no one particularly cared when they were gone."

Ashby had moved back to them, he was brave enough to lean against the building as he crossed one leg over the other. "Those first humans, the ones immediately after the war, must have had a tough time," Aria mused.

Braith had never thought about the humans after the war, never thought about how they had adjusted to their new, and far more brutal, lives. But he had also been newly blinded at the time, (by the jackass leaning against the garage that Braith hoped would crumple under his weight), and trying to adjust to his own difficulties. Turning his thoughts from the past, he grasped hold of her hood and tugged it back into place. She smiled at him; her eyes sparkled as he tucked her hair away and caressed her cheek.

"I'm sure they did," he agreed.

"Was it really so different?" she asked.

"It was." She peered up at him as his hands lingered on the hood of her cloak.

William took a step closer, curiosity evident in his eyes that were the same bright shade of blue as his sister's. "Why did it change so much?" William questioned.

Braith shrugged. "Technology was never a real necessity for us. I spent seven hundred years of my life without it. Don't get me wrong I enjoyed some of it, but I didn't mind seeing most of it go. My father and a lot of the others felt the same way. They didn't overtly try to get rid of most things, but they didn't try to maintain them either."

"What else was there besides automobiles?"

"There were trains and planes, computers and TV's; there was the internet and game stations, cell phones…"

"I never did like those things," Ashby muttered.

Braith silently agreed. "There were so many new things developing every day that at times it became impossible to keep up. We didn't get rid of it all. Indoor plumbing stayed, as did electricity, but that's mostly around the palace now. The outer areas didn't, and still don't, have the resources to sustain the upkeep for it.

"The golden chain," Aria's nose scrunched, resentment burned in her eyes at the reminder. "It's also part of that technology. It recognizes fingerprints, and only responds to the prints of the one that owns it. That's why only the owner can remove it from their slave. There is also a device in it that allows a slave to be tracked if they escape while wearing the chain."

"It should be done away with," Aria said fiercely.

He didn't argue with her, he'd never thought about it in the same way she did until he'd met her. She was the only person he'd ever put the chain on, and she still bore the faded marks on her wrist from that debacle. If they were successful he'd have a bonfire using the chains as fuel. "It will be," he promised. The way she smiled up at him would have made him promise her the moon too if she asked. "It will go the way of the automobile and guns."

"Guns?" William inquired.

"They were weapons," Ashby answered.

"And these weapons would kill you?"

"Not necessarily. They fired metal bullets, but we know you're ingenious little critters." Ashby informed William as he nudged his shoulder. "It was only a matter of time before you designed some type of wooden bullet. The king seized all guns and had all manufacturing plants razed.

You're deadly with those bows and arrows, but they aren't nearly as fast as a bullet was."

"They sound interesting." Aria bit on her bottom lip as her eyebrows drew sharply together.

"I guess you could say that." Braith soothed the taut line in her forehead, tracing it with his finger until she smiled once more.

Even though he began to whistle, Ashby's eyes were hooded and guarded as he moved away from the building. They walked across the sand coated streets that had once been ribbons of asphalt that wound through the abandoned town. He remembered what it had been like before the war but he'd never seen the aftereffects of what his father had done until now. Beyond the acres and miles of woodlands and towns, there was nothing left of the earth, nothing inhabitable anyway.

He'd heard the rumors of the aftereffects of the war, the whispered talk of the empty lands, but he'd honestly thought that a lot of it was just rumor. Looking at it now, he realized just how wrong he'd been. The extent of the damage that had been done was devastating, and as he took in the vast Barrens he began to realize that his father had not shut down technology and advancements because he didn't need it, but because he had taken it and ruined the world with it. The king had been terrified that the same technology would one day be used against him.

For the first time he wondered if the rumored aristocrats were even still alive, or if they had perished in these forsaken lands as his father had intended.

"Was it better?" William asked.

"Depends on who you ask," Ashby replied. "Some vampires preferred the way things were, others wanted more." Ashby had preferred the way things were, while Braith's father had wanted more, much more, and he had gone to great lengths to get it. "I don't think there were many humans that preferred the way things became, but it wasn't all roses and candy back then either."

"Candy?" Aria inquired.

Ashby shook his head. He shoved back strands of shaggy dark blond hair as it fell across one of his bright green eyes. "Just something humans used to enjoy eating."

"Oh. Did you like it back then?" Braith glanced down at Aria as she gazed up at him from beneath the hood.

"I never really minded it." In fact, there were a few things he actually missed.

"I've heard stories about it," William mused. "It seemed fantastically extravagant. I've heard there was plenty of food, homes everywhere, and that people had everything they required."

"Depends on who you were, where you lived," Ashby informed him. "Not everyone was so lucky, but there were many people that had such things, and many that didn't. Like I said, it wasn't all roses and candy."

"But it *was* better," Aria pressed.

"It was," Ashby finally agreed.

Braith stopped abruptly; pulling Aria up beside him he searched the stark landscape. Dilapidated buildings dotted the desert area. They were hollowed out remnants of what they had once been, with gaping windows and doorways. Most sagged beneath the weight of disuse and abuse.

The wind howled around them, blowing sand up, coating his glasses with fine particles of dust. They were deep into The Barrens now, far from the fertile lands they all knew well. Survivors out here were unpredictable and remorseless.

And there was something out there right now.

"Ashby," he said tensely.

Ashby had already stopped too, his head tilted to the side as he listened. Braith's hand tightened briefly around Aria's as he drew her back another step, pushing her behind him. It would do little good, he knew that she wouldn't stay there, but for now he was at least mostly in front of her. He heard the rustle of her cloak as she pulled her bow free.

"Aria," he growled in warning.

She didn't say anything but there was a low clink as she rested an arrow against the bow. The explosion of motion seemed to come from nowhere and everywhere at once. He didn't have time to alert Ashby and William, it was too late anyway. Braith grabbed hold of Aria, spinning her out of the way as the first vampire slammed into his back. Braith was knocked forward beneath the impact of the weight; he braced himself as the creature tore ferociously at him.

Aria grunted as his arms momentarily constricted before he was forced to release her. He grasped at the creature clawing up his back, spilling his blood. Teeth snapped as it reached his neck, the scent of it was fetid and harsh. He finally managed to seize it; clutching its head as he pulled it over his shoulder and threw it away from him. The creature squealed, squirming on the sand as its attention was torn from him and focused solely upon Aria.

She took a startled step back. Her hand shook on the bow as the vampire launched to its feet and rushed at her. All of her fear vanished as she straightened her shoulders and lifted the bow. Her hand was steady as she released the arrow.

The vampire fell back beneath the impact of her clean shot, its hands clutched at its chest as it gurgled and squealed. Braith seized the creature, determined to spill its blood as rage overtook him. Fury swelled through him, ripping through his cells, and enhancing his strength. For a moment he teetered on the edge of madness, for a moment it felt so unbelievably good that he almost let go completely, almost gave in and let the monster take over.

And then the smell of her blood hit him. She pressed flush against his back as she sought to protect *him*. A shudder rocked through him as she brought him back from the brink he'd been standing upon. Even though it was dying, the vampire launched itself back at him.

He felt her elbow against his back as she took aim again; he was keenly reminded that there were more creatures out there as she let another arrow fly. He seized hold of the creature, and with swift brutality, finished it off. Aria let out a startled cry. Terror shot through him as he spun around. One of them had reached her, but not before catching her arrow in its shoulder.

She caught the creature under the chin as she swung her bow up, but it was too late. The pale, thin monster was already upon her, its hands grasped at her arms. The hood of her cloak had fallen back; her hair was the color of blood in the bright light. That ominous sign terrified Braith as the sweet scent of her blood hit the air.

The creature, enthralled by the prospect of fresh food launched itself forward. Braith wrapped his arm around Aria's chest, pulling her back as he seized the creature by the throat. It squealed as its hands swung in the air trying to grab hold of her again. He was going to kill it, going to destroy it, but he couldn't bring himself to release her, not quite yet. Her chest heaved against his arm; he could feel the rapid staccato of her heartbeat. Even over the squealing noises coming from the monstrosity he held, he could hear the subtle splash of her blood as it hit the sand.

She was bleeding, this creature had caused it.

Fury tore through him. His hand on her chest tightened, pulling her further back. In one violent motion he snapped the creature's neck and shoved it back. It was not dead, but for the moment it was disoriented by pain. Braith was more than happy to put it out of its misery.

And then he heard it, the stutter in her heartbeat.

His head snapped around, she was still standing in his arms, but her face had gone deathly pale, her lips were nearly white. The sleeves of her cloak had been shredded; the cloth hung in tatters. Blood slid down both arms, pooling at the ends of her fingertips before dripping onto the sand. Her arms were laid open nearly elbow to wrist.

Panic tore through him; he grasped hold of her, spinning her around as she staggered a little. Her normally bright, crystalline blue eyes were dull, almost lifeless.

He bit deep into his wrist, catching her as her knees buckled. He was shaking as they slid to the ground. He didn't even care about the creature still staggering before them, didn't look up to see if there were others coming. "Blood Aria, drink it!" They were the only words he could get out through the constriction of his chest and throat.

She closed her eyes for a moment before they sprang open. It seemed as if she was having difficulty focusing on him. "I'm fine Braith, the others. There are more of those things."

"I don't care."

He didn't wait to hear more of her protests; she was stubborn enough to keep offering them. He shoved his wrist into her mouth, desperate, praying that this would be enough to stop the flow of life he felt rapidly seeping from her. There was a moment of nothing, and then he felt her teeth nipping at his skin. Despite their circumstances, ecstasy tore through him at the sensations that suffused him. Her hands clenched around his arm as she drank deeply.

He couldn't stop the low moan of pleasure that escaped him as he leaned over her, embracing her against him. "Stay with me," he breathed into her ear.

She nodded as her eyes dazedly met his. The creature was already healing as it staggered back toward them, its eyes a vibrant red in its hollow face. Its sagging skin had taken on a yellowish, sickly hue. Lack of food and the sand and sun had turned this creature into a morbid version of a normal vampire; one that apparently had no sense of self-preservation anymore.

He pulled her against his chest, cradling her with one arm as he tried to shift himself into a better fighting position. It wasn't much use; he couldn't pull his arm away from her. If there was any chance for her survival, she would require his blood.

The creature was only feet from them when Ashby rammed the bony thing from behind, flinging it a good ten feet through the air. Ashby didn't hesitate as he rushed after it. William was suddenly before them; his upper lip was cut and bleeding. One of his eyes had already started to darken, and the sleeve of his cloak had been ripped, but otherwise he appeared uninjured.

Unable to stand the thought of someone else touching Aria, Braith almost ripped her away from William. He stopped himself from doing so, but couldn't stop the low growl that escaped him. William leaned back as he studied Braith warily. Aria tried to tug his wrist from her mouth as she squirmed against him in an attempt to get to her brother.

"It's alright," Braith grated through clenched teeth. "I won't harm him. Stop. Please Aria, you need my blood, he's safe I swear."

Aria relaxed against him but there was a lingering tension in her body. William continued to watch him suspiciously as he leaned forward. He pulled Aria's arms toward him, finally looking away from Braith as he focused on her. Braith couldn't bring himself to look at her damaged and battered flesh again. The smell of her blood was enticing enough without seeing it too. Neither he, nor Ashby, had been feeding well; he shuddered, his fangs elongated instinctively. He closed his eyes as he fought against his baser, more driving urges.

"William, wrap her arms," he managed to grate out.

Sand and dust kicked up around Ashby as he slid to a stop before them. His eyes flashed red as the scent of her blood hit him, something dark flickered over his face. "Get away Ashby!" Braith snarled. Ashby remained where he was, his shoulders heaving as his fangs sliced into his lower lip. William's hands had stilled on the cloth he was trying to rip into shreds. Aria was immobile against him, her breath frozen in her lungs. "Now Ashby! Now!"

His brother-in-law shook his head; his fangs retreated as his eyes flickered wildly between red and green. Ashby managed a small nod as he took a step back, and then another before he finally turned away. Relief filtered through Braith; he didn't want to have to kill Ashby but he would to keep Aria safe. He wanted to try and regain his trust in Ashby. Jack and Melinda trusted him, Aria and William seemed to, but Ashby was the one that had blinded him, and Braith was still uncertain about him.

William shredded the rest of Aria's ruined sleeves and began to gingerly wrap her brutalized arms in the coarse material. She squirmed in his lap; her eyes squeezed shut as her mouth twisted. Braith bent closer to her hair, inhaling her sweet scent as he tried to calm himself. As her pain suffused him, he kept reminding himself that William was helping. Even though Braith told himself this, his emotions were swinging on a precarious pendulum between rage, dread, and famine. He was unstable, deadly if unleashed, and the only thing that helped to soothe him was her. He savored her scent, the feel of her teeth against his skin, the gentle pull of his blood seeping into her system. His blood would heal her, it would be enough. It had to be, there were no other options. She would die if it didn't.

Aria jerked against him. Braith's head snapped up, an involuntary snarl escaped him. William flinched but continued to wrap her arms in the cloth. "I'm sorry," he whispered his gaze worriedly darting to Braith.

William tied the last knot and sat back on his heels as he studied his sister. Aria squeezed William's arm briefly before slipping lifelessly away. It took Braith a frantic moment to realize that her chest was still rising and falling.

Her heart was beating, sluggishly and far too erratically for his liking, but it was there and it was getting stronger.

Braith was painfully aware of the fact that she had managed to stay conscious long enough for her brother to finish what he was doing.

# CHAPTER 3

"You're awake."

Was she awake? Aria took stock of her body as she tried to figure out exactly what had happened. She blinked at the ceiling, an actual ceiling; she couldn't quite remember the last time she had seen a ceiling over her head. Where was she? She turned her head carefully, her muscles throbbed; she felt drained, tired and a little nauseous. William blurred before her, there were two of him at first but the more she blinked the clearer he became.

"I am," she confirmed.

His shoulders slumped in relief, his hand rested lightly upon her upper arm. "You had me worried."

Her throat was dry, it was difficult to swallow but she finally managed to form words. "I feel awful," she admitted.

"That's because you almost died, and you would have…" William's voice trailed off, his gaze drifted somewhere behind her.

"William?" She was worried by the perplexed look on his face.

"He gave you some of his blood." He sounded almost as equally disgusted as awed.

Aria sighed, she wanted to stay where she was, wanted to lie on the cool floor forever, but she had a feeling she had been out for awhile. It was time to get moving. William lurched awkwardly forward as she braced herself on her forearms. Pain instantly tore through her, she nearly fell back to the ground but he grabbed hold of her and helped her into a seated position. She sat for a minute, panting as the copper taste that preceded vomit filled her mouth. She shuddered, swallowing heavily as she struggled to keep her stomach from revolting.

After a few moments of taking deep breaths, she was finally able to gain enough control to realize she was not going to toss the meager contents of her stomach all over the floor. William looked like he was about to cry, his hand on her back had begun to shake, and she had never seen a look of such abject terror on his face. Not even when their mother had been killed. Then, they'd had no time to react, and had been too shocked and horrified to show any real emotion. Now he'd had plenty of time to sit here and agonize about what had happened, and what *might* become of her.

"I'm fine William, really." She squeezed his hand, trying to reassure him with her strength, but it seemed weak even to her. "Just a little disoriented. But that's better than the alternative."

She'd hoped to elicit a chuckle from him, he only stared stone faced back at her. "The blood..."

"He's given it to me before when I was wounded. It won't hurt me."

His gaze darted behind her again as he leaned closer. "But won't it, you know..."

Aria frowned at him. She started to shake her head but realized the motion would only bring on another bout of nausea. She forced herself to remain still as she swallowed heavily. "No. I don't know. I'm not entirely sure how that all works."

"You've never discussed it?"

She lifted her hand gradually; trembling as she wiped a strand of hair back from her face. "Not that part."

"Huh, I had assumed that you had." William sat back on his heels; his eyes inquisitive as he studied her.

"William?" she asked worriedly.

"He really *does* love you."

Aria started in surprise. "Did you think he didn't?"

He shrugged; his fingers tapping against the floor alerted Aria to the fact that it was not solid wood beneath her, but worn carpet. The carpet was beneath her too, but she couldn't feel it as her fingers were somewhat numb at the moment. It was an unsettling feeling not to have the full sensation of touch. She hoped the numbness went away soon. "I don't know what to think," William admitted. "I'd like to believe it, but it's all *really* strange Aria."

She wasn't going to argue with that. "But seeing him today, the way he was with you, I don't doubt it anymore. All I can do is wonder why?" Aria glared at him, but she couldn't hold up the pretense of being mad at him as he finally managed a smile for her. "You had me worried kid."

"You're all of an hour older than me."

"But it was a glorious hour of solitude," he quipped.

"Jerk."

"Brat."

She awkwardly embraced him with her injured arms. "Where is Braith?"

William exhaled noisily as he pulled back. "They had to..." His gaze traveled to her wrapped arms. "Go outside."

Aria nodded, sorrow and regret twisted her insides. "This is difficult for them."

"It's difficult for all of us."

She tilted her head, her heart picked up as her body instinctively began to react. "Help me up."

"Aria…"

"He's coming William, I can't be sitting down."

"How do you know that?"

"I just do, please William."

He was about to argue further but decided against it as he slid his arms under her and gently lifted her up. He was steadying her when Braith appeared in the doorway. A muscle twitched in his cheek, his shoulders were rigid, but those hated glasses were in place so she was unable to see his eyes, unable to get a read on what he was really thinking, what he intended.

"It's ok William," she told him, sensing that her brother was hesitant to leave them alone as Braith seemed unstable.

William stood uncertainly before bowing his head and leaving them. Braith's broad shoulders almost filled the entire doorframe as he watched her in silence. Aria swallowed nervously, shifting slightly as she tried to gather what little strength she had left.

"You're not sending me away Braith." The silence was killing her. Braith was not the strong, silent type. When he was angry or when he was upset or frustrated, he didn't hide it, especially not with her. "You're not going to stash me somewhere either," she blurted when he remained frustratingly mute.

"No, I'm not." His voice was hoarse, grating.

"But you said before that you should have left me behind."

"I was wrong." She didn't know what to say. "You nearly died."

"I'm fine."

"If I hadn't been there…" He broke off as he shook his head. Her heart ached for the anguish she felt twisting through him. "I won't send you away Aria. I won't leave you somewhere I think might be safe because there is nowhere safe for you, and I can't take the chance of something happening to you while I'm not there to possibly save you. This never should have happened."

"This isn't your fault."

"Isn't it?" She was thrown off by his words. "You shouldn't be in danger."

"I've always been in danger."

"But I want more for you!" he exploded. Aria was startled by the devastation behind his words. He was in front of her in an instant, his hands grasped hold of her arms as he smoothly turned them over. She stared down at the makeshift bandages, disturbed by the amount of blood that coated the rags. *Her* blood. *Her* life. "Don't you understand that? I want you to be safe; I want you to know peace for once in your life. I don't want you to know fear and death anymore. And I've thrust you into even more jeopardy; I've brought this upon us. These lands, they aren't good Aria."

She swallowed heavily, her hands flipped within his as she grasped hold of him. The feeling in her fingers was slowly returning. "One day Braith, when all of this is over, we'll know peace."

His head was bent as he studied their hands. She knew he was thinking what she couldn't say, what she didn't even want to consider. *If* they made it to the end, *if* they won, *if* they were even still together.

"Let's get these off and see how your arms look."

"I can have William do it."

His head came up to hers as his nostrils flared. "I can take care of you Aria."

What had happened to her had rattled him even more than she'd realized. He was off balance, edgy, and uncertain in a way that she'd never seen before. "I know that Braith."
And she did know that, but he was unpredictable right now and her blood was a torment she wanted to spare him from.

His jaw was clenched so tightly that she could practically hear his teeth grinding together as his fingers nimbly undid the knots William had tied. The rags fell away, sliding from her skin to slither silently to the floor. At first Aria couldn't look at what had nearly killed her, but his stillness and the slight tensing of his shoulders, told her that she would have to.

She braced herself as her gaze slid to the arms he held so delicately within his large hands. The gashes were vivid against her pale skin but not as deep as they had been. The ones on her left arm ran from elbow to wrist while the ones on her right arm were below her elbow but just as wicked looking. She was shaken as she stared at them, lost in the realization that she had nearly died, that these marks represented what could have been her end.

Though she wasn't bleeding anymore, there was still some dried blood on her skin. Her hand trembled as she pulled the glasses from his face; she needed to see his eyes. The small white scars around his eyes weren't as visible; his face had paled considerably from the restraint he was exerting over himself. At first he wouldn't look at her, at first his gaze remained focused upon her brutalized arms. Then, his eyes met hers. Her breath froze in her lungs; her heart fluttered like a trapped bird as it beat against her ribcage.

The beautiful gray eyes with the bright blue band she had come to love were gone. They were as bright as rubies now, gleaming at her from the depths of his striking face. He was hungry, he was savage, and right now all he yearned for was her. She would give her blood to him willingly, but he wouldn't take it, she knew that. Not now, not after today. But it was unnecessary torture for him to be here when William was perfectly capable of re-bandaging her arms. "Braith…"

And then he was on her, over her, nearly inside of her as his mouth seized hold of hers with a tenderness she had not expected given his mood right then. His hands were on her face, stroking her cheeks as his tongue flickered against her lips. She felt the press of his elongated fangs as she opened her mouth to let him in. A low moan of pleasure escaped her as he invaded all of her senses. All she could feel was him, all she could smell was him. He was inside her soul, so much a part of her. She could barely breathe as his hands slid away from her face. His arms wrapped around her waist as he lifted her, pressing her back against a wall. His body was hard against hers, impassioned beneath her hands.

Her legs instinctively wrapped around his waist, pulling him closer against her as he groaned low in his throat and nipped at her lip. Her mind and body spun out of control. She was in over her head, but she found she didn't care as she gave herself over to the emotions running wildly through her.

She squirmed against him, aching and unfulfilled as her body longed for more. She couldn't breathe, and she didn't care as his tongue slid into her mouth, becoming more fervent and demanding as he caressed her. Aria moaned in delight, her still somewhat numb fingers curled into his back. She wanted to cry, she wanted to scream with joy, she simply wanted to never have the moment end, to forget the world around them and just *be* with each other. Buttons slid free as he pushed her shirt aside to press his hand against her breast. Pleasure swept through her with the consuming intensity of a wildfire. She didn't care where they were or what was happening around them, not anymore.

"Braith." At first, she was so lost in him, so swept up in the surging needs of her body that Ashby's voice barely penetrated her mind. "Braith." Loss, acute and profound, filled her as Braith's hands stilled on her and he pulled a little away. She stared breathlessly up at him. Joy and love filled her as she saw the beautiful gray of his eyes once more. He stared at her with a mix of awe and love that caused her legs to quiver around him. "Braith."

His eyes flashed briefly red again, his hand slid free as he moved her into a position that protected her from Ashby's gaze. Aria felt her face heat at the thought of what Ashby may have seen as she quickly re-buttoned her shirt. "So help me Ashby if you don't leave us be for five minutes…"

"There's someone coming."

In a split second everything about him changed. Gone was the laziness of his posture along with the small half smile that had curled his mouth. Before her now was the man that would one day rule if they succeeded. He lowered her slowly and turned away. "Who is it?" he inquired as he replaced his glasses.

Ashby shook his head appearing disconcerted as he glanced between the two of them. "I don't know. A figure just appeared over the horizon. I'm not sure if there are others with it."

Braith glanced back at her, for a moment she thought he was going to order her to stay, but then he held his hand out to her. Relief filled her as she slid her fingers between his and he led her from the room. Aria was able to get a good look at her surroundings as they stepped into the hall. The room she'd been in had no windows in it, and it appeared that none of the other rooms up here did either.

Braith led her down a rickety set of stairs that seemed to drop from a hole in the floor. She stopped at the bottom, staring up as she examined the darkened area above her. It took her a moment to realize that it was an attic, she hadn't seen one in years.

His hand squeezed hers as he led her down another set of stairs to the first floor. Unlike the attic, this area was covered in dust and sand. It coated what remained of the furniture and was piled against the back wall. William turned from the doorway as they crossed the room.

"It's alone, as far as I can tell," William informed them.

Braith squeezed Aria's hand before releasing her. "She has to have her arms wrapped back up."

William stared at him for a long moment, his eyebrows furrowed questioningly before he nodded. William glanced at her arms, shaking his head as he pulled the remains of her ruined cloak from the bag on the floor. "Leave it to you sis to nearly get killed by one vamp and make out with another." Braith shot him a lethal glare as Aria felt her face flame red again. She remained silent though as William tore pieces of cloth with his teeth and hands. "We should find something to clean it with."

"It won't get infected," Ashby assured him as he moved unhurriedly past them.

"And how do you know that?" William demanded.

"Infections don't live in us."

William and Aria studied him. "You don't get sick?" Ashby shook his head in response to William. "Ever?"

"No."

Aria stood in stunned amazement, lost in thoughts of the rebellion she'd been a part of since birth. "We never had a chance did we?" she asked.

Braith finally turned toward her but he didn't respond. He didn't need to, she already knew the answer. William had become still, his fingers were wrapped around the scraps of cloth in his hands as he looked between the two of them. "Aria isn't one of you though."

"No, but Braith's blood has already accelerated the healing process; it will boost her immune system also. The cuts will not get infected."

She met her brother's worried gaze for a moment before he finally turned his attention back to ripping the pieces of cloth. He bandaged her arms with fingers that quivered against her skin. She knew how he felt. She was just as rattled by the realization that not only were the vampires faster, stronger, and possessed enhanced senses, but they apparently had never even had one freaking sniffle in their lengthy life spans.

William tied the last knot, squeezed her hand and then stood. Aria was drawn to the doorway, curious about the new arrival as she picked up her bow and arrows. "Is it human?" she inquired.

"It is," Braith confirmed.

The figure had gotten close enough for Aria to realize that it was a woman. She appeared to be about five years older than Aria with long brown hair that flowed around her shoulders. She wore a dress that hugged her curves and swayed about her feet as she moved. The woman was beautiful as she flashed a bright, disarming smile. Braith was wooden beside her, his hands clenched upon the doorframe as he studied the woman with a flare of his nostrils that caused a knot of apprehension to form in Aria's stomach.

*Here* was the food source they'd been lacking.

Aria thought she might be sick as Ashby stepped beside her, practically salivating. Aria remained unmoving, struggling to breathe normally as her heart lumbered. They wouldn't force this woman to provide blood, or at least Aria didn't think they would, but she wasn't entirely certain just how much the depravation of blood may have affected them.

If this woman was willing, then she knew they would have to use her as a food source. They were both hungry and therefore unpredictable and extremely treacherous.

"Gideon sent me."

Braith's need for blood seemed to vanish the moment he heard the name.

# CHAPTER 4

"What did Gideon send you for?" Braith grated from between clenched teeth.

The woman's smile widened, she provocatively stuck a hip out as she grinned at them. "What do you think?" she taunted as she pushed her hair back to reveal her slender, unmarked neck. "I was instructed to provide you with anything you might require, and then bring you to him afterward."

She ignored Aria with an ease that was astounding, and infuriating, as her gaze wandered lustfully between Braith and Ashby. "You can take us to him now."

The woman was taken aback, her eyes finally focused on Aria for a brief moment before she shook her head, obviously finding nothing remarkable in her. Aria was half tempted to hit her. "Braith," Ashby hissed.

"If you'd like to feed from her go ahead." Braith's words were clipped and harsh. His body vibrated with tension. Ashby was staring at him as if he'd lost his mind. "Do what you must, but do it quickly. I plan to leave before nightfall."

Braith turned away, leaving them staring questioningly at his retreating back as he moved deeper into the dwelling. Aria remained unmoving, dismayed by what had just happened. "Aria." She couldn't turn her head to look at Ashby, couldn't bring herself to meet his gaze as she stared at the doorway Braith had disappeared through. "Aria you have to talk to him."

Finally she was able to look away long enough to meet Ashby's fevered gaze. "He needs to feed Aria, he's weakening and he's becoming more unbalanced. Giving you his blood drained him further. He *needs* this Aria."

She managed a small nod as she finally closed her mouth. "He has to understand that you *can't* be his only human supply, it's not possible." He was right, she knew he was right, but it caused a physical ache in her chest to even think about another woman nourishing Braith. "I don't like to do it either, it's most certainly not something I enjoy, but I must, and so must Melinda. Maybe if there were more animals around and you hadn't been wounded it would be different. He's not going to put up much of a fight if he's malnourished, he'll get injured."

It was those last three words that spurred her forward. She had to go quickly, or she wouldn't go at all. If she stopped to think about it…well no, she couldn't think about it. She just had to focus on getting him to feed, getting him strong again and making sure that he didn't get hurt.

She found him outside, leaning against the house, his arms folded over his chest and his legs crossed before him. "Braith." She broke off, unable to get the words out as her chest and throat constricted. It took her a few tries before she was finally able to speak. "Braith you must." He kept his head bowed, refusing to look at her. "Braith…"

"And you would approve of this?"

She swallowed heavily; her eyes burned. She tried to tell herself it was from all the sand and dust, but she knew it was from the tears she was struggling not to shed. Not in front of him anyway, not if she had any hope of convincing him to do this. "I don't like it." She hedged, unable to lie to him. "But you're weakened, and you need blood. If it can't be mine…"

"Then it will be no one's."

"You can't deny yourself. You need it to survive."

"I need you more."

"Braith…"

"I'm not arguing with you on this Arianna. It won't do any good anyway."

She started in surprise. "Of course it will."

He lifted his head and finally looked at her. "No Aria, it won't. Yours is the only blood I crave. None of them, *none* of those blood slaves after you satisfied me." The words were almost purred; they caused the hair on Aria's arms to stand up.

"Then take mine."

Though she had sensed his interest in the woman, it was nothing compared to the blast of hunger that vibrated from him now. Her mouth went dry. She thought self-preservation should kick in, that she should run screaming back into the house and away from him, instead she found herself wanting to run *to* him. She was losing her mind, and it was all because of him.

"No."

She inhaled deeply, straightened her shoulders and thrust out her chin. "If you're going to be stubborn about feeding from others, then you can't be stubborn about this. You don't have to take much, just enough…"

"It's never enough!" he snapped. "That's what you don't understand. It's *never* enough. Every time I taste you I think maybe my thirst for you will weaken, that maybe it will ease, and I won't crave you so badly. But the yearning only increases and I find myself insatiably craving more and more."

She was stunned speechless. She hadn't known, she hadn't understood, she *couldn't* understand, not as a human anyway. But she did know one thing, he needed nourishment, he was stubborn, and she was here. Without thinking, she pulled at the knots on her arm as she stalked toward him. The cloth fell free, exposing the gashes as she thrust her arm out to him. Yes, she had completely lost her mind, tempting him like this, but there were some things that needed to be done, even if he couldn't see that. His weakness could get them all killed, it could get *him* killed. Her life was a small thing compared to their far greater goal, and the lives of so many others.

"You being unable to fight won't do us any good. I will not stand by and watch you starve yourself because you think you will hurt me. You will *not* hurt me. It's either me or her Braith."

Though shadowed by his glasses, she knew his eyes were latched onto her arm, and the droplets of blood that glimmered on her skin. "Either way I upset you Aria," he grated.

"I am offering my blood to you and so is that woman. You have to pick one." She tried to keep her face impassive, tried to control the beat of her heart as she stared stubbornly up at him. She couldn't reveal how much it would upset her if he went to that other woman, it would only stop him if he knew, and he couldn't be stopped. Not this time.

He clasped hold of her wrist, his long fingers gentle as they wrapped around her. He could kill her; with a simple flick of that hand he could kill her so easily, but he would kill himself before he ever injured her. She waited breathlessly to see what he would do, as he bent his head and licked the blood from her arm. A shiver raced down her spine, her breath was frozen inside of her as he pressed his lips against the inside of her elbow and rose over her.

She thought that she had won, that he was conceding defeat as he brushed the hair back from her neck. His fingers lingered upon his marks still on her skin, pressing ever so briefly against them. Then his hand entwined in her hair as he rested his forehead against hers. "You really are reckless," he muttered.

She managed a wan smile as he kissed the tip of her nose. "And you are stubborn."

"Soon," he said tenderly. "When you're stronger…"

"The woman."

"When *you* are stronger. Let this go, it will not happen."

Aria gave the battle up on a sigh. She leaned into him, simply enjoying the feel of him as they stood together in a stolen moment of peaceful silence.

***

He was starving, simply on fire with the necessity to feed. His veins felt as arid as the desert surrounding them. His body was sore, muscles he hadn't known he had burned from the blaze licking through them. It was shear willpower that drove him forward now. He should have fed, he knew that, he *needed* it so badly right now but he'd sensed Aria's unhappiness, sensed her anguish over the idea. She wouldn't deny him the woman, she would understand, but he couldn't bring himself to do that to her.

Instead, he was walking a thin line, bordering on complete loss of control. He was becoming even more of a threat to her with each passing moment. It didn't help that Ashby looked far better than he had before. The color was back in his face and the spring was back in his step. He was whistling merrily, and annoyingly, as they followed the woman across the desolate landscape. The woman was a little paler but appeared otherwise uninjured. He could smell the fresh blood from the bites on her inner wrist, but it was nowhere near as sweet and potent as the scent of Aria's blood on the rags covering her arms.

She was wearing William's cloak now, the hood pulled over her bent head shadowed her features and hid her hair. He felt that simply touching her might help to ease the fire inside him, but he didn't dare touch her in front of the woman that obviously held some loyalty to Gideon. Gideon may very well have been one of the strongest, and most human rights friendly aristocrats that Braith had known before and during the war. He'd fought adamantly against the enslavement of the humans, but Braith had no idea what a hundred years of living in these Barrens had done to him. He wasn't entirely certain what to expect from Gideon, but Braith wasn't going to alert Gideon to the fact that Aria was his biggest weakness. Not until he knew if he could trust the once powerful aristocrat.

They rounded the top of another dune and like a beautiful mirage a town came into view. Heat rose from the sand in waves that made everything shift and blur. But the town was there, green and lush for as far as the eye could see. "How is this possible?" Awe laced Aria's voice as she gazed over the town.

"At one time all of these lands were lush and fertile." Braith forced the words out. "It was the war itself that left everything so desolate. Gideon must have found a water supply out here, probably deep within the earth."

"Amazing, simply amazing," she whispered to herself.

He gazed at her for a moment before turning his attention back to the town before them. There were already vampires lining the streets, waiting for them as they moved down the dune and onto the main thoroughfare.

For a moment he hesitated. He should have fed. It was too soon for Aria, and the thought of feeding off the woman was enough to make his stomach turn, but he was in no condition to fight if that was what this became. Aria went to touch him, but her hand fell limply back to her side. He almost grabbed hold of her hand to make it abundantly clear that she was off limits to everyone in this town. He didn't want any more talk of someone possibly buying her, or her brother. However, he also had to keep her alive and there was no way to know what they were walking into.

He shouldn't have brought her here, but in the end there had been no choice. They would need help if they were going to take down the king, and there was no one that hated the king more than the aristocrats that had stood against him during the war. Aristocrats that had power and followers of their own, or at least they used to, and judging by the growing crowd, they still did. The people and vampires all appeared healthy, the buildings were in good repair, and it was obvious that they had established some sort of unbiased system here as human and vampire stood side by side. There was astonishment on some of the faces surrounding them, a couple of which he vaguely recognized from the years before the war.

They were almost to the end of the street when a figure separated themselves from the crowd. Braith's growing need for blood diminished under the shock of seeing a face he had never thought to see again. Uneasiness twisted through his gut. It took everything he had not to grab hold of Aria and shove her behind him, but though there was no surprise on Gideon's features, there was also no hostility.

"Braith," Gideon greeted blandly.

Braith stepped in front of Aria as Gideon's gaze slid over them. He didn't miss the flicker in Gideon's hazel eyes as his attention momentarily focused upon Aria and William before moving dismissively away. His eyes gleamed with amusement as they landed on Ashby, and a disbelieving smile curved his thin lips. He shook back his light brown hair and studied them over his hawkish nose.

"Well, if nothing else, it looks as if I'm in for an interesting story. Come along."

They followed silently behind as Gideon led them down the streets and into a home that, while it was not opulently furnished, was appointed nicely. Aria pressed closer to him as her horrified gaze slid over the brutal scenes of death and violence depicted on the numerous canvases lining the walls. It was the first time he sensed any true fright from her as she fidgeted nervously with her hands. This was a world she didn't understand and probably never would.

"Are those human?" William's eyes were narrowed as he stared at a shelf displaying jars full of teeth.

"Some," Gideon replied flippantly. "Others are vampire."

William looked horrified as his head turned slowly toward Gideon. Aria's lips parted, a small breath escaped her as her hands pressed against her belly. Even though she'd worn a hood throughout most of their journey the sun had still caught her face and reddened her cheeks and nose.

At the moment she was deathly pale beneath her sun kissed skin.

"Why?" she breathed.

"Souvenirs," Gideon answered with a negligent shrug.

Aria took a small step back. She looked ready to bolt as her gaze darted wildly around the room before landing on her brother and the jars. "Don't look at them," Braith told her.

She couldn't seem to stop looking at them though, as her eyes were riveted upon them. "Souvenirs of what?" William demanded more angry than mortified.

"Better times."

"Gideon," Braith hissed.

Gideon met his gaze head on. "This is *my* home Braith, you came here. I won't put on airs for two humans that you've brought along as your food supply." Braith bristled, his hands fisted at his sides. Aria tugged on his shirtsleeve as she shot him a reproving look. Gideon rested his fingertips on his desk as he pinned Ashby with his unyielding gaze. "Some of us didn't exactly enjoy the war, or the outcome, right Ash?"

Ashby shook his head, his lip curled in distaste. He hated to be called Ash, he always had, always would. "Whatever you say, Giddy."

"Did you enjoy my gift?" Gideon inquired, refusing to acknowledge Ashby's dig at him. "Was she to your liking?"

"She was fine," Ashby answered absently. "How did you know where we were?"

Gideon grinned at him, his fingers bounced lightly on the desk as he pushed himself off of it. "I have eyes all over these lands; a man in my position must always be alert. So, to what do I owe the honor of the heir apparent and the fallen brother-in-law coming into my humble town?"

"We've come to gain your support," Braith informed him bluntly, knowing that Gideon didn't do well with subterfuge.

Gideon was thoughtful, his eyes doubtful and questioning as he frowned at Braith. For the first time he didn't appear even faintly amused or smug. In fact, he seemed almost hopeful. "Support for what?"

"To overthrow the king."

Gideon released a low curse; his fingers stopped their incessant moving as he leaned forward. "You're serious."

"I am."

Gideon was speechless, he gawked for a moment. Then his jaw snapped closed, and his dark eyebrows drew sharply together as his focus became riveted upon Aria. He came out from around the desk, striding forcefully toward her. Braith instinctively stepped in front of her, pulling her back as Gideon reached for her. "Don't!" Braith snapped slamming his hand into Gideon's chest and knocking him back a step.

Ashby seized hold of Gideon's upper arm when Gideon lunged at Aria again. "Are you an idiot?" Ashby demanded.

"Let go of me," Gideon snarled as he shoved Ashby's hands away.

Braith widened his stance, bracing himself for Gideon as the vampire spun back on them. He was prepared to kill the man they had come to seek help from. Gideon's eyes were fevered as they raked Braith from head to toe. Aria's head popped out from around him, the hood had fallen back from her face to reveal her cascade of auburn hair and the paleness of her features.

Braith was afraid to take his focus off of Gideon for even a moment to pull her hood back up. "You can *see,*" Gideon said in amazement. Braith remained silent, he wasn't going to respond to him, wasn't going to relax until Gideon moved away from them. "And it's because of *her.*"

"Gideon," Ashby cautioned.

"You did not feed from my gift."

"We are not here to discuss this," Braith informed him.

"Have you lost your mind!?" Gideon exploded. "She's a *human* Braith."

"We are *not* here to discuss this!" Braith roared trying to control his rising temper as Gideon focused on Aria again. "This topic is off limits, for now," he amended, knowing that it would have to be addressed one day, but not today.

Gideon stalked back to his desk. "I should just have you all killed now," he muttered. "Save myself the aggravation."

Fury boiled through Braith at the mere thought that Gideon might do something to one of them, to *her*. It took everything he had not to leap over the desk and beat Gideon into a bloody pulp, but beating him senseless, or just flat out killing him, wouldn't do any of them any good.

"If you think you could," Braith grated.

Gideon glared at him. "You're in *my* world now Braith, *I* rule here!"

"And just what do you rule?" Braith demanded. "Some brothels and bars, farms, a trade ring, a smuggling business? You rule *nothing* Gideon. This is a poor substitute for the life you used to have and you know it. With your help Gideon, we may be able to get that life back for you. But don't think I won't destroy you if you try to harm one of us. You don't have to help us, but you will *not* threaten us."

Gideon turned back to Braith, but it was not Braith he focused on. His fascination with Aria was pushing Braith closer and closer to a deadly precipice. "What is it that you require?"

"You must still have friends; you must have stayed in contact with the other collaborators that were against my father."

Gideon grunted in displeasure and slid into the chair behind his desk. "I may still have contacts, but what exactly is your plan here Braith? What do you propose?"

"To take control from my father."

Surprise flickered briefly over his features. "And you are going to lead? *You* are going to be the man that rights the wrongs?" Gideon's tone was sarcastic, almost hostile as his gaze focused on Aria again.

Braith pressed Aria against the wall, pinning her against his side. Her displeasure was obvious as she tried to push away but he was not going to let her out. "It doesn't have to be me."

Gideon motioned to someone behind them. Aria inhaled sharply as a servant girl hurried passed them wearing almost no clothing. Bite marks marred her neck, but she didn't seem overly used as she flashed a smile at Braith and Ashby before bending to pour a glass of liquor for Gideon. Gideon smiled at her and lifted the glass in salute. "Thank you Dara, my friend here might like to meet with you later."

"Anything he desires," she replied with a saucy smile that lingered on Braith. Aria shot the girl a dark look that would have amused Braith at any other time. Right now though, he was too hungry and too tense about this situation to find anything humorous.

"I'm fine Gideon," Braith grated.

"Oh not you Braith, I can tell you're not relinquishing your meal anytime soon. I meant Ashby."

"I'm fine also," Ashby assured him.

"Oh well then, perhaps the young human, he seems rather interested."

William closed his mouth as he ducked his head and blushed just as vibrantly as Aria suddenly did. Her discomfort was nearly palpable as her fingers curled into his shirt. Braith hated this, hated that she had to be in this awful place, exposed to some of the worst forms of debauchery he knew. But for all of his numerous faults and all of his sinful tastes, Gideon was a strong vampire and a natural leader. At his core he was not an evil being. It wasn't easy to discern that at first glance but Braith had known Gideon for a lengthy amount of time. He knew what resided inside of Gideon, or at least what *had* resided inside of him.

If Gideon was anywhere near the vampire he had once been than this servant girl was here willingly and was not abused.

"Gideon..." Braith started.

"Perhaps I can even introduce him to some of the things that we used to enjoy," Gideon continued as if Braith hadn't spoken. He idly twirled his goblet and watched Aria intently as he weighed her reaction to his words. "Or perhaps you would like me to teach *her*. That is, of course, unless you haven't already."

"Enough!" Braith snapped as Aria went completely still. "If you mean to punish me for the past hundred years, then so be it. But unless you would like to stay here for another hundred years than you need to get over it, or I'm going to rip out your damn tongue so you can't say another word!"

Gideon became thoughtful again, staring at Braith from under hooded lids. "Protective aren't we?"

"Gideon." This time it was Ashby who spoke in a low, warning tone.

"Oh, it's all in fun. Dara why don't you show our two young humans to a room so they can get cleaned up?"

"They aren't going anywhere alone," Braith informed him.

"Lighten up Braith. You're nowhere near as much fun as you used to be. Why don't we all take a small break and meet back in an hour then. You can replenish." Gideon's eyebrows quirked as his gaze ran pointedly over Aria. "And clean yourselves. How does that sound?" It really was taking all Braith had not to punch Gideon. His increasing need for blood wasn't helping the situation much. He didn't have the patience to deal with Gideon's taunting and candid manner. Not right now. "Show them to the guestrooms upstairs please Dara."

Braith held tight to Aria as they followed the semi-nude woman up the stairs. He led Aria into the first bedroom the girl pointed to, eager to get her away from the girl and Gideon, eager to have just a moment alone as he closed the door and leaned against it. "Can we trust him?" she blurted instantly.

Braith closed his eyes and rubbed the bridge of his nose. "I still think we can, he's far more bitter than I had anticipated, but I don't think he's dangerous."

"Maybe we should leave Braith. This place…"

For the first time she glanced at the walls, relief filled her as she realized that they were free of the "artwork" that the downstairs possessed. "This place is awful, and strange. We're going to bring these creatures back to help us, and then give them positions of power? What would they do to the rest of us?"

"At one time these were the vampires that fought for human equality. No matter Gideon's anger, I believe that he still wants that equality. The people in this town are amongst the vampires Aria, they are living *with* them. It won't be easy, but it can and *will* be done."

She stared inquisitively at him. "Is this what you liked? That girl…"

"I was never like Gideon, or even Ashby, and most certainly never like Caleb. I've never stooped to rape, even after you left the palace and I thought I'd lost you. Though, I suppose taking someone's blood by force is a form of rape." The color drained from her face, her lower lip trembled slightly as she took a small step back. Any reminder of his past was distressing to her, especially that one. He hated doing this to her, but she needed to hear and understand some things. "As far as I know neither Ashby, nor Gideon, has ever done such a thing either.

"If Gideon is anything like he used to be, that girl is here willingly. He never abused a human that didn't agree to it and he never would have possessed a blood slave. His tastes are more salacious than most, but he was never cruel."

"Those teeth, the paintings…"

"I'm sure there's an explanation, and perhaps he will eventually give it to us, but until then you need to be a little more understanding and open minded. Though there may be things in our pasts that we are not proud of, we are not all monsters. If you are willing to look past my faults and the sins of my past, you should be willing to at least give Gideon and the others a chance.

"I wouldn't have brought you here if I thought Gideon was dangerous."

"Vampires and people change," she whispered, her eyes raking over him.

Self-hatred blazed through him, he shook his head as he looked away from her. "I don't think he's changed as much as he's trying to portray. That girl is not unhappy here Aria."

She shook her head as she turned away. Her fingers trembled as she untied the knot of her cloak. Though he wasn't sure if she wanted his help right now he pulled it free of her. The material slithered to the floor; she didn't bother to pick it up. He watched her as she placed her bow and arrows by the bed; he was disturbed by how thin she had become again.

"Oh, a shower!"

With those excited words, she was gone, vanishing through the doorway in a flash. He couldn't help but smile as the sound of running water filled the room. He admired the delight she found in things that he had taken for granted. He remained by the door as she moved around the bathroom gathering soaps and shampoos in her arms with an eagerness that caused him to laugh softly.

His laughter vanished in an instant as she shed the bindings from her arms and dropped them to the floor. The smell of her blood assaulted him. She disappeared from sight again, the water flow changed as she stepped beneath the shower head. He hurt. It was a physical ache so intense that he couldn't focus on anything else. She was humming in the shower, a melodious sound that drew him forward a step, and then another, and another. He was trembling, trying so hard to stop moving that his muscles throbbed from the restraint he tried, and failed, to exert over himself.

The water turned off. She was wrapping a towel around herself when he stepped into the bathroom doorway. He didn't know what he was doing, didn't know what it was he intended as she finished tucking the towel into place. Her back was to him, her head bowed as her dark hair tumbled about her shoulders in curly wet waves. He could hear the beat of her heart and smell her blood in the cloying steam that filled the air.

She grabbed a brush then wiped the mirror with the palm of her hand. Her eyes widened, she jumped in surprise as she spotted him in the reflective surface. There was a brief moment where her surprise turned into a small smile, which rapidly faded away. Her hands grasped the towel as she turned toward him, her heartbeat accelerating.

He should leave, but instead he found himself drawn toward her like a moth to a flame. He found himself standing before her when he'd had every intention of turning away and leaving the room. He should get as far from her as possible until he was well fed and stable enough to trust himself in her presence again. His hand trembled as he brushed the hair back from her very fragile, very delicate neck. Her pulse leapt wildly, a subtle breath escaped her as his fingers pressed against the previous marks he'd left upon her.

His fangs sprang forward; his vision was clouded by the hunger pulsing through him. "Yes," she breathed.

"Too soon." They were the only two words he was able to choke out.

"It's been almost a day, I'm fine. Your blood strengthened me." She pulled his hand away, tilting her neck so that he had a better view of his marks on her.

He wanted to fight, wanted to tell her no. But it didn't matter, he was no longer in control of himself, no longer sensible enough to tell her no, to tell himself no. He was tempted to lurch forward and drive his fangs into her as he bit deep, finally easing the fire that had almost consumed him. He somehow found the strength not to give into that urge; he couldn't injure her in such a way. She shuddered as he pulled her against him; darkened by desire her eyes were fearless as her arms entwined around his neck.

She clung to him, so trusting and giving, so unknowing of the ferocious thirst clamoring through him as she offered her vein to him. He was braced against her as he struggled to find the strength to pull away, to walk out of this room and find someone else. But there was no one else, there was only *her*.

The scent of her blood engulfed him; her heartbeat invaded his body and took over his senses. As he bit deep, her sweet life giving blood surged into his mouth, flowed through his body and filled his dehydrated cells. Instantly the clamoring that had encased him began to ease. A groan of ecstasy escaped him as he became lost in her.

# CHAPTER 5

It was sometime later before Aria stirred. She was drowsy, her muscles felt weak, but the strange sensation of being sated clung to her. Her fingers curled, she had expected to find the unyielding bite of the ground but instead she felt the solid muscle of Braith's chest, and the yielding give of a mattress. She was momentarily confused, she barely recalled the last time she'd been in a bed, or the last time she had awoken with Braith still beside her.

But he was beneath her now.

She allowed herself to simply drift in the pleasure of that realization and managed to doze off once more. He was still with her when she woke again feeling more refreshed and a little livelier. She lifted her head, blinking down at him as she found him staring back at her. The glasses, thankfully, were not in place.

Though his eyes were filled with concern, the lines around his lips and eyes had nearly vanished. The strain he had been exhibiting, the nearly mechanical movements he had been going through were gone as he gazed at her. Her blood had revitalized him, his body had been nourished. She stretched and pressed closer to him as she was swamped with the realization that she had been the one to give him what he so desperately needed.

"How do you feel?"

"A little tired," she admitted. "How long have I been out?"

"A while."

Uneasiness filled her. "We were supposed to only be an hour Braith."

"It's fine."

"But Gideon is waiting for us and he doesn't seem all that patient. William…"

"I took care of it Aria, and William is with Ashby, you don't have to worry."

Of course she had to worry, her brother was stuck in this place and she was curled up sleeping with Braith. "We should go."

She went to climb out of the bed but he grabbed hold of her, pulling her back. "Braith…"

"Wait Arianna, just wait." His left hand entwined in her hair, she became acutely aware of the fact that she was only wearing a towel as it dropped a little. "It shouldn't have happened like that. I was out of control."

"You can't keep denying yourself, and I'm fine."

His fingers brushed nimbly along the top of the towel. Her heart lurched as excitement pulsed through her and her mouth went dry. Her skin tingled and heated everywhere he touched. "You're fine this time, but next time…"

"Next time I will be fine too because you are going to start feeding better. If you insist on not using other humans as much, fine." That was just fine and dandy with her also, but she couldn't stand to see him suffering anymore. "But you're going to have to use them more when animals aren't readily available."

His jaw clenched and unclenched as he studied her. "How are you so accepting of all of this, of me? I hurt you."

She tilted her head to study him. "You didn't hurt me."

He pushed himself up, launching to his feet as he stalked across the room. She watched him, sensing something more beneath the tension radiating from him. "Not just today Aria, but the first time I took your blood, in the woods, the fact that I was previously engaged. The other blood slaves."

She recoiled at the reminder of all of those things. She felt the blood drain from her face but somehow managed to keep her chin up as she glared at him. "And I left you in that palace Braith. My pride wounded us both when I left with Jack. I didn't believe in you, and because of that I drove you to those slaves; I drove you to your lowest depths of depravation. How do you forgive me for that?"

"You didn't almost kill me."

"I shot an arrow at you!" she snapped.

His head tilted to the side, his dark hair spilled across his forehead. "That hardly counts."

Irritation shot through her, she clasped the towel to her as she knelt on the bed to face him. "Then give me another one and this time I'll *make* it count!" His grin infuriated her. Huffing a little she clutched the towel as she shimmied her way inelegantly off the bed.

He grasped hold of her arm before she disappeared into the bathroom; he held it tenderly as she glared angrily up at him. "Aria…"

"Love isn't about perfection Braith! It's about understanding and forgiveness, it's about giving and taking in equal measure. I *gave* my blood to you. I forgave you for things that you are struggling to forgive yourself for, because I love you. I know that you have done some awful things, and you *have* hurt me, just as I have hurt you. You gave up a life of opulence, grace, and a vast supply of blood for a life of deserts and fighting and starvation for me. I willingly gave you my blood because I would do anything for you also.

"*That* is love Braith. I'm seventeen and even *I* know that. Maybe you should learn."

She jerked her arm free of his slackened grasp and didn't look back as she stormed into the bathroom and slammed the door. She gasped in a breath as she leaned against the door; all of her pleasure from earlier had evaporated. He was such an infuriating *ass* sometimes.

She realized only too late that there were no clothes in here for her. Crap, she thought as she released an aggravated breath. She had just blown up on him, and now she was going to have to go back out there to ask him for clothes. It was humiliating.

She remained leaning against the door, reluctant to face him again. A low knock reminded her that it was impossible to hide. She opened the door to find his large and imposing frame standing before her holding a dress which looked tiny in his hands.

"I thought you might require some clothing."

She scrunched her nose as she nodded. "I do."

"Gideon had it sent up while you were sleeping." She eyed the dress warily as he stepped into the room. She hadn't worn one of these horrible garments since her time in the palace, and had hoped to never have to wear one again. She took the dress from him, barely meeting his gaze as she draped it over her arm. "I'll button it for you after you slide it on."

He turned away as she dropped the towel and slipped the dress over her head. His fingers were gentle as he buttoned the back with surprising ease. Pulling her hair over her shoulders, he covered the fresh marks upon her neck with it as he turned her around to face him.

"I need you to know I'm not a complete monster."

She started in surprise, *that's* what this was about. "I know that Braith, I never thought you were." She sought to give him comfort as her fingers wrapped around his wrists. "The past can't be undone, but it doesn't define you. It's our future actions that will show who we really are, what we'll become."

"I hope so."

"They will," she promised him. "I'm sorry I yelled at you."

He smiled wanly. "I deserved it." She wasn't going to argue with that. He kissed her forehead soothingly. "I never had anyone to teach me about love before."

Her hands constricted on his forearms, tears burned her eyes. He was stronger than her, faster and more powerful, his life had been one of pleasure and luxury, hers one of struggle and starvation, yet she realized now that she had gotten the better deal. She knew what it was like to have people that loved her. His siblings, at least Melinda and Jack, seemed to care for each other, but they weren't anywhere near as close as she was with William and Daniel. Yes, her mother had been killed, but she had died for her children. Her father had never hidden the fact that he loved his kids, even if he had never been overly affectionate with them, and even when the rebellion had too often come first. Her entire life had been about love, his had been about cruelty. It was amazing he had turned out as wonderful as he had.

"I'll teach you," she vowed.

"You already have." Tears spilled down her cheeks as he lifted her face and kissed her tenderly. She embraced him, reluctant to have the moment end, but knowing that it must. It was time to return to reality. "We have to go downstairs."

"I know."

He gently wiped the tears from her cheeks before taking hold of her hand, and following the sounds of voices back to Gideon's study. Ashby looked up from his place by the window where he had been staring outside, a drink in his hand as he spoke quietly with Gideon. He grew silent the minute they entered the room. Gideon was sitting behind the desk, his feet propped on top and his hands folded on his stomach.

"Where's my brother?" Aria demanded.

"Relax Aria, he's fine," Ashby assured her.

"Where is he Ashby?"

"Dara took him on a tour of the town."

A cold chill crept down her spine, she nearly sputtered in disbelief. "You let him go alone?"

"There's no need to fear anything here, your brother is safe."

Gideon's smug tone irritated her as she turned her glare on him. "I don't fear anything," she retorted sharply.

Gideon quirked an eyebrow as Braith shook his head. "She's a feisty one."

"She is," Ashby agreed. Though Ashby was smiling, and Gideon seemed somewhat amused, they were both studying her with an intensity that was a little unnerving. "I wouldn't let him go anywhere if I thought he was at risk, I promise. Besides, he's with a human."

Aria refrained from saying that didn't mean much, especially not in a vamp ruled world. She didn't think William should be wandering around alone; she tried to control her panic at the mere thought of it. "I'd like to find him," she said softly.

"Of course," Gideon purred. "I can have someone take you to him. We have some things to discuss anyway, don't we Braith?"

Braith shook his head. "Aria will be here for that discussion. We'll find her brother first."

Gideon contemplated this before he dropped his feet down and rose with an easy grace. "Why not?" he asked nonchalantly. "I'd like to show you around anyway. I think there is much you'd like to see here."

A small chill of apprehension raced down her spine, she wasn't sure she cared to see much of what this town had to offer, but her need to find William outweighed her trepidation. Gideon handed Braith a cloak, this one the same deep blue color as her dress. "It gets cold at night around here," Gideon explained as she studied it. "The color doesn't denote any certain position. Not in these lands."

She nodded and slipped it around her shoulders. Braith tied it for her and pulled the hood up. She was grateful the cloak hid the fresh bandages on her arms, and even more grateful for its warmth as they stepped outside. After the intense heat of the past week, the sudden chill was shocking to her burnt skin. Goosebumps instantly broke out on her flesh, her teeth chattered as she wrapped her arms around herself.

"The water in the area causes the nights to be colder here," Gideon explained.

Braith slid his arm around her waist, pulling her firmly against his side in an attempt to offer her some warmth. It did little good as the icy air licked at her. "Moving will help," he told her, seemingly unfazed by the sudden chill.

They made their way through the cobbled streets of the loud and boisterous town. People and vampires littered the crowded streets. They passed by bars and a theatre, and a dimly lit brothel that caused Aria to blush as one of the women called out to them.

Then they were moving out of what seemed to be the party area of the town, and into an area of subdued streets and dimly lit homes. Though the houses were small, they were all in well repair, and it seemed as if the owners took pride in them. She had been unnerved by the seedier parts of the town, but she was surprisingly charmed and a little fascinated by this area. Did humans and vampires actually live side by side in these homes?

"Let's rest here for a bit." Aria frowned at the building Gideon had stopped in front of. Large windows in the front revealed the people sitting inside talking as they ate in a cozy, candlelit ambiance she found intriguing. Gideon held the door open, allowing the gentle aroma of food to waft out as he waited expectantly for them to follow him.

Braith kindly nudged her forward into the entrance of the building. People glanced up at them, momentarily riveted as Gideon led them easily through the crowd of tables. Aria's stomach rumbled far more loudly than she would have liked. Gideon spoke softly with a woman. Aria found it impossible to decide if the woman was human or vampire as she flashed him a smile and nodded.

"This way." They followed the woman through the room to a booth hidden within the dark shadows at the back.

"We should find William first," Aria said, trying to ignore the increasing rumble of her stomach as she studied the plate of crackers already on the table.

"Relax young human," Gideon chided. "I can hear your stomach rumbling from a mile away. Besides, if we are going to fight a war together than at least some level of trust should be formed, don't you think?"

There did have to be trust and her hunger was making her lightheaded, but she was worried about William.

"I'll find him Aria, sit and eat," Ashby assured her.

Relief and gratitude filled her as she nodded. "Thank you Ashby."

He grinned at her before disappearing into the crowd. Aria slid into the booth, she almost grabbed the plate of crackers and pulled it over to her, but managed to restrain herself from acting like a complete ruffian as she eagerly ate one.

"What is this place?" she inquired as she studied the people, or vampires, gathered in the booths surrounding them. Some were eating, some were leisurely sipping wine. There was a faint melody playing in the background that lulled her, and to her surprise she found herself swaying along with the music.

"It's a restaurant," Gideon told her.

Aria blinked out of her strange reverie. "It's where people gather to eat," Braith explained further.

"They just feed you here?" she asked in surprise.

"For a price," Gideon explained. She frowned fiercely at him. She could well imagine what that price might be. Gideon held up a hand, chuckling as he shook his head. "The only price here is our form of currency."

"I see." Aria's gaze drifted over the strange place again. It was such an oddly amazing thing. Braith handed her a piece of paper, her stomach lurched as she read over the list of food.

"Choose what you want."

She wanted *everything*. It all looked so yummy. A young woman appeared at the booth; Gideon spoke to her before they all turned their attention to Aria. Her hands were trembling, her stomach was rumbling so loudly that mortification was starting to take hold of her. Braith leaned over her shoulder to study the paper in her hand. He leaned away, talked briefly with the woman, who nodded and disappeared.

"Let me see the menu," Braith said. "Menu?" she croaked. Her head was spinning, this town and everything in it was far different than anything she'd ever known. It was overwhelming and so out of place with the jars of teeth and scenes of death she'd seen in Gideon's study.

Braith pointed to the paper she held before smoothly taking it from her hands. A feeling of uncertainty seized her; there was still so much she didn't know. Braith's hand took hold of hers; he gave her a reassuring squeeze as he nudged the crackers toward her. Gideon was studying her in a strange manner that flustered her even more. Instinct made her want to pull her hand away from Braith's, but it was already too late to hide what was between them from Gideon.

"These are all humans?" she inquired as she studied the shadowed room.

"No, there are vampires here too." She started in surprise as her focus shifted back to Gideon. The woman reappeared, placing two goblets before Braith and Gideon, and a glass of water before her. Aria's throat was dry, but she was far more interested in what Gideon had to say at the moment. "Braith and I can tell the difference."

As she looked around the room again, she realized she could pick out some humans also. The one's that appeared to be over thirty and eating were most certainly humans, but the rest were more difficult to discern. She didn't ask how the two of them could tell; she assumed all vampires could tell the difference. "They get along together?" she asked.

"Of course they do, why wouldn't they young human?"

Aria shot him a dark look, not at all liking his placating tone, and the young human nickname was beginning to grate on her last nerve. "You have jars of human and vampire teeth on shelves in your home," she retorted. "That's why."

Gideon just grinned annoyingly back at her as he reclined in his seat. He swirled the contents of his goblet before taking a small sip. "Those humans were just as culpable as those vampires during the war, sweetheart."

"Watch it Gideon," Braith growled.

Gideon's hooded gaze flickered briefly to Braith; he looked about ready to say something more but seemed to think better of it. "What do you mean?" Aria inquired.

"Do you think it was just vampires that were fighting on the side of the king? No dear, there were also humans involved."

Surprise flooded her, her gaze flew to Braith, looking for denial of Gideon's words but he just squeezed her hand. Anguish filled Aria; her shoulders slumped as she forgot about her crackers. "Why?" she breathed.

"Who really knows why?" replied Gideon. "Some wanted to be on the winning side while others wanted to be in the king's good graces should he be the victor. You know the saying 'to the victor go the spoils?' Perhaps some of them were even offered the chance to survive the change. No matter their reasons, unfortunately, they chose correctly and it paid off. Their offspring, and their offspring's offspring, are still amongst the higher-ups of the human race within the palace."

"Oh," Aria breathed, her hand pressed against her lips as the full horror of his revelation sank in. She'd known that the humans within the palace were more than willing to sell them out now, and in the past. She hadn't known it had gone all the way back to the war, and that they had actually fought *with* the vampires.

"I keep the teeth of the ones I killed, and their vampire brethren as a reminder."

"Why would you require such a reminder?"

"To keep the fire for revenge alive." Gideon leaned across the table, for the first time his flippant air vanished. His hazel eyes burned forcefully as he studied her. "I keep that whole room like that to remind myself every day of my hatred of that place, of the betrayal, and the destruction. I fan the fires everyday in the hopes that one day, just *one* day I'll get a chance for payback."

The ardor with which he spoke, the fire in his eyes ignited an answering spark inside of her. "I escaped that palace, and that war, and I fled to safety. My family was not so lucky. They were already gone, already massacred when I escaped, but I vowed that one day I would avenge their deaths and it appears that day has finally come."

Aria swallowed heavily, she didn't know what to say to that. She knew how Gideon felt and understood the urge that drove him forward. She had hated the vampires for as long as she could remember, had wanted their deaths more than anything, until she'd met Braith. And now she realized that her kind was just as culpable for the fall of her race as the vampire's were. She should be relieved to see this side of Gideon, to know what drove him, and finally understand why he had that hideous room; however, she didn't like the way Gideon was looking at Braith.

She didn't like the stiffness, the rigidity she could feel taking hold of Braith. The tension was nearly palpable in the small booth. The woman reappeared, seemingly oblivious to it as she placed heaping plates of food before Aria. She laid utensils down, utensils that Aria hated but had grown accustomed to in the palace. Her stomach rumbled at the sight of the food, but she couldn't bring herself to move toward it as she warily watched the silent war of wills going on beside her.

Braith looked away first, not because he was capitulating to anything, but because he realized that she was not eating. His glasses were back in place but she knew when his eyes latched onto hers, she would always know. "Eat Aria." She swallowed heavily, her gaze darted nervously to Gideon. Braith grasped hold of the fork and pressed it into her palm. "Eat," he urged.

She hesitated before digging eagerly into the plates of meat, potatoes, and vegetables before her. She thought he might have ordered everything on the menu. It was delicious and she couldn't stop the small moan of pleasure that escaped her as she devoured it. They didn't speak again until she had finished every last morsel on her plate.

"Are you still hungry?" Braith inquired.

She did want more, simply because it had been so good, but she was completely stuffed. "No, I'm full." He squeezed her knee gently as she focused on Gideon again. "Humans and vampires live together in peace here?"

Gideon signaled for the woman who reappeared with a bottle of something. She topped off Braith and Gideon's drinks, though Braith required far less of a top off than Gideon did. "They do," Gideon confirmed when the woman was gone. "We do not have blood slaves and we do not force people to give their blood."

Gideon's gaze latched onto her neck. She hadn't realized her hair had fallen back until Braith tugged it over the marks he had left upon her.

"Most give it willingly, either by allowing us to feed from them or by donating their blood. Just as most vampires don't like the intimacy and vulnerability that the exchange of blood can produce, neither do some humans." Braith didn't move his arm, but his firm jaw flexed as Gideon's gaze dropped to the bite marks on his inner wrist. Gideon's left eyelid ticked. "Though, the connection between a human and a vampire is never as strong as it is between two vampires. I've never allowed another to feed from me, and I have never fed from another. I don't know many vampires that have."

"What do you mean by donate?" she inquired. She knew what "donating" meant in her world. The people who were not purchased as blood slaves were taken to be drained of their blood, and their bodies were callously discarded afterward.

"It is given willingly here. If they do not care to give, they do not have to." A small smile played at the corner of Gideon's mouth as he lifted his goblet and swirled the liquid inside. Aria frowned and leaned over Braith's shoulder to peer at the contents of his goblet. It was the color and viscosity of blood as it gleamed in the candlelight. She glanced up at Braith, who nodded briefly, confirming what she suspected. He didn't seem to be enjoying it very much though as he'd only taken a few small sips. "There is enough for everyone to go around here, and we live in easy, relative peace."

Aria sat back. "Relative?"

Gideon frowned as he nodded firmly. "There are always those that break the rules. I think you encountered a few of them on your way here." He glanced pointedly to the bandages on her arms showing from the edge of the cloak that had slid back. "Humans are not to be hurt here, not unless they ask for it, of course."

"So those humans in that section of town back there, and that girl at your home, they were… ah…"

"They are willingly there. We do not force humans to do anything they do not want to do, some simply have lustier needs than others, and they like to fulfill those needs. Besides, most of them are vampires, not humans, and we have far lustier needs, don't we Braith?"

Aria fought against the blush creeping up her neck and across her cheeks. She was well aware of Braith's needs, even if she hadn't satisfied all of them yet. "Gideon," Braith warned.

"She's a big girl Braith, she can handle it, stop being such a bear." Braith's jaw clenched, his hands fisted on the table. Aria grasped hold of his arm; his biceps bulged beneath her hand as he fought the urge to punch Gideon. "There is a no tolerance policy here against hurting humans that are not willing and eager. Those offenders are dealt with swiftly. We do not kill our own kind, but we do not allow them to stay either. Although, most of them would probably prefer death to the banishment they are given."

Aria glanced at her bandaged arms. Gideon was probably right, those pitiful creatures probably would have preferred death to the life of starvation and struggle they now endured. "And what are the rules for the humans?"

"They are the same for both species. Do no harm to others, no stealing, and no false accusations are to be issued. Our justice system is speedy and decisive. The humans are also banished; most of them end up in the border towns where their rights are stripped away by the vampire's presiding there. Some of us didn't care for the king's new rule, and fought to keep things the way they were. Others liked the idea of no longer hiding, of letting their cruelty reign, but they didn't like the rules and tyranny of the palace. Those vampires reside in the border towns. You passed through one such town before arriving here, that's how I knew you were coming.

"We trade human food, clothing, and other goods with them and in exchange they alert us when anyone may be coming to look for us. Though we do not actually hand them the humans that are banished from here, or deal in slavery, it doesn't hurt that most end up seeking shelter and protection in the towns.

"The vampires within the towns are used to dealing with The Forsaken Ones, as we have started to call the banished, and are usually able to avoid them in order to reach us, though sometimes they do get lost. However, if they hope to keep receiving food they have no choice but to aid us. We need to know when someone is coming, or when the king has sent one of his raiding parties to attempt to find us. The Forsaken Ones are hazardous, and we've been having increasing problems with them lately, but they come in handy as a defense against the king's soldiers, and other unwanted guests."

Aria hadn't realized what that town had been; it was a little unnerving to know they had been being spied on, and monitored, the entire time. "They asked to buy me though," she blurted.

"No dear, it was Braith they were interested in. It's been awhile since they've seen the prince, and they were a little surprised by his appearance. Though, they would have taken you if Braith had been willing." Aria sat back, she was flabbergasted by this revelation. "Truth be told, we had once hoped that Braith would come here to do something about his father's policies. We had given up that hope though."

Gideon's gaze was irritated as he turned his focus to Braith. "Why would you think I'd come at all?" Braith's voice was hoarse, grating.

"You were never a malicious bastard like your father or Caleb. I thought you would eventually grow tired of the brutality, the unfairness of it all."

"You could have started your own rebellion."

Gideon shook his head, though he tried to appear casual, tension hummed through his shoulders. "Not many of us escaped Braith, certainly not enough to challenge the king again, not with the power he wielded. The number of vampires was just as badly decimated as the number of humans, especially vampires that didn't agree with your father. We would have been massacred.

"It was a long time before we were able to establish this town. The first twenty or so years after the war were spent moving constantly, trying to avoid the hunting parties he sent after us, but eventually he grew tired of hunting us and became more concerned with the rebellion brewing in his own backyard. We continued to move about for a few more years, but there's nothing out there anymore. *Nothing* Braith."

Braith shook his head almost sadly and took another sip of blood. "We eventually found an underground water supply here that we were able to tap. It took a lot of work but we established an environment where humans and vampires could coexist peacefully."

"We never knew much about The Barrens, but none of us suspected *this* existed amongst them," Aria murmured.

"Nor did we want you to." Gideon idly twirled the goblet in his fingers, his gaze pensive as he stared at the shiny metal. "The last thing we needed was an influx of humans leaving the woods to come here. We may not have everything we once had, may not live in the lap of luxury, but look around you, these people are happy."

Aria studied the occupants of the restaurant. They were smiling and they were *healthy*. They weren't dirty and bedraggled, they weren't too thin or sickly like some in the woods. They weren't pale and drained like the blood slaves. The most amazing thing though, was that they weren't afraid. They weren't hiding and screaming, they weren't struggling to survive, they were sitting in the open, surrounded by vampires, and they showed no fear. It was amazing.

"We weren't going to let the word out until we were ready."

"Ready for what?"

"For a revolution," Braith informed her.

Gideon shrugged as he leaned forward. "Perhaps, but it still would have been a long time coming. Our numbers are not as strong as we would like, and to reach out to your little rebellion would have been risky."

"*Little* rebellion?" Aria demanded in indignation.

"Even you must admit that you don't accomplish much more than being a thorn in the king's side."

Aria's jaw clenched as she leaned across the table. "At least we're not hiding in the middle of the desert!" she snapped at him. "We're there, we're fighting now, and we've come to *you* to join this fight!"

Gideon arched a brow at her as he leaned closer. Braith rested his hand on the table, twisting so that his shoulder was in between them. Aria sensed no hostility from the man across from her though, just a desperate need for her to understand something. "You have no idea what the king is capable of, what *humans* are capable of when their livelihoods are threatened. Rushing into something, and getting ourselves killed, wouldn't do *anyone* any good.

"The king has a way of drawing everyone in, of making them *believe* things that they wouldn't normally believe. It is how he was able to wrest control, how he was able to inflict the damage upon the world that he did. By the time any of us realized what he had in mind, and the lengths that he would eventually go to, to get it, it was too late to stop him. We were outnumbered and overpowered, getting ourselves killed by rushing heedlessly back in would not help us one bit. Of course not everyone was on board with the king at first, which is why your mother was killed, something I think you now realize was your father's doing."

"Yes," Braith acknowledged.

"Vampires gobbled up the crap the king was spewing, bought it hook, line, and sinker. Even then the king was the most powerful, the oldest, and though he didn't control everything, we looked to him for leadership and guidance. We were fools. He took everything. And when he was done with the humans, he turned on his own kind. There were those of us that disagreed with what he was doing all along, and those that realized to late what he intended. The world had gone to shit, blood and death ruled. Though I do enjoy my fair share of blood, killing indiscriminately was never my forte, or anything I took pleasure in.

"These people, and these vampires," he gestured around the restaurant, "Are the survivors, and their offspring. The factions surrounding us are led by the other aristocrats that escaped, and the humans that fled from the fallout of the war. Some of the humans are descendants of the early escapees from the palace."

"My great grandfather escaped the palace when he was thirteen, he started the rebellion," Aria muttered.

"So you've always had rebel in your blood?" Braith inquired as his finger briefly rubbed the back of her hand.

She smiled as she shrugged at him. "I guess so."

Gideon shook his head as he took a sip of blood and looked at Braith thoughtfully. "If it hadn't been for Ashby's bomb, I think you would have come to see what your father was a lot sooner. I still can't believe you survived that thing. You were a mess; your arm was barely attached, your torso... We all thought you were as good as dead."

Aria didn't like the picture that Gideon was painting. She couldn't imagine Braith so vulnerable and broken. "So did my father," replied Braith. "I think surviving it in the first place, even more so than mastering my blindness, was the thing that convinced him to let me live."

"Your blindness?" Gideon inquired, though his gaze was focused on Aria.

"Don't play stupid Gideon, I heard you questioning Ashby about us." Braith's body vibrated like a tuning fork as his chest pressed against her shoulder. His hand fell to her waist, pulling her possessively closer to him. "I think you've figured out the extremes that I will go to, and that there isn't anything I won't do, any one I won't destroy, to protect her."

The words, growled and cold, caused the hair on her neck to stand on end. Gideon quirked an eyebrow, a small smile of amusement flickered over his full lips. "Easy there watchdog, I mean no harm, to either of you. Like I said, we've been waiting for your arrival. I'm not going to ruin that now. Yes, I already figured out that there's something going on between you two. I'm not exactly sure what, but I'm guessing that it's far more than you're willing to tell me right now, and that it has something to do with the return of your sight. Though, I think it will be best if this is kept from the others, at least for now."

There was something more beneath his words. She suspected the "for now" was just to appease Braith, and that this was really something Gideon meant to keep secret for good. A part of her knew he was right, and that part terrified her.

"And you truly think things will be so different if you return now?" Aria inquired, proud her voice remained strong.

"I know they will be," answered Gideon. The way he stared at Braith made it clear why he believed things would be different.

"Why would you even go back?" Aria gestured around the restaurant. "Everyone seems happy here, you've somehow managed to find a way for humans and vampires to coexist in peace."

"Let's be clear here, before the war we all lived in relative peace too. Most humans were oblivious to us, and we liked it that way. There were some that were a threat, some that hunted us. For the most part other humans thought those that hunted us were crazy, and there were so few of them that they weren't all that threatening to us anyway. Some of the humans actually enjoyed our world, enjoyed sharing their blood with us. It was actually an agreeable time and place. The king forced us into the border towns and The Barrens. He ripped our world away from us and he slaughtered our families. I want revenge, I want *my* life back just as much as you want freedom and security."

Aria hadn't seen Gideon move until his hand was resting casually upon hers. She jumped slightly, as did everyone around them, when Braith's hand slammed down upon Gideon's. "I'll only tell you this once, do *not* touch her."

Gideon winced as Braith's grip tightened on his wrist. "Braith," Aria said softly.

He lifted Gideon's arm from her and threw it back at him. Though he tried not to, Gideon finally gave into the urge to rub his brutalized wrist. Aria almost apologized to him but she remained silent as Braith smoothly moved her hand off the table. "Touchy aren't we," Gideon muttered.

The people around them gradually went back to eating. "I'm not saying it's going to be easy," Gideon continued. "It took awhile for the humans to trust us, years and a couple of generations to forge the easy coexistence we have now, but it works well for us. It will probably take even more time with your people. They've been even more oppressed, even more beaten and broken than the ancestors of the people here. However, their offspring, and future generations, won't even know what it was like to be oppressed."

Aria was breathless, her hand clenched around Braith's as hope filled her. "The same way I don't know what it feels like not to be oppressed," she whispered.

Gideon offered a sympathetic smile as he nodded. "Exactly. If it wasn't for our aversion to having children our numbers would be even stronger, but some things don't change."

"Your aversion?" Aria asked in surprise.

"Most vampires don't like the thought of having children," Braith explained.

"It's not that we dislike them," Gideon continued. "In fact I tolerate them well enough; I simply do not have the patience or the time to take care of them. It's too much work and not enough play. Nor do we want a vast group of immortals running around the planet; it would only be a matter of time before we outnumbered humans. That would be a nightmare for *everyone* involved so we've always kept our numbers in check. Braith's father is one of the few that had more children after a son was born."

"To make it look as if he cared for my mother," Braith told her.

"I think he was also hoping that he would have a built in, powerful unit of protection. Though he did get two junior psychos out of the five of you. Luckily the rest of you were born with a conscience," Gideon continued. "Most of us accept that offspring will be required of us at some point in time, but we are also aware of the fact that if we are lucky enough to beget a son on the first try, we can consider ourselves successful."

Aria scowled at him as she folded her arms over her chest. "I can assure you that a woman is a success too!" she snapped.

Gideon grinned at her as he raised his goblet in a salute. "I'm sure, but they do us little good for continuing our line."

"You're an ass."

Gideon shrugged, not at all offended by her words. "Simply the truth, our heritage and our ways have been like this for thousands of years. Though we have adapted and changed greatly over those years, there are some things that simply don't change. Perhaps if I cared for the woman it would be different, but I know the hag I was supposed to be saddled with despised me as much as I despised her. Believe me, a son would have been a miracle for both of us. I didn't mourn her even a little when she was killed during the war."

Aria seethed as she continued to glare at him. Screams erupted in the night, pulling her attention away from Gideon as she searched for the source. A chill swept down

Aria's spine as more shouts pierced the air. On the street, people began to run; their heads were barely visible through the glass as they bolted forward.

Both Braith and Gideon leapt to their feet. "Stay here," Braith commanded.

Aria sat for a bewildered moment, disoriented by what was going on, confused by the sudden eruption of chaos into this peaceful setting. She remained still for only a moment before she jumped to her feet and followed quickly behind the two vampires. They had to push and shove their way through the confused and frightened crowd packing the building. Being smaller, she was far more adept at moving in and out and around the people and things.

They were stepping onto the street when she arrived at the door. Standing behind the glass, she watched as more people fled past, some were bleeding, others were carrying their children and still more were stumbling around and disoriented. Aria was nearly taken out as two people slammed into the door, shoving it open as they tumbled inside in a breathless heap.

She grasped hold of the man's arm and helped him to his feet. "What's going on?" she demanded.

His eyes were wild, rolling in his head. Blood trickled from his forehead and into one of his eyes. "The Forsaken Ones," he gasped.

Dread trickled down her back as one ran past the building. It appeared more grub-like than man-like with its nearly translucent skin, hairless body, and nondescript features. It was in much worse condition than the ones they had encountered in the desert. Is this what happened to the vampires after *years* of banishment and starvation? A shudder rippled through her, nausea twisted in her stomach at the thought.

More of the creatures appeared, their heads swiveled sluggishly back and forth, their nostrils flared as they scented blood in the air. They were twisted and demented in a way that not even Caleb had been. And they were heading straight toward Braith.

Her breath exploded out of her. She released the young man as she leapt over some broken dishes on the floor and shoved through the door. The chilly air hit her but it didn't rob her of her breath anymore. Braith was about fifty feet away, his head swiveled toward her, and his jaw clenched as he came back at her.

"Get back inside Aria!" he shouted.

"You need my help!"

"You don't even have your bow, get back inside! We'll be fine!"

"I'll get it!"

"What?"

Lifting the hem of her dress, she tucked the ends of it into the attached belt. Braith, seeming to sense her intent, started for her. She didn't have much time. Running, she bolted up a set of stairs next to the building, jumped onto the railing and leapt at the top of the wall. Her fingers scrambled, and nearly lost purchase. By sheer luck and pure determination, she was able to keep her hold and pull herself up. Panting for breath, she knelt on the roof and peered over the side.

Braith was standing on the street below, fury radiated from him as he stared up at her with clenched fists. She was going to get an earful later, but she didn't care. "I'll be right back!" she called to him as she rose to her feet and raced across the roof of the building. She jumped onto the wall and leapt across the space between the buildings. They weren't the same as her trees, but she was able to navigate them with relative ease as she raced back to Gideon's house.

Some of the creatures started to follow her, but the others continued to filter through the streets hunting for prey. The screams of the maimed and frightened increased as she moved deeper into the fray.

# CHAPTER 6

"*What* was that?" Gideon's amazed whisper was close by his ear.

Braith was seething, his hands fisted as he watched Aria leap from one building to another. "I'm going to kill her myself."

"Well let's worry about *getting* to her, in order to kill her first," Gideon muttered.

Braith's attention was brought back to the street and the creature's filtering down it. He would have to get through them in order to reach her, and he had no problem doing just that. They were the sickliest looking vampires he'd ever seen, but their desperation made them far more volatile than many things he had encountered.

The streets echoed with screams, the scent of blood hung heavily in the air as the creatures stalked through the town, looking for more victims. Most people had already fled to safety, taking shelter in the buildings. Some still scrambled to get out of the way, others had not been fortunate enough to escape. Some of the creatures were trying to drag their victims behind them.

Their eyes were a glowing red. Braith assumed it was a permanent condition, one caused by their desperate need for sustenance. Two charged at him, one broke away, squealing as it raced down an alley after some unknown quarry. The other one was so pale that it was nearly transparent. These creatures seemed to no longer move about in the day, but remained hidden until nightfall when they searched out whatever kill they could find in these desolate lands.

It launched itself at Braith with an eager screech; its overgrown fingernails were hooked into lethal claws. Braith managed to catch its arm and pull it down. It bounced off the roadway with a sickening crack of bone.

He found no pleasure in the mewl of pain it released; in fact he was hesitant to kill the thing. He didn't know what it had done to merit banishment, knowing Gideon the punishment had been deserved, but this thing was pitiful.

And it was deadly.

Bracing himself, he knelt to drive his fist through the creature's chest for the final blow. Its ribs gave way far too easily. He didn't know that it had been a woman until he felt the clammy fleshiness of her breasts against his wrist. Disgust curled his upper lip as he ripped the heart from her chest.

He rose slowly, standing over the remains of the unfortunate creature. He didn't have time to process the fact that this was what they could all become as more were already emerging. They ran down the streets in a savage frenzy, clawing over top of one another in their enthusiasm for blood. Panic tore through him as he threw himself into the madness, fighting his way toward where Aria had disappeared.

Gideon stayed close by his side as they grappled to control the melee around them. Braith caught glimpses of other vampires in the crowd, Gideon's vampires, trying to control the chaos, but the creatures kept coming. It was a never ending wave of pale, almost slimy bodies with vivid red eyes. Aria was fast, she was resourceful and a fighter in more ways than most humans, but she was also just that, human. And there were so many of these things.

If they got their hands on her…

He shuddered, breaking the thought off. It wasn't possible; he would *not* allow it to happen. He shut down all his pity for these creatures and turned to deal with the commotion at hand. Braith heard Gideon grunt loudly, he realized that they had been separated and Gideon seemed to be the main focus of the creature's attention. Gideon had been the one to banish them, the one that had forsaken them and now they required payback.

Gideon was being pushed back, swamped by their weight as they piled on top of him. Braith grabbed hold of the shoulder of one and pulled it back. Animalistic sounds ripped out of its throat as it fought to get back at Gideon. He drove his fist through its back, and crushed its heart within his grasp. Gideon was fighting to get out from beneath the crush upon him. Though as one fell, another one swiftly took its place.

He heard the whistle of the arrow seconds before it shot a hairs width past his ear. Gideon let out a gurgled shout of surprise as it pierced through the skull of the creature that had just sprung up to grab hold of him. The thing squealed; horrible sounds of distress tore from its throat as it reeled back. Able to get in a better shot, the second arrow pierced through its heart, effectively putting the thing out of its misery.

Braith turned; relief filled him as he spotted Aria. She was standing on the roof of a bar, her bow raised as she released another arrow that soared past Braith's shoulder with a sharp whistle and dull thud that indicated it had hit its target. He was given only a brief moment to savor in the sight of her though as another creature came at him and he had to destroy it.

Ashby was shoving his way toward them; he had never been much of a fighter and he'd been doing more of it than he liked recently, that was made obvious by the grim set of his shoulders and the clench of his jaw. The remaining creatures began to scatter, sensing a shift in the tide as more of Gideon's vampires emerged. Braith and Gideon managed to grab hold of a few more, but the rest were fleeing, escaping beyond the town. Gideon gestured to some of his men, pointing down the road as he ordered them to follow and bring back any survivors.

Another arrow knocked a straggling creature over as it jumped toward him. Gideon had worked his way free of the group surrounding him, he was bloody and his clothes were torn, but otherwise unscathed. The whistle of another arrow pierced a creature that had been lurching awkwardly at Gideon. Gideon didn't flinch at the sound again, but his head fell back as he looked toward where Aria stood. Surprise and amazement filtered over his features.

"Let's hope she never aims that thing at you," Gideon muttered.

"She already has," Braith admitted.

Gideon's eyes widened and then he burst into laughter. "Ah, it is amazing what life throws your way, is it not?"

Braith pondered the truth of those words. Life had been so different just a few months ago, he had been blind, alone and content to simply go through the motions of what he now realized was an empty life. Then he'd seen her standing on that stage, filthy and proud, and forcing him to see in more ways than one. "It is."

Braith took in the destruction littering the street, the mess of bodies surrounding them. Not all were those of the strange creatures, nor were they all human, some vampires had fallen here too.

He turned bracing himself as he looked up at Aria. Her bow was at her side, she had tucked the long ends of her hair into the collar of her dress. The hem of her dress was still tucked within her belt, revealing her legs to her knees. She looked wild, almost savage, but beneath it all he sensed her sadness as she stared at the carnage of the streets.

His remaining annoyance with her faded as her eyes met his. He had said once that he would not chase her into the trees she moved through with the ease of a monkey, he had assumed that would extend to rooftops as well, he'd been wrong.

He grabbed hold of a ladder, pulling it down with a clatter of metal. She was standing at the edge of the roof when he arrived at the top. He clutched her against him as he sought to ease her sorrow.

\*\*\*

"Is she sleeping?"

"Finally," Braith answered in response to William's question.

William nodded as he ran a hand through his disheveled hair. "She's been through so much that I sometimes forget she's not as tough as she acts." His eyes were so similar to his sisters, but they were also harsher. "She's always hated to kill things, she'd do it, but she hated it. I should have been there."

Braith bit back on the retort that William was right, he should have been there. He could smell the alcohol, and the woman on him, but this hadn't been William's fault. None of them had expected the events of this night.

"How often does this happen?" Braith inquired as he accepted a glass of whiskey from Gideon.

Gideon shook his head, he was still bruised and bleeding from his split lip, but he was healing quickly and the marks would fade within the hour. "It used to happen once every couple of years, but this is the third raid in the past eight months."

"What caused such an increase?" William asked.

Gideon was thoughtful. "In the beginning there weren't many of them, but over time more have been banished. They've grouped together, they're angry, and they're taking that anger out on the one's that put them in this situation. The other factions are experiencing the same problems with The Forsaken Ones."

"How many are out there?" Braith asked.

"I don't know for sure, like I said there are other towns that work under the same rules. We've banished six out of here over the years. Some towns are rigid in their rules, others are less strict, but after the ones destroyed tonight I would guess that there are approximately twenty five to thirty of those creatures left."

"Why didn't you just kill them?" Ashby inquired.

"No one here wanted the king's rules, at all. We thought we would give them a fair shot at survival."

Ashby quirked an eyebrow, he downed his drink in one long swallow. "I'd rather be dead."

"If it hadn't been for Melinda that very well could have been you," Braith reminded him.

"And as I said, I would rather have been dead. Those things are a monstrosity Braith. They are a shell of what they used to be." Ashby shuddered. "I would have much preferred to be put out of my misery."

"It's too late to change the punishment that has been handed to them and perhaps the time has come to take care of them. If we are successful in the endeavor of war, they will not be necessary as a security measure anymore, and perhaps death would be kinder. I can get you support Braith. There are four other aristocrats that survived and have their own villages, and the fifth village is solely human."

"Who are the four survivors?"

"Xavier, Saul, Calista, and Barnaby."

"Barnaby," Ashby groaned. "I hate that self pretentious ass."

"As do we all," Gideon agreed. "And though I wish it had, a hundred years hasn't changed him much. He is somewhat more humbled by his circumstances, but you wouldn't really know it to talk to him. He does well with his village though, and I haven't heard anything bad about him although I've tried to stay away from him as much as possible."

"Who wouldn't?" Braith muttered as he downed the remains of his whiskey. William stood silently by, frowning as he tried to follow the conversation. "Barnaby was a jerk, he's always been a jerk, and I doubt there's much that could change him. He didn't even choose a side to fight for, but stood idly on the sidelines to see who would win the war before he chose. My father was not oblivious to this fact and evicted him from the palace as soon as the war was over. I don't see him being much help now Gideon."

"He has followers that are not as cowardly as he is, and you know as well as I that this is not the life of luxury that Barnaby covets. We are not without here, but it is far less than he once had. He won't stand on the sidelines this time Braith."

Braith wasn't so certain, he wasn't even certain he wanted Barnaby involved at all. He would take Saul, Calista, and Xavier though. Saul and Calista had fought with Gideon, had chosen the losing side, and had just barely managed to escape when the war had taken a turn. Xavier had stood by the king's side, had been rewarded when the war was over and given the opportunity to remain in the palace. He had, however, disagreed with the king's policies toward humans and fellow vampire's. Fearing for his life, he'd fled within a year of the king's new rule. Xavier had always been an honorable man and Braith admired the fact that he had stood up to the king, even after he'd been rewarded. Xavier was also the only history keeper left as far as Braith knew, and that could come in very handy for them.

"Can we do this without Barnaby?" Ashby asked.

"I think we need as much help as possible," Gideon remarked. "But it's up to Braith."

"We'll take him, for now. But we'll keep a close eye on him, I trust him about as much as I trust those *things* that came in here tonight."

"That can be done. I've already sent word that I would like to meet with the other leaders. I think the human leader, Frank, is a good, upstanding man. I'm not sure what his response will be though. Their greatest concerns now are the creature's out there."

"Those creatures must be handled," Braith muttered. He agreed with most of what Gideon had done here, and understood his aversion to handing out the death sentence, but those things were not rational, thinking beings anymore.

"There is something else we must discuss Braith." Ashby and Gideon exchanged a look that caused Braith to stiffen. Whatever Gideon was about to say, he wasn't going to like it. "It's about the girl."

"She's not open for discussion," Braith stated flatly.

William took a step forward, drawn by the topic of his sister. "Braith you must understand…"

"What I understand Gideon, is that you better think about what you are going to say before you continue."

Gideon swallowed heavily; his hazel eyes were turbulent. Braith thought he'd finally gathered enough sense to remain silent. He was wrong. "I understand you care for this girl, love her even," he amended quickly when Ashby shook his head. "But you must understand that no matter how powerful you are vampires will not accept a human as their queen."

"They don't have to."

"You plan to try and change her then?"

William inhaled sharply, his eyes were questioning as his gaze bounced between them. Braith shook his head sternly. Something shifted and twisted inside of him, it curled through his belly, and clutched at his chest. He would love nothing more than to spend eternity with her, to give her the strength that came with immortality, to protect her from her own recklessness, and to ease the instability the thought of her death created in him, but he couldn't take the chance. He would not be the one that destroyed her.

"No. I will not risk her life in such a way."

Gideon and Ashby shifted uncomfortably, William's eyes were beginning to resemble an owl's. "She is strong, she's brave, and she has earned my respect, but you cannot rule with a *human* Braith. The others will not fall in line for a human, and they will *not* follow your children."

"Is that even possible?" William blurted in surprise.

Braith shot him a dark look as the boy gaped back at him in something akin to horror. "It is," he sneered.

"The child will be either vampire or human," Ashby elaborated. "The vampire children are often ignored, exiled, or ridiculed. The humans don't fare any better, but some are given positions as servants within the palace. It's always been that way, even before the king ruled."

"There are some of those children here, they were either created here, or they fled the persecution they received while in the palace. Here, no matter what they are, they are treated as equals, but we still wouldn't accept them as a ruler unless they were full vampire. They are slightly stronger than a human but not as strong as a full vampire."

"Does that include you Gideon?" Braith sneered.

He shifted nervously. "You can't hold the truth against me Braith. We are just here, give us credit for that, but do not blame us for the truth. Unless she survives the change, she will not be accepted, and neither will your children."

Braith shifted as he folded his arms over his chest. "*If* Aria and I have children then I can assure you they will meet no such fate."

"Life in the palace…"

"They will not be raised in the palace."

Gideon gaped at him. "What do you plan on doing with them Braith? With *her*? Perhaps you could marry another…"

"No."

"Braith, be reasonable," Gideon urged.

He *was* being reasonable; he wasn't beating the shit out of them right now. He considered that pretty damn reasonable considering the burgeoning rage he felt. "Ask Ashby to marry another."

Ashby paled, he shook his head fiercely as he took a step back. "No."

"Ashby doesn't *have* to marry another!" Gideon snapped. "His marriage to Natasha is over. No one will question him if he takes Melinda. She is your sister, her blood is pure. It's a fine match. She's not a *human* Braith!"

Braith moved so rapidly that Gideon didn't have time to react before he seized hold of Gideon's neck. He slammed him against the wall with enough force to crack the plaster. Gideon's eyes bulged; shock caused his face to go slack as Braith squeezed hard enough to draw blood. "I told you to watch what you said, you were warned, and this will be your final one. This topic is *not* up for discussion. There will be no other woman, there will be no talk of changing her, and our children will *not* know the life that you have described. I will fight with you, I will even help lead this battle, but someone else will rule. When this is over I am taking her and we are leaving that place. I promised her a life of peace and I *will* give it to her!"

He slammed Gideon against the wall again before shoving him violently and finally releasing him. Gideon's hand flew to his throat; he bent over as he watched Braith warily. "Who do you expect to lead?" he choked out

Braith shrugged. "I don't particularly care. You do it, or even Ashby, you said yourself that my sister is of sound bloodlines. Perhaps even Calista or Xavier would be a fine choice. I don't care who you pick, just as long as we are left alone."

"She will still die."

"And I'll be there beside her, and I will find a way to go with her."

Gideon was completely flabbergasted; his mouth opened and closed a few times before he was finally able to speak again. "*You* are the next in line Braith, the one that *everyone*, including the humans, has expected to take the throne. The infighting that such an abdication would cause…"

"I'm sure that it will all work out," Ashby inserted quickly. He shot Gideon a silencing look as he stepped forward to break up what was sure to be a battle if it continued. "We must win the war out there first, let us not start one here."

Braith waited for Gideon to say more, but he finally just shook his head and took a step back. Gideon turned back, opened his mouth to say something more, but Ashby grabbed hold of his arm and pulled him back. William remained silent as he leaned against the wall.

"This child thing, a baby…"

"I'm not sleeping with your sister!" Braith's temper had hit its boiling point, he'd had enough. The remaining color drained from William's face, and then it flamed bright red. Ashby and Gideon's mouths dropped. "I don't want to hear one word from any of you again tonight," he grumbled as he stalked from the room.

# CHAPTER 7

Aria stood silently in the corner of the room. Thankfully they had not retreated to Gideon's "study," but to a large dining room in the back of the house. Braith sat at the head of the large table, his hands folded before him. He was leaning forward, his tone low and fervent as he spoke with the vampires gathered around him. They listened to him with rapt attention, ensnared by his words and the aura of power he emitted. A lump formed in her throat as pride bloomed in her. It was amazing to watch him like this.

She knew he didn't consider himself a leader, but he already was. And they would follow him, she was certain of it.

Her gaze scanned over the group gathered around him. They were an eclectic lot. Gideon and Ashby sat on each side of Braith, beside Ashby sat Barnaby, a vampire even fairer than Ashby. His hair was nearly white, his eyes a washed out watery blue. Tall and thin he possessed a regal air that marked him every inch the aristocrat he was. Xavier sat beside Barnaby; he was leaning forward as he listened to Braith. His head was completely bald and his dark skin gleamed in the light filtering through the windows. Tattoos marked the backs of his hands and ran up his solid arms before disappearing beneath the sleeves of his shirt. Strange designs and flames reappeared at the side of his neck before ending at his right ear and the bottom of his chin.

Xavier might have been one of the most intriguing looking men she had ever seen, with his eclectic tattoos, but it was Saul that she found her gaze drawn repeatedly toward. Unlike the others, who all appeared to be under the age of thirty, Saul had salt and pepper hair that fell around his sharp face. His nose was hawkish, his eyes a darker shade of gray than his hair. She knew that Frank was the human leader, but what was Saul? He was the first vampire she had ever seen that appeared aged, at least fifty judging by the lines around his eyes and the corners of his mouth. Had he been human once? Had this man survived the change? She wanted to ask Braith about it, couldn't wait to get him alone to find out the details, but it would be awhile before that happened.

Calista sat regally beside Saul, her head held high on her slender neck. Her skin was not as dark as Xavier's, but a soft brown hue that matched her eyes. Her hair was cropped close to her skull, highlighting the intriguing angles and planes of her features.

"He reminds me of father," William whispered. "People listen to and follow both of them."

Besides being a little disturbed by the association William had just made, Aria couldn't help but smile as she nodded in agreement.

"They will follow him." Aria turned toward William as she caught the hint of something in his tone. He seemed to have come to some sort of realization, one that saddened him. He smiled wanly at her, but it was forced, awkward and uncertain.

"William, what is it?"

He shook his head, looking like he was about to say something, but Braith interrupted him. "Arianna, William." Forcing her face to remain impassive, she straightened her shoulders and appeared indifferent toward Braith as she moved unhurriedly toward him. She was well aware of the fact that they were all watching her and William questioningly.

"Their father is the leader of the rebel cause closest to the palace. David is gathering support there for what we are about to undergo." Aria met each of their gazes as Braith continued on. "Jericho, who now goes by the name Jack, has been working with David for awhile now and is helping with this undertaking. Melinda has returned to the palace to be our eyes and ears on the inside."

"Will the humans follow this David?" Xavier inquired.

"People will follow our father," William informed him. "They've followed our family in one form or another for almost ninety years, and they will continue to do so. Especially if there is a chance to end the fear, starvation, and death we live with everyday."

"I met your father once," Frank said as he ran a hand through his dark hair. "It was years ago but he was a good man and I remember being impressed by him. I think your mother was pregnant with you both at the time. He is right; David will be able to rally many to the fight."

"Are you willing to fight?" Gideon inquired.

Frank was fixated on a spot behind Braith's shoulder. Then he looked at William and finally her. "I'm not sure how many of my people will be willing to jump into this fray. We don't know what you know; we've never experienced the life that you have. Though, it would be nice to put an end to the apprehension that the king may one day discover us."

"What about you Frank, will you join us?" Braith pushed.

"I am willing to help. I can't say how many will come with me but my second in command, Marshall, can run things while I'm away. I'd like to move the rest of my people into the vampire towns until this is over, and I'd like to keep them all together, if possible."

"There will be room for them here," Gideon offered.

Frank nodded. "Thank you."

"There will be the matter of the king himself," Saul said. "It will not be easy to remove your father Braith. He's the strongest one of us; he hasn't managed to stay alive and retain such an iron tight hold because he is weak. I don't know anyone who could take him out one on one…"

"Braith can," Ashby interrupted.

Aria's breath froze in her lungs; every muscle in her body went rigid. There was no love lost between Braith and his father, but for the son to destroy the father…

It was unthinkable. And she wasn't sure that Braith could do it, that he could survive the consequences of it. Their probing gazes latched onto Braith. "Braith is powerful, yes, but the king has years on him, experience and cruelty, and a viciousness that none of us possess. Those are all driving motivators that make the king the deadliest one of us," Saul continued.

"They are," Braith confirmed. "We'll just have to make sure that more than one of us goes after him when the time comes."

"Even then…"

"Braith can take him," Ashby cut Saul off firmly. Aria shot him a dark look, irritated that he kept pushing the issue. She ground her teeth, clenching her jaw as she bit back a sharp retort.

"It's his father," William blurted.

"And he wouldn't hesitate to strike down his son," Ashby reminded him.

William looked sickened by the thought. "First we have to worry about getting into the palace, and then we will worry about my father."

"There is also the matter of The Forsaken Ones," Calista inserted, her hooded gaze was wicked as she stared at Braith. "They have to be stopped before we can leave our towns. We cannot leave the ones that remain behind susceptible to them."

"Yes," Frank agreed emphatically.

"We'll try and group these creatures together and destroy them. It needs to be done quickly before they cause more damage." Braith spoke the words flatly, but his muscles flexed briefly beneath his shirt. Anxiety trickled through her; no matter how many went out there after them, those things were unsafe, deadly. "I would like to do this tomorrow, if at all possible. We'll move out as soon as we can."

Aria kept her face as emotionless as possible. She was acutely aware of the fact that Xavier's deep brown had fixated upon her. His dark brows drew sharply together over his broad nose. Something slithered down her spine, something cold and numbing as his eyes swung toward Braith.

"Why now?" Xavier inquired a little too loudly. "Why do you desire to overthrow your father now?"

The coldness spread to her belly, she couldn't breathe. "I have learned of my father's plot against my mother."

"How did you come to learn of this?"

"Melinda, fearing for her life after Jack's defection to the rebellion, came to me and told me the truth. I was able to find Jack afterwards, and was finally led to David and his children. I may not have known my mother well, but such a deception cannot go un-avenged. I'm sure you all understand how I feel as most of you are here to avenge your own families, though none of you were ever close with them. It is the principle of the matter."

They all nodded eagerly along to Braith's very abridged and not entirely true version, Xavier remained unmoving as he stared at her.

\*\*\*

Aria was beginning to hate The Barrens with its endless sun and sand. The woods were cool even on the hottest of days and shady when the sun was at its brightest. She missed the smell of them, that invigorating blend of earth, fresh air, and wilderness. There was nothing like that here.

Sweat trickled down her back, her forehead, and in between her breasts. The thin, tan shirt she wore adhered to her back and shoulders. She pulled it off her skin, fanning herself with it as she pushed her braid over her shoulder. Shielding her eyes, she stared across the endless brown, searching for any sign of life, all she discovered was a dizzying sense of unreality and a slight headache.

"How will we ever find them out there?" she asked.

"We won't," Braith confirmed. He tugged lightly on the end of her braid, smiling for a brief moment as he wrapped it around his finger. "They'll find us."

That didn't sound like a better option. The desolate town was depressing, but she would rather be here than left behind as she had greatly feared Braith intended to do. Instead, he had been uncharacteristically reasonable about taking her with him, a fact that astounded her until she realized that he didn't feel Gideon's town was any safer than here.

Aria wiped the sweat from her brow, wrinkling her nose in disgust at the smell that wafted from her. "I miss the woods."

She hadn't meant to say the words out loud, hadn't meant to reveal her melancholy to him, but they popped out before she could stop them. Braith's hand stilled in her hair, his body was still as stone. "I know. I'll get you back to them."

She grabbed hold of his hand and squeezed as she forced a smile. "I know."

He brushed his finger over her cheek, trailing it down her throat, pausing briefly upon the marks on her neck. She felt his rising thirst, but he promptly buried it. "You won't ever have to leave them again when this is over."

She frowned as she pressed his hand more firmly against her face. "But you'll need to be in the palace in order to rule."

"I don't plan on ruling anything Aria."

Shock shimmered through her, her fingers convulsed on his. She didn't understand what he was saying. Of course he was going to rule, who else would do it? The people would follow him, he was the next in line; it was obvious that it *had* to be him. "But you have to."

He shook his head, opened his mouth to respond but a shout interrupted his words. Aria wanted to pull him back, wanted to demand that he explain his statement to her but he was already releasing her, already moving out of the small room they had been standing in. There was a large group of men outside the door, most of them were vampires, but a good amount of them were also humans armed with bows and stakes. Sadly, stakes would be a last resort, if a vampire was that close it was more than likely the human would not survive the encounter.

There were other women with them, but she didn't think any of them were human, and in all honesty she wasn't entirely certain if they were there to fight, to keep the men entertained, or to try and get their hooks into Braith. She was acutely aware of the fact that they watched his every move with interest. They wore make-up, had their hair styled, and smiled flirtatiously at him whenever he was near. Many of them believed her to be the meal that the prince had brought along with him for the journey, even if her father was the rebel leader, she was of little consequence to them. Vampire or not, they were making her mad enough to take them down.

She refused to look at any of them as she followed Braith to the door of the house they had taken shelter in. She needed a thicker skin if she was going to have to deal with these people for the rest of her life or eternity? Either way it was going to be a long time, because no matter what Braith thought, she *knew* he was the one that was going to lead them out of this mess. He would be the one to end all of the brutality and oppression they'd experienced for the past hundred years.

He was the only one that could.

It was almost impossible to discern one thing from another in the shifting sand and wind. She didn't see what had caused the shout, what had drawn the attention of the group surrounding her. Idle talk and gossip broke off; the laughter faded away, what had apparently been some sort of titillating social event to them finally became something serious.

Then through the shifting sand and blinding light, she saw movement. Braith stepped outside of the building, the wind rippled across his hair, blowing it around his face and causing it to stand on end. Sand trickled over him, coating his clothing and broad shoulders.

He seemed oblivious to the hideous weather conditions surrounding him as he studied the horizon. Figures slipped through the sand, moving as swiftly as wraiths through the hostile environment they knew so well. Braith made his way back toward the house, he didn't say anything as he gently grabbed Aria's arm. He pulled her back into the small side room, gesturing for Ashby and William to follow them.

Pushing the door closed with his foot, he turned to her. "I need you to stay here." He held up a hand, forestalling her protest. "I can't have you out there Aria; there's enough to worry about without having to worry about you too."

"But your vision…"

"I'll be close enough to you so that it won't be affected drastically. I'll be fine, but you have *got* to stay here." Her eyebrows drew together; she folded her arms firmly over her chest. She was a fighter, she belonged out there, and she didn't want him out there alone. "Don't fight me on this, please."

It was the please that was her undoing, the please that melted the fight from her. The vulnerability that radiated from him for that brief moment was almost more than she could stand. Swallowing her pride and her need to be part of the fight, she managed a small nod. Relief filled him; his hand wrapped around the back of her neck as he pulled her against him and kissed her forehead for a fervent moment. She hugged him, savoring the moment.

"Come back to me," she whispered.

"Always." He kissed her again and reluctantly released her. "Stay with her," he ordered Ashby.

Ashby nodded, William glanced between them but his unasked question was answered when Braith handed him an extra quiver of arrows and gestured for him to follow him from the room. Aria fought the urge to go after them, to race out the door and follow them across the desert. She was shaking with the impulse, struggling not to succumb to the urge. She could be of help, she knew it, but she also knew she would be a huge distraction for Braith. Her hands fisted in frustration as a feeling of helplessness flooded her.

Ashby watched her with a wary expression that alerted her to the fact he was well aware of what she was thinking. "You know he'll kill me if I end up having to tie you up," he warned her.

Aria couldn't help but give him a feeble smile as she shook her head. "He wouldn't kill you."

"Like hell," Ashby muttered.

Aria crooked an eyebrow at him but refrained from arguing. "I'm going to watch."

"I didn't expect anything less."

Though Ashby said the words, he still looked guarded as Aria popped the door back open. She was about to stick her head out when Ashby grabbed her shoulder and pulled her back. "Ashby..."

"Let me go first."

She frowned at him in displeasure, but relented as he pulled her away from the door. The chatter hit her instantly; she could practically feel the excitement palpitating through the room. Ashby took hold of her arm and turned her in the opposite direction of the crush trying to work their way out the door.

Ashby kept her behind him, using his body to shield her from the stragglers drifting through the house. He shouldered aside a questioning young man that eyed Aria with interest. A low growl emanated from Ashby's chest, the color drained from the man's face as he hurried on down the stairs.

"Idiot," Ashby mumbled under his breath.

Aria craned her neck to watch the young man. "Is he human Ashby?"

"He is."

"Why is he so interested in us?"

"Because he's an idiot." Aria turned back around as Ashby placed a gentle hand in the small of her back, urging her on before quickly removing his touch. Aria forgot all about the young man as she hurried up the last few steps, she nearly bolted to the broken window at the end of the hall. She placed her hands against the sill, leaning out to watch the group spread out across the sand. She searched frantically for Braith, but he was nowhere to be seen amongst the crowd and run-down structures surrounding them.

Panic seized hold of her, her hands curled around the ledge as she bent further out. It was bad enough not being able to be with him, but not being able to see him was a thousand times worse. Ashby grabbed hold of her shoulder, pulling her back as he pried her hands from the sill.

She was stunned to see blood welling up on her palms and fingers. There had still been glass in the frames, but she hadn't felt the bite of it against her flesh. "How did you manage to stay alive this long?" Ashby inquired as he tore the edges of his shirt and used the rags to wrap her damaged hands.

"I didn't feel it."

"I know."

She turned eagerly back to the window as he released her hands. "Where is he?"

Ashby's shoulder pressed against hers as he peered out the window. "There."

She followed his finger to a building about four hundred feet away. She could just barely make out the form of someone standing in the doorway of a small shack. He was half hidden amongst the shifting sand, and blinding light. Though it was difficult to discern the figure completely, she knew instantly that Ashby was right, it was Braith.

Her fingers twitched, she pulled the bow from her back and propped it on the floor before her. It would be tricky to get a clear shot with so many below, but she was going to do her best to take out as many as possible. Braith may not want her down there, but he hadn't said anything about her taking position right here.

She watched as more figures crept forward. Gideon had said that they were drawn by the presence of anyone in the desert sands, they did not discriminate, they were hungry and they didn't care how many were awaiting them or how powerful they were. The promise of blood was a strong motivator to these lost, ravenous souls.

"Do you think we can get on the roof?" she inquired.

"Do you want to see me dismembered?"

Aria chuckled as she shook her head. "I don't think he's quite as volatile as you make him sound."

"No Aria, he is. The only thing that might keep him sane if something were to happen to you is the fact that you have not done everything necessary to completely form the link. But don't doubt for a minute that he is capable of far more vicious and brutal acts than anything you've ever seen. I've come to realize that he is capable of anything when it comes to you, maybe even beating his father. I know what I would do if Melinda were threatened."

Aria swallowed heavily as she fought the blush trying to work its way up her neck and through her face. It didn't sit well that he knew such an intimate detail of their lives. "But your link with Melinda is complete."

"Yes, and that does make some difference, I think. How much of one I don't know. No one does."

There was something about Ashby's tone of voice, something secretive and fevered about his bright green eyes that caused a deep feeling of unease to form in her stomach. A shout from outside drew her attention, her hand constricted around the bow. The fresh cuts on her hands ached but they were not deep or overly painful. She drew an arrow from its quiver, knocking it against the bow without a sound.

The creatures were closer now, blending with the environment. They moved as swiftly as the dust particles dancing through the air. Her eyes found Braith, her heart beat against her ribs with loud thumps she was certain everyone could hear. William stood behind him, his hair far too noticeable for her liking.

The attack was faster than she had expected it to be. She didn't think the creatures had much use for logic, at least not anymore, but she hadn't expected this suicidal rush into the town. It was as if they didn't care, as if they welcomed the thought of death as much as the promise of blood.

Braith tried to coordinate the attack but she wasn't sure he could coordinate anything against these mindless creatures. How could he plan against something that had lost the ability to reason, something with no sense of self-preservation? But somehow Braith did it as she watched the vampires, along with some humans, split and flow in different directions, effectively encircling and trapping the creatures between the buildings. She was well aware that Braith was at the center of the attack, even through the shifting conditions she could see the blood that coated him, the speed with which he moved, the deadly precision with which he carried out the death of these things.

She knew he took no pleasure in the killing, or at least she tried to tell herself that because at the moment she wasn't so certain. The ease with which it was done, the brutality of it all was mind numbing. She was so focused upon Braith that it took awhile for her to realize that though the group had encircled the creatures, Braith was the only one fighting.

"What are they doing?" She spun away from the window, determined to get to him. Ashby stepped abruptly in front of her. Gone was the good natured vampire she knew, instead he was a massive hulk of annoyance as he effectively blocked her way. "Move!"

"No."

For a moment she was speechless, then her mouth snapped shut and she glowered at him as her fingers curled around her bow. "They're not helping him!"

"I know."

"I have to!"

"No."

Aria's nostrils flared, she was fuming as she pushed against him. He was like an impenetrable wall and he didn't even have the decency to pretend her shove affected him. "So help me Ashby if you don't get out of my way I'll shoot you!"

"No." If he said no to her one more time she really was going to shoot him. "Braith suspected this might happen."

Her anger deflated instantly. "What?"

"They have to see if he's strong enough to lead. This is a test and he needs to pass it."

"There's too many of them, he needs my help!"

Ashby shook his head. "No, he needs to concentrate and you will be nothing but a distraction to him right now. He can do this Aria, you know it and *I* know it. You need to stay here. Why do you think he left me in charge of you instead of William? He knew your brother wouldn't be able to stop you, please don't make me force you to stay."

She didn't know which feeling was worse, the anger or the terror. Braith had suspected this, he'd set her up, the three of them had plotted against her and unless she really did injure Ashby, she wasn't getting past him. Though she would hurt him if Braith required help, and there was a definite possibility she would shoot her brother when this was over. He had it coming anyway; he'd been tormenting her since he could talk. Rushing out there, being reckless and not trusting Braith could put them all in even more danger. She could get them all killed.

"Damn him!" she snapped as she spun back to the fight. "And damn you!"

She thought she heard Ashby mutter, "Too late," but she became so focused on the fighting again that she couldn't be sure, and she wasn't in the mood to push it.

Her stomach twisted as the bow fell limply back to her side. There was no need for it now. Her interference would not be appreciated. She slipped the bow onto her back and replaced the arrow. She couldn't stand the spectacle of the bloodbath anymore but she couldn't turn away, not until it was over and she was certain Braith was safe.

Death, those creatures welcomed death. The realization left Aria hollow and shaken. These were not the king's soldiers; these were lost, starving souls. Souls, she reminded herself, that had done something to warrant such a fate. The reminder did little good. There was so much blood and rage that she was frightened she might be sick.

She leaned forward as two of them launched at Braith. Her breath was frozen in her chest as he fell back, struggling beneath the weight of one of them. She barely had time to blink before he grabbed hold of the back of its neck and ripped it off of himself. No matter how much she yearned to turn away, every ounce of her was focused upon Braith.

Ashby's hand suddenly slid around her mouth. She jumped; a startled cry escaped her as he pulled her firmly against his chest. A finger appeared in front of her face, held up before her as he pulled her back a few steps and maneuvered her into a side room. Aria caught only a brief glimpse of pale dirty feet appearing at the top of the steps before Ashby slid the door silently closed.

# CHAPTER 8

Ashby released her as he strode across the room. Broken pieces of furniture were stacked in the corner, buried beneath years of dust and sand. Dismay filled her as her gaze drifted down. Their shoes left footprints in the sand; no matter how silent they were there was no hiding.

"Ashby." He turned to her, placing a finger against his lips as his eyes narrowed into a glare. Impatience filled her as she pointed angrily at their feet and then the trail of prints they had left behind. Apparently being banished to a tree house for the past hundred years had dulled Ashby's senses as it took him a few seconds to understand what she was trying to convey. His mouth dropped at the same time the knob began to rattle.

Aria lurched forward, thrusting her weight against the door as it started to creak open. It slammed back closed. There was a hushed moment of silence and then excited grunts and squeals began to issue from the other side. Ashby was instantly beside her, his body weight shoved against the door as the creatures began to push and pound eagerly upon it. Between the two of them one was easy to take care of, Ashby could do it himself, but judging by the sounds, and the force with which they pushed against the door, there were at least three out there.

Her fingers itched for her bow as a crack appeared at the top of the door. It was old, it would not hold against the force of these creatures. Aria's gaze fell to the pile in the corner, but even if they stacked it against the door it would do little good. Then, she spotted the window.

"Stay here."

"What!?" he gasped, struggling to keep the door closed when she released it suddenly. "Aria! *Arianna!*"

She didn't hesitate as she raced across the room, grasped hold of the windowsill and plunged onto the porch roof. It creaked beneath her weight, and for a moment she hesitated, uncertain if the old wood would support her. It wouldn't do either of them any good if the thing collapsed beneath her. It groaned again but held steady beneath her weight. Using her arms, she was able to maintain her balance on the steep pitch of the roof as she hurried to the back of the house.

She heard something beneath her and looked down to find two more creatures following her movements, eagerly jumping up and down as they waited for her to fall.

Reaching the backside of the house she plunged into another broken window. She was in another room which had a broken shower. She gave little thought to her favorite contraption as she pulled the bow from her back. Knocking two arrows against it, she used the tip of one to nudge the door open. She was able to stick her head out enough to see that there were four of them down the hall, beating on the door, pushing and shoving and grunting eagerly as they jumped on top of each other in an attempt to be the first one in. They would turn on each other if given the chance.

She turned the bow sideways, she had no clear shot at any of their hearts, and with two arrows she was unlikely to hit the heart anyway. But at least she would impair two of them, and perhaps the scent of blood would help them turn on each other. Aria used her elbow to open the door the rest of the way. Four heads snapped toward her as she stepped into the hall, took aim and fired.

A squeal erupted from one of the creatures as it stumbled back, an arrow imbedded firmly in its throat. Another one was brought to its knees by the arrow in its shin. Blood spurted forth but the other two did not go after their fallen brethren like she'd hoped. Instead, they focused more intently upon her; their eager eyes were like glistening rubies, their fangs hung over their lower lips as one of them shoved aside the creature she'd shot in the neck.

Aria pulled two more arrows and fired them rapidly. One was caught in the upper arm, it didn't slow him even a little, the other arrow slammed uselessly into the wall. It quivered there for a moment, a trembling reminder of her error. Aria took a step back, needing to put more distance between them if she was going to get off another round. They raced at her as she fired. This time she hit them both, one was a deathblow that sent the creature scrambling back, howling in pain as it thrashed upon the floor. The other one was nicked in the ear, it didn't even recoil as it launched at her with clawed fingers and an eager hiss.

She barely had time to toss her bow aside and grab hold of her stake before it was upon her. She fell back, bouncing across the sand as they skidded into a wall. The breath was knocked from her, stars burst before her eyes as her head crashed against the wall. Struggling to remain conscious, she managed to get her hands up between them as the thing lurched forward. It snapped at her, just inches from her face. It was strong, far stronger than her, and she could already feel the weakening in her arms as it lunged at her again.

Her fingers scrambled over the stake as she tried to twist it into an angle that would be beneficial for her. It was nearly impossible as the thing clawed eagerly in its excitement and bloodlust. Adrenaline coursed forth; her survival instinct took hold of her, giving her a strength that enabled her to get the stake fully twisted around. The creature's lurching momentum drove it into the sharp weapon.

Its scream pierced her eardrums, blowing her hair back as it wailed in agony. She turned away, horror filling her as it began to convulse before finally falling away from her. She couldn't move, her back was pressed against the wall as her fingers curled into the thick sand.

As it went still, behind the revulsion and terror a strange sense of exhilaration flooded through her. She had just beaten a vampire in hand to hand combat. Granted it had been an emaciated, weakened vampire but she had still defeated it, and she was *alive.*

She pushed herself up on the wall as Ashby yanked the arrow from the throat of the other one she had shot and drove it into the creature's chest. He shoved the thing away and Aria was able to see that he had already dispatched the other one. Ashby's gaze latched onto her, his eyes were red, and blood marred his right cheek.

"You ok?"

Aria managed a small nod. "Yeah."

He wiped the blood from his face, shaking his head as he surveyed the damage around him. "Impressive, but let's not tell Braith about this."

A low laugh escaped her; she sat up straighter against the wall. She was about to agree when a growl from her left froze the words in her throat. "Too late."

The color drained from Ashby's face as he took a step back. The hair rose on the nape of her neck as she slowly turned toward the stairs. She could practically feel the fury radiating off of him as her eyes latched onto Braith's. He was imposing; his broad shoulders took up most of the stairwell. He was coated in blood. It stained his shirt and pants, streaked through his hair and was splattered across his face.

Aria was immobile, terrified by what she sensed inside of him. She knew he was wild and hot-tempered, but now he seemed utterly savage. His glasses were in place, but even behind the dark lenses she could see the shadowed hue of his crimson colored eyes. Xavier stood just behind him staring at her in amazement. Behind Xavier she could see William and then Gideon as he fought to shove his way past her brother.

It was the alarm on Gideon's features that drove her to her feet. Unfortunately, she forgot about the blow to her head and became somewhat dizzy as she rose. She took a staggering step before falling against the wall. Ashby retreated further as Braith came out of the stairwell. She didn't blame Ashby, she'd never been afraid of Braith before, was certain he would never harm her, but in this moment he was terrifying in his anger. That fury was not directed at her, but it was explosive and it was looking for a release.

Aria pushed herself off of the wall as Gideon reached Xavier. Gideon's eyes found hers as he rested his hand against Xavier's shoulder. Xavier wasn't moving though, he was too focused on the events unfolding in front of him.

"I'm fine Braith." His jaw clenched and unclenched, the red of his eyes deepened. Aria gulped as she held her hands up before her. "See, I'm fine."

"You're bleeding." The words were grated behind his clenched teeth.

She'd forgotten about the broken glass. "It's from the windows Braith. I didn't realize there was glass still in them."

It didn't seem to matter though as his head twisted toward Ashby. He was like a wolf stalking its prey. Ashby took another step back as Braith came further into the hall. He was only two feet away from her now, but the distance seemed far more immense and she was scared she wouldn't be able to cross it in order to reach him in time.

What was wrong with him?

She didn't know the answer to that but it seemed as if he was directing everything at Ashby. "You had one job, *one* thing to do." Ashby took another step back as Braith honed in on him. Panic filled her as she realized he was going to attack Ashby. It didn't matter that she was fine, that they had succeeded in killing four of them. "All you had to do was make sure she stayed safe."

Aria shoved off the wall. If Braith rushed Ashby, there would be no stopping him. Xavier had taken a step into the hall to watch what was about to unfold. Gideon tried to get past him but Xavier thrust out his arm, blocking his approach. "I want to see what happens," he murmured.

Aria was confused by the vampire's words. Gideon looked as if he was going to protest but remained silent as he took a step away. William was ashen, he too tried to get past them but Xavier and Gideon blocked his attempt. Weren't they going to help her? At least help Ashby?

She didn't have time to contemplate the answer as Braith continued to prowl toward Ashby. Melinda! She barely knew Braith's younger sister, but she'd felt a bond with the proud, beautiful woman. If Ashby was destroyed, then Melinda would be also. Plus, she'd kind of grown attached to the cocky vampire who was currently backed into the corner at the end of the hall.

Scrambling forward, Aria threw herself in front of Braith, flinging her arms wide as she strained to get air into her suddenly constricted and panicked chest. "I'm fine!" she wheezed. "Look at me Braith. *Look* at me!" It seemed like forever before those red eyes shifted toward her. There was no softening in them though, no acknowledgement of her words. Without thinking, she ripped the bandages from her hands to reveal the shallow cuts that had only slightly bled. His eyes blazed even brighter as they latched onto the drops of blood glistening on her skin. Was he hungry? Was that the problem? No, this was something more. He was caught up in something, and for the first time ever she wasn't sure that she would be enough for him.

"Braith." It was a low plea, a desperate whisper. He grabbed hold of her arms as she reached for him. His body was rigid, his muscles locked but his grip was surprisingly gentle. She hoped for a moment that he had come to his senses, but then he was moving her out of the way. "Braith, wait."

Aria strained in his grasp trying to get him to snap out of whatever had him ensnared. Her fingers shoved aside the sleeves of his shirt, she needed to feel his skin; she hoped the contact would bring him back to her but it didn't seem to be helping.

"Here," she breathed fervently. Grabbing hold of his hand she pressed it against her chest, over the spot where her heart beat. She had no idea what she was doing. "Here Braith, feel, I'm fine."

Recognition seemed to shimmer through him, there was a wavering, a softening that sparked some hope inside of her. His fingers splayed against her, they twitched faintly and then curled into her shirt, into her flesh. Pulling her against him, his forehead fell to hers. Relief flowed through her; she clutched his hand as air rushed into her empty lungs.

"Alive," he breathed.

"Yes, of course."

Then, before she knew what he was doing, he wrapped his hand around the back of her neck and pulled her close. His mouth was in the hollow of her throat, his lips pressed against his marks on her skin. Aria went completely still, she would give him whatever he needed, but she sensed more behind this. She sensed something dark and desperate as his lips pulled back. A shiver worked through her as his fangs skimmed over her flesh, pressing against her. His arm latched around her waist, dragging her against him, pressing her body flush to his.

Her heart leapt wildly as she waited for his bite. She yearned for this so badly, perhaps even more so than him. Her fingers curled into his back, she forgot about the others within the hall, she didn't care about them anymore. She was too swept up in him, too caught up in the teasing pressure of his fangs.

And then, just when she thought she might scream from the longing building within her, he finally bit deep. A gasp, more of pleasure than pain escaped her. Her fingers curled into his hair, she held him tighter against her as she felt the tantalizing pull of her blood in deep, leisurely waves. Her head fell against him, she clung to him as beyond the concern for her safety, the pleasure her blood gave him ensnared them both.

She had just started to lose herself to him when he severed the bond between them. She felt the loss acutely as he cradled her against him. "You terrify me," he breathed.

She managed a small laugh. "The feeling's mutual."

She realized she'd said the wrong thing as he stiffened against her. "I would never harm you Aria," he grated.

She was not surprised to discover that they were alone in the hall; Ashby had been smart to use Braith's distraction as a chance to escape... so had the others. "I know that." She ran her fingers over the firm planes of his face as she pulled the glasses away and dropped them into the sand. "I know you would never hurt *me*," she assured him. "But Ashby, what was that? What were you thinking? You were going to kill him."

He opened his mouth; she thought perhaps to protest her statement. Instead he closed it again and tenderly rested his fingers over the fresh marks he'd left on her neck. "I would have, yes," he admitted.

She was not taken aback by the admission. "Why?"

He shook his head; his eyebrows drew together as a brief look of confusion crossed his face. "I don't know." She knew it killed him to admit that, but there was no denying it. "I saw you, on that roof, bleeding. I thought you were going to die. I left you with him, to protect you, and..." His voice broke off. Aria stroked him, looking to calm him as his distraught eyes met hers. There was so much anguish and confusion in his gaze that it robbed her breath. "I just lost it."

He hated acknowledging any weakness, and that's just what she was, a weakness that he couldn't keep completely protected no matter how much he tried. And no matter how strong or how fast or how capable she was, she was also a mortal. She had a lifespan clock that she suddenly heard ticking very loudly within her chest.

"There's so much risk for you here. I shouldn't have left you, but I trusted Ashby to take care of you…"

"It wasn't his fault Braith, he *did* protect me."

"You were on the *roof* Arianna."

She forced a smile, hoping to ease him in some way. "It's not that different than a tree, little more of a pitch, little less bark but still wood."

He wasn't amused. "You could have broken your neck."

She quirked an eyebrow at him. "Hardly," she snorted.

"That wood is over a hundred years old…"

"I know where to put my feet," she interrupted sharply not at all phased by the irritated look he shot her. "You have to stop treating me like I'm incapable. I may not be as strong as you, I may not be immortal, but I am far more capable than most of taking care of myself. I just beat a vampire in hand to hand combat. *No* one does that Braith, *no* one. And you shouldn't talk; you left me in the dark about your suspicions for you out there! You put yourself at risk also!"

His jaw clenched as his teeth ground. She was braced for a fight. She was not braced for the brush of his lips against hers, or the surge of heat that pooled in her belly, causing a small sigh to escape. "I need Ashby, Jack, and Gideon, and yes I trust Gideon enough to trust him with you, to help protect you. When they fail…"

"Ashby didn't fail. We were ambushed Braith, there was no way for anyone to know that they would sneak up behind us like that. He saved me."

"I'd say you saved him," he retorted.

Aria smiled as she poked him in his rigid stomach. "Who knew that *I*, of all people, would have a habit of saving vampires?"

She was finally able to coax a smile from him, one that melted her heart and caused her own grin to expand. It was so rare that he smiled. It lit his flawed eyes and eased the hard angles of his face. If the smile were big enough, every once in a while a dimple would appear. She was the only one that ever got to see him like this, relaxed, almost vulnerable, and oh so wonderfully, *almost* trouble-free.

"Certainly not me."

"I didn't think so."

She was saddened when his smile faded and his face became tense again. One day, she vowed, one day he'll smile more often. She'd make sure of it. And he'd laugh, at least once a day, preferably more. "Is it always going to be like this Braith? Ashby said you were volatile, I told him no, but he was right wasn't he?"

"I think he is."

She peered up at him, hoping he would say more but he remained silent. "Because of me?"

"No." He frowned, shaking his head. "Well, yes, but it's not like you think Arianna." He grasped hold of her hands, pressing them flat to his chest. "Here, my heart may not beat but it's there, I'm aware of it now *because* of you. I can't stand the thought of losing you, it just…" He broke off as his gaze drifted to the window at the end of the hall. "I would die for you and not think twice about it. I won't, I *can't*, risk losing you. I need you to stay with me."

She was awed by his words. "Of course I will."

"*Alive* Arianna, I need you alive and there are so many things against you staying that way."

"If I became a vampire…"

He stiffened so suddenly that she stopped speaking mid-sentence. "No."

"But…"

"I said no. It's too much of a risk, I won't take it."

He went to turn away from her, but she grasped hold of his arm. "Braith, I'll die no matter what."

He flinched as pain flickered through his eyes. "Most humans do not survive the change."

"But some do," she pushed.

He ran a hand through his thick hair in aggravation. "Yes, of course, some do."

"What makes them different?"

He shrugged and took hold of her hand. His thumb ran leisurely over the back of her knuckles, causing shivers of delight to run up and down her spine. She didn't think he was aware of the effect he was having on her though as he seemed distant and remote. "I don't know. No one really does. Perhaps it's just sheer strength."

"Strength?" she prodded when he didn't continue.

He shook his head; his eyes finally seemed to focus on her again. "It's extremely painful for a human Aria. I've only seen it occur once and the man did not survive it. I won't put you through it."

"Who did you see it happen to?"

He waved a hand absently. "Some young peasant that a vampire was playing with. It was years ago, before we had even taken control."

Aria swallowed heavily. "But there *is* a chance…"

"No."

"I'm strong Braith, stronger than most. I can handle pain…"

"This is more than just pain, this is *death*."

"Better than most people," she continued as if he hadn't spoken.

"Your insides twist into something different, your heart ceases to beat; your body goes into rigor mortis…"

"I'm stronger than most people! I just beat a vampire in hand to hand combat. I *can* survive this."

"You won't have the chance to find out."

Aria sputtered as indignation filled her. His stubbornness was truly beginning to grate on her nerves. "If Saul can survive…"

"Saul?" he asked in surprise.

She folded her arms over her chest and began to tap her foot. "Yes, Saul. I assume he was once human, he's older."

Braith's full lips quirked in a small smile. "Saul was never human."

"I don't understand. He has gray hair, wrinkles. Do you eventually age?"

His thumb stopped stroking her skin, his hand turned in hers as he held her. His gaze was focused on her hand for a moment. He was studying it as if he had never seen it before. Aria leaned forward to peer up at him, surprised by the distant look on his face. He moved her fingers apart, deliberately tracing the bones of each one.

"Braith," she whispered, fighting against the reaction her body had to his tender touch.

"No, we don't age," he finally stated. "At some time in our twenties we reach maturity, and we stop aging. I was twenty two when it happened. For some reason, Saul didn't stop aging until he was almost fifty. It's happened before, rarely, but it has occurred."

Aria's mouth parted on a small breath, what a strange and oddly fascinating bit of information. She never would have suspected that such a thing could occur. "Has there ever been one that has just never stopped aging and died?"

Braith shrugged, his hands moved leisurely up her arms as he pulled her a step closer to him. "It's a possibility, there were *some* before me," he said with a teasing smile that melted her heart. "I suppose it could have happened then, but since I've been alive I've never heard of it. One aged until he was almost seventy before stopping, but that's the oldest I know of."

"How is that possible?"

"Do you know the legend of the vampire race?" She shook her head no. "Have you heard of God?"

She frowned, confused by the question. "I've heard of him, it, her? Some of the people in the woods would talk of God, they even had ceremonies, but most didn't really understand what it was."

"That's one thing that hasn't changed in a hundred

years." Dry humor that seemed oddly out of place tinted his voice.

"Was it supposed to?"

"No."

"Then what does this God have to do with anything?"

"It's said that God created the first man, humans, in his image. God also created angels to serve him, and to protect and guide the human race, but between the two, man was God's favorite. One such angel, Lucifer, was cast out of heaven because he didn't want to play second fiddle. It is said that on his way to Hell, in order to punish God, and inflict pain and fear amongst the human race, that Lucifer also created something in his own image to walk the earth. A demon that looked like man but had the vast power of the angel's, and fed upon man. He created the first vampire."

"Your speed and strength," she muttered.

"Yes, our immortality, our thirst for blood is all said to be tied to the demon that Lucifer became. The quirks that sometimes affect our race are supposedly because there is also man within us."

Aria's head was spinning. "You believe this?"

He shrugged absently. "It's what has been told over the years, but I don't know for certain, no one does."

"And if you change me, you believe I will become a demon or the demon is what will kill me?"

"You already are a little demon." He chuckled at the stern look she shot him. "But no, I don't believe that. I believe that the loss of your blood, and the sudden influx of mine, is what will kill you. I believe the trauma to your system, the changing of your system into ours is what will kill you, but I do not believe you will become a demon, or become infected by one. Most of us are colder and more callous than humans, we feel things more acutely, our needs are more intense, but we control our actions and we are not ruled by some demon inside us. It is why Ashby loves Melinda, why my mother died for Melinda, why Gideon has established a system of equality. It's why I love you. If we were ruled by a demon none of that would be possible. Some of us seem to relate more to their angel or human side, and some to the demon one though."

"I see." Though she was fascinated by what he was telling her, she was barely paying attention to the conversation anymore as his hands clasped hold of her face and he kissed her lightly.

# CHAPTER 9

Braith stood silently, his arms folded over his chest as he watched Aria move about the room with subtle grace. She didn't know he was there as she studied the bindings of the books with interest. Her hands were folded behind her back as she leaned back on her heels before tilting forward again. There was a wistful smile on her face that enchanted him.

He didn't think he would ever get over the powerful effect she had on him. The sway she had over his deadened heart. She leaned back on her heels again. "Are you going to stand there all day?" she asked.

"I didn't realize you knew I was here."

The sunlight lit her features as she tilted her head to study him. "I'd know you anywhere." For a moment he was robbed of all sense of reason. His fingers ached with the need to touch her, to hold her. Standing on her tiptoes she pulled a book from the shelf. "Would you like to read with me?"

He would like nothing more than to curl up and read with her, but that was not why he'd come here. She seemed to sense that as her smile slipped away and she tucked the book under her arm. "What is it?"

"They're going to vote on whether or not they're willing to join us. I thought you would like to be there."

"I would," she agreed. Her hand slid into his extended one. He held her for a moment, simply savoring in her as she watched him. "What do you think they'll vote?"

Braith shook his head. "I don't know. Those creatures have been taken care of, there may be a few left out there, but they're not much of a threat. I think I passed their test. I think I proved that though I was blinded, I am still deadly enough to lead."

"Do you think they suspect you can see when I'm near?"

He shrugged. "I don't think so, though Xavier saw far more of our relationship than I intended for him to. I don't think he will say anything. For now he prefers to watch, listen and learn."

"What does he want to learn?"

"Everything and anything. Xavier's bloodline has always been the record keepers; he knows more of our history than anyone. His leaving was a huge blow to my father. Xavier sees far more than most, he processes things differently. He'll keep what he saw to himself until he can figure out what to do about it."

"Do you think he'll do something bad with it?"

"Not if he wants to live. Xavier, though his original loyalty was to my father, is a man of thought and learning, not one of action and violence. He is logical and fair. He will come to me when he is ready to confront me about you, before he goes to them. He'll look for answers first."

"I think you're right, he seems very curious about us." She rocked back on her heels again. "They will agree to help us."

"And what makes you so certain?"

"Because it's impossible not to follow you."

He chuckled as he folded her arm within his. "I'm glad you believe so."

She tugged on his arm for a moment, causing him to stop in the doorway of the library. Her hand tightened around his arm, her eyes were filled with determination. "I don't *believe* so Braith, I *know* so. They'll follow you because they know strength when they see it, because they'll believe in you, and you'll win." He was awed and humbled by the amount of faith she had in him. She grinned at him, a smile that lit her face and caused her eyes to sparkle as she playfully bumped his hip. "Just don't let it go to your head when you become king."

He couldn't find the words to remind her that he had no intention of becoming king; he was too stunned. She turned away from him, her gaze darting toward the dining room that they had been meeting in. She squeezed his hand before reluctantly releasing it and nervously tucking the book under her arm. "You can do this Braith," she whispered.

He was pretty sure he could do just about anything if she was standing at his side. He wanted to reach for her again, wanted to pull her back against him, wanted to walk proudly into that room with her, but he knew he had already allowed too much to slip in front of Xavier.

Aria entered the room first and walked to her brother's side. William studied her before nodding to Braith. The others had already gathered around the table, the chair at the head was empty as it waited expectantly for him. Braith rested his fingers on the top of the table as he faced the powerful people whose help he desperately needed if they were going to have any shot of winning this war.

"You've all made your decisions?" he inquired.

"We have," Xavier confirmed as his dark eyes flickered briefly to Aria. Frustration filled Braith; his momentary loss of control in the hallway earlier had placed Aria in even greater peril. She met Xavier's inquisitive glance with a lift of her brows that somehow managed to make her appear even more innocent and unknowing. But Braith could see that Xavier didn't buy it, not for an instant.

"I'll fight with you," Xavier confirmed. "You've proven that you are capable enough to earn my allegiance, and I have never agreed with your father's policies. I believe yours will be more just." His eyes flickered briefly to Aria again.

Braith had to force himself not to look at her. "They will be," he assured him.

"I will also fight with you," Barnaby confirmed. Braith felt a momentary tug of apprehension, he still didn't know how to feel about Barnaby, but at least this time he was actually taking a stand instead of cowardly waiting until the end. Perhaps the past hundred years had actually changed him. Ashby made a slight face but remained silent. "I've been waiting for this moment for a very long time."

"I would like to confer with my people, but I believe they will agree to help." Saul folded his hands into the sleeves of his cloak, his head was bowed. He had always been tranquil, reserved, with an air of dignity that was enhanced by his seemingly vast years, even though he was almost two hundred years younger than Braith. "We've built a good home here, but we are well aware of the fact that it is tentative at best. The king still randomly sends search parties after us, there is no guarantee we will not be uncovered and ousted at some point. War offers no promises, no peace or stability, but the hope of a future filled with security will probably sway them, as will the chance to leave The Barrens and return to a home that most of us still miss."

"I was in even before we went after those creatures," Calista said. "I want my homeland back. We've established a good system here, but I'm sick of dust and heat and sand. I assume that those of us who join with you will also be rewarded."

"Your wealth will be returned to you. The Council will be established as the ruling body again, you will be returned to your seats upon it, you will have equal say within it and the majority will rule," Braith assured them.

"Even the humans?" Frank inquired.

Braith nodded. "What you have established here will be the model that the new rule will be based upon. Humans will rule with us, vampires and humans that do not follow the rules will be punished accordingly."

"And blood slaves?" Frank pressed.

Despite himself Braith felt his gaze flicker to Aria as she shifted uneasily. Though few people in this room knew she had once been his blood slave, it was still a touchy subject with her. "If we are successful, no human will *ever* be forced to be a blood slave again."

It was only the slight tremor of Aria's chin that hinted at any sign of distress from her. He couldn't take those days away from her, even if he could, he wouldn't. If she'd never been captured, if she'd never been brought to the palace as a slave, he never would have met her. He wouldn't be standing here right now and neither would she. She was in danger now, but her life up to this point had been nothing but danger. He hated it but for the first time he saw things from her perspective, for the first time he understood her total lack of fear toward anything.

She feared nothing because she had lived with the constant threat of death every day of her life, it remained the same now, but there was finally hope for her. Finally there was a light at the end of a tunnel that before had only been dark. She would do anything for that light, *anything*. She had been trying to tell him this, trying to make him understand that this was a battle she embraced wholeheartedly, enthusiastically, and with a determination that may even exceed his own, but he had been too stubborn to listen. He needed to give her more freedom or he would crush the beautiful spirit he had fallen in love with in the first place.

The thought of losing her was almost enough to drive him to his knees, but he realized he'd rather see her dead than destroyed by his inability to let her be who she was.

He almost took her hand, but thankfully he came to his senses before he did something careless. Her life may not be any more precarious now than it was before, but if he revealed his feelings for her any further, it would be.

He turned forcefully away from her as he focused on Frank once more. "You and David will have a say in how things are run afterward. You will both have seats on The Council to represent your people. If there are other human leaders amongst the rebels I'm sure David will bring them to my attention."

"There aren't any others," William informed him.

"The humans will have the same say as vampires?" Frank persisted.

"Yes, humans will have an equal say," Braith assured him.

"And a leader will also need to be appointed." Gideon's hazel eyes were turbulent as they met his.

"There isn't truly a need for a leader." Braith stared at Gideon, silently warning him to back off.

"There is always a need for a leader. A leader will have to carry out the results of any vote, and they will have to squash any inner squabbling. A leader will be needed to make sure that justice, *fair* justice is carried out. And everyone, people and vampire alike, will need someone to follow. There *is* a need for a leader, a strong one that can rule and see over what will be a difficult time of transition for everyone involved. They will be required to put an abrupt end to the uprisings I am sure will follow this overthrow, and to make sure that all traitorous persons are hunted down and dealt with appropriately.

"There is a need for a leader if what you envision, what we *all* envision, is to be successful. We will need the strongest among us to carry out this vision. Someone who is just and not simply seeking power, someone who knows how government and politics works, someone that is recognizable to *everyone,* as there are many of us that would not be known among the humans anymore. "

Braith was silent, astounded by the fervor of Gideon's speech, frightened by the sway he felt in those words. Aria gazed at Gideon for a long moment before turning to Braith. It was the pride gleaming from the bright depths of her beautiful eyes that caused his gut to clench. He knew what she expected of him, but if he rose to power she would never be accepted, never be welcomed at his side.

He would give up anything for this cause, except for her.

Beside her, William looked just as amazed as she did. His gaze moved from Gideon to Braith and then finally to his sister. An almost painful look crossed his face before he turned away.

"We should select a new leader, a new king so to speak, here, now, amongst the leaders that our people have elected to speak for them."

"Not all of them are here," Braith reminded them, unable to keep the aggravation from his voice as Gideon tried to railroad him.

"Either I, or William, can vote for our father, for now," Aria amended quickly. "I'm sure he would trust our judgment, and if he doesn't then he can have his say when we reunite."

He wanted to tell her no, that there would be no vote now, but the others were already nodding their agreement. A cold chill swept down his spine. He was not a coward, he had never shirked his responsibilities but he did not want this. Maybe he was getting ahead of himself though; they had not elected him yet. Gideon had just given a rousing speech that had swayed everyone in the room. After Braith, he was the most elder vampire within this room. They all knew Gideon well, had worked well with him over the past hundred years. All Braith had was his older age, his power, and his pedigree.

"I think that's fair," Xavier said. "They came as representatives for their father after all." His gaze fixated on Braith. "I'm sure he would respect their vote."

"He would," William confirmed.

"Jericho is also an option as a leader," Braith reminded them. "My brother has lived amongst David's rebel faction for the past six years. He is part of the royal bloodline, David's people trust him."

Saul chuckled as he shook his head and spread his hands before him. "I'm sure Jericho has matured greatly over the years Braith, but I do not believe he is up for this responsibility. Nor was he ever groomed for it. We represent our families now because most of our family members are dead. Barnaby's youngest cousin, and my sister, are the only others that survived the war, subsequent slaughter, and exile. Neither of them is prepared to lead, and neither is Jericho."

"That is yet another thing we can discuss when we're all united," Xavier said. "I'm sure that Jericho is not the boy we remember, and if there is to be true equality amongst us than we should consider him. *If* he wishes to be considered."

"Then we are in agreement, for the most part," Gideon asserted. "We'll vote now. Ashby?"

Ashby was pensive as his eyes flickered briefly between Aria and Braith before his shoulders slumped a little. "Braith started this, he has led us this far, united us, and defeated most of your enemies. He'll see us to the end; he'll take down his father. My vote is with him."

Braith remained silent, unmoving, his body becoming steadily colder as Gideon went through the room. He somehow managed to remain impassive and unflinching every time his name was said. William and Aria were second to last. They spoke briefly with each other before Aria quietly said his name. It was like a stake to his heart, she didn't know what she had just done.

"It seems as if we have had our first unanimous vote." There was no satisfaction in Gideon's tone. In fact he seemed resigned, saddened yet sturdy as he met Braith's gaze. "Will you accept the decision to run the form of government that *you* would like to see carried out in the future?"

Braith's jaw clenched, his teeth ground as he nodded. "I will."

He left out the words "for now" as he gave his response but they were there and Gideon and Ashby were well aware of it. He would lead them into this war, he would help to see them established, and then he would disappear with Aria leaving Jack or even Gideon in his place. They may be unsure of his little brother; to a certain degree so was he, but Jack would at the very least be a fair king.

"You have two days to gather your people. We'll move out on the third to rejoin with David."

"How will we find him?" Barnaby inquired.

Aria grinned. "Oh we'll find him."

The sinking feeling in Braith's stomach had nothing to do with his recent election, and everything to do with the unruly air suddenly surrounding her. He'd never inquired how Aria and William would find their father again; he'd simply assumed they had a way of relocating each other after all their years of moving and separating so often. He was beginning to realize he wasn't going to like the answer.

# CHAPTER 10

*Her* forest. She'd missed it so much, the sweet scent that filled her nostrils; the cool shade that hid the heat of the sun. The sounds of the animals were familiar and soothing. The tension in her body eased, her heart beat seemed to slow to match the melodious rhythm of the world around her. A rhythm that enveloped her within its comforting embrace, and held her close as she picked her way through the natural obstacles with the ease of an expert.

An ease that a lot of their group did not exhibit. Though their predatory vampire nature made them stealthier than most, they were not accustomed to the sticks, leaves and fallen debris that littered the forest floor. And they were obvious about it. Aria flinched at every snap of a twig or branch. She was doing a lot of flinching.

Braith finally stopped, his impatience was apparent as he turned to face the massive troops gathered behind them. Though most of the women had remained in The Barrens with the children or the elderly, there were a couple hundred of them mixed in amongst the men and looking just as ferocious and annoyed by their surroundings.

She was leading an army of deadly vampires, humans, and weaponry straight into the heart of her world. Aria swallowed the lump of trepidation that lodged in her throat. What they were doing went against everything she had ever known, ever fought against.

They were on *her* side, she reminded herself severely, but she still couldn't shake her lingering concerns. She had absolute trust and faith in Braith, in his ability to succeed, she had grown to like Ashby, had forged a small amount of trust in Gideon, and there was something about Xavier that intrigued her. But even so, she didn't really *know* these vampires, and she sure didn't know the thousands following behind them.

There were too many of them and she knew it. They couldn't continue on like this without being caught. *Her* people knew these woods, they moved through them with ease but this mass would never make it through unnoticed if they continued to stomp through the woods like a herd of elephants.

Braith seemed to sense this as he turned to her. "How long do you think it will be before you are able to find your father?"

"Stay here."

Braith lurched for her, but she was already scrambling up the closest tree. It was the only way she knew he wasn't going to be able stop her. She imagined it would be amusing to watch him attempt to chase her through the trees, but she doubted she'd ever get the chance. She wasn't at all surprised to see him following her as she leapt, jumped, ran, and swung easily from limb to limb.

Climbing steadily higher, she swiftly made her way up a small hill where she paused to skirt to the top of a large maple. She hoped she was near one of the areas she used to communicate with her father when they were separated, or that he had even moved through this region. There was a chance she'd have to go a couple miles to the west before finding another place that would help her. It could take days before she located one of his markers; she hoped that she would get lucky now.

"Arianna!" Even though the snarl had been low pitched it drifted up to her.

She didn't look down, she didn't have to. She knew his look of displeasure and annoyance well. The thinner branches bowed beneath her weight, but she'd done this since she was a child, she knew exactly how far she could go before the tree wouldn't support her weight. Pausing, she spread her legs, bracing her feet against two branches that bent to the side. Between the two of them she was able to distribute her weight without snapping them as she poked her head over the top of the leaves.

She moved slightly, adjusting so that she could see the forest from different angles. It spread out before her, an endless array of shimmering leaves, deep green conifers, and a spattering of red maple groves that added sporadic color to the landscape. For a brief moment she allowed herself to savor in the view.

Then she spotted it, a small glimmer halfway up a tree about two miles away. Her father didn't climb as high as she did, but he could also navigate the trees well. Smiling with satisfaction and relief, she was about to shimmy back down the tree when something to the right snapped her head around. Eyes narrowing, her hands dropped down to grab the two branches supporting her weight. She brought them sharply together, lifting herself higher and earning an angry hiss from Braith.

She didn't care though. She didn't even care that she was pushing her luck as she scooted another foot higher. Only about a mile away there was a movement in the woods that was not made by any animal, but she couldn't be certain if it was human, or something else, until a break in the trees revealed the group of men. Though they were too far away to discern much about them, they were all wearing the royal colors of the king.

Aria's heart leapt into her throat, panic flashed through her body as two of the men turned to scan the horizon. She didn't move, didn't even breathe. They turned in a complete circle, seemingly oblivious to the brim of her head over the tree as they bent to confer again.

They had more soldiers on their side right now, but if things went wrong, and one of the king's men happened to escape back to the palace, everything they had worked for would be ruined. They needed to stay hidden until Braith decided it was time to make their presence known. But that would be impossible with the herd following them.

With their attention distracted, Aria plunged rapidly out of the tree, dropping from branch to branch until she released the final limb and plummeted toward the ground. She would have been fine if she'd hit the ground, but she didn't mind at all when Braith's arms wrapped around her. He held her for a brief moment, cradling her within his embrace. She allowed herself to relax, to feel the strength of his body beneath her hand before he set her smoothly on her feet.

Ashby was gaping at her, his bright green eyes astonished as he looked from her to the top of the tree. Behind him Gideon and William were watching her anxiously. "Dad?" asked William.

"That way, about two miles there's a marker." Taking a steadying breath, she turned and pointed to the west. "That way about a mile, are the king's men."

Braith's hand stilled in the hollow of her back, his eyebrows drew sharply together over the bridge of his nose as his nostrils flared. "Are you certain?" Gideon asked.

"They're wearing his colors."

"What are we going to do?" Ashby demanded.

"There are caves." William inhaled sharply at her words, his eyes darted uncertainly toward her. She stared hard at her brother, understanding his trepidation and hesitance. But it was too late for that, they had brought these vampires into their world, there was no turning back now. William looked hesitant for a moment more before he nodded. "Less than a mile from here. They're large enough to hold everyone but with so many it will be cramped."

"They're not going to like being forced into those caves." Aria started in surprise as Xavier separated from the shadows of the trees. She hadn't seen him standing there, but Braith seemed to have known as he didn't react to Xavier's sudden appearance. She was even more surprised when Braith didn't remove his hand from her back, didn't separate himself from her. A tremor of trepidation shuddered down her spine as Xavier pinned her with his dark, knowing eyes.

"They knew this wasn't going to be an easy undertaking," Gideon stated. "That there would be sacrifices when we left. This will be one of those sacrifices. It's painfully obvious that we cannot move them all through here, this hasn't been their environment in a hundred years, and some have never experienced it."

"These caves will be safe?" Braith inquired.

Aria forced herself not to shudder at the thought of the darkness, the confining space, the chill that came with the underground hollows she had grown to hate after nearly being trapped in a separate system with William and Max. "All the cave systems have iron gates, some sort of alarm, and traps in them," William explained. "Though there is no way to know if they have been discovered since we left."

"I don't think we have a choice," Ashby said.

Braith was silent as he pondered the situation. "Neither do I. Gideon and William go back to round them up, try to get them to be a little quieter if it's possible. Don't engage with my father's troops, but if it becomes necessary make sure there are *no* survivors. Xavier, Ashby, Aria and I will go to the caves and make sure they are safe."

Aria remained silent, she didn't want to go to the caves, didn't want to step foot in them but she had no choice. "Go," Braith commanded. Gideon nodded and slipped silently into the woods with William. "Get us there quickly Aria."

She swallowed heavily and nodded firmly. "Follow me."

*** 

Braith followed silently behind Aria as she led them with an ease that was fascinating. She was quiet, far more so than Xavier as she moved like a wraith through the trees. She covered the distance to the caves in less than ten minutes. Standing at the edge of the woods he studied the cliff face twenty feet away that appeared entirely impenetrable to him.

"That's them," she stated.

"Where?" Xavier inquired in disbelief.

Her jaw clenched, there was a darkening of her eyes that only he would have recognized as fear. The last time she'd been in the caves, he had taken her from them. Just when he thought she was going to balk against telling them exactly where the caves were, she slipped silently from the woods.

They followed her, fanning out around her as she knelt before the rock wall. Her head tilted as she examined a cropping of bushes against the rock wall with an intensity that was a little unnerving given the fact it was simply a group of ferns and wild scrub. Then her small hands slid forward and parted the brush to reveal a sliver in the rock wall that was nearly indiscernible even without the brush covering it.

"No one has been here in months."

"How do you know?" Xavier asked her.

Her smile was fleeting. "I know."

Ashby looked about ready to protest but Xavier simply nodded. "Lead the way then."

"I'll lead the way," Braith told her. Xavier quirked an eyebrow at him, his head tilted to the side.

"I know the system Braith. Its fine, I'm certain no one has been here, at least not through this entrance, and the only other one is two miles from here."

"But there could still be someone in there," he asserted, pressing closer to her.

She shook her head as her eyes darted to the opening and then back to him. "It's unlikely. The other opening is in a meadow at the top of a hill. If it's even spotted, it appears to be more of a foxhole than an entrance to anything significant underground. There's no one in there Braith."

"Except bats," Ashby muttered not looking at all pleased by the notion.

"I'm still going before you." She opened her mouth to protest further but he cut her off. "You can guide me through Aria. Tell me which way to go."

"Ok," she agreed; her voice a little tighter than normal.

Her fingers brushed over his, before they wrapped around his index finger for a brief moment. His heart swelled with love. To hell with Xavier, it was too late anyway. He pulled her into him, cradling her as his fingers splayed across the back of her neck, savoring in the silken feel of her hair, and the suppleness of her body. Bending low, he pressed his lips to her ear. "Will you be ok in there?"

She nodded, her head turned toward his, her mouth brushed enticingly against his as she spoke. "Yes."

"We can find…" he started before she cut him off.

"I'll be fine."

Her hand flattened against him, a small exhalation escaped her as she closed her eyes and pressed closer to him. Time seemed to slow as she lifted her face to him, and her lips parted beneath his. He didn't care who was there with them, forgot about the reason that had driven them here as he lost himself to the soft pressure of her lips, the sweet taste of her mouth, and the quickening of her heartbeat.

For one long moment the only thing that existed was her, and then reality returned. It took everything he had to pull away. He pressed his lips to her forehead as he held her for a lingering moment. "I'll lead the way," he whispered.

She relented with a nod before she reluctantly released him. She didn't meet Xavier's gaze, but Braith did. Xavier's eyes were hooded with a gleam in them that Braith couldn't quite place. The wheels in Xavier's mind were turning, but it was impossible to decipher what it was the powerful vamp was thinking as he examined the two of them. It would only cause friction among the factions, but he would kill Xavier if he made one move toward Aria.

Taking hold of her hand, he turned sideways in order to fit through the small crevice in the face of the rock wall. For a moment he wasn't sure he would fit as he pushed himself further along. "It's cramped for the first hundred feet or so, but it opens up in a little bit." Aria seemed to have read his mind.

Ashby grunted in response, Xavier remained silent in the back. Aria's hand trembled in his, her palm was sweatier than normal but she forged steadfastly on behind him. Relief filled him when the walls released their grasp. Even with his enhanced night vision he had to strain to see the pathway before him as almost no light penetrated the thick rock walls.

"Wait." Aria released his hand suddenly. He grabbed for her as she moved forward, intending to pull her back, but she returned to his side almost immediately. "Hold this."

She thrust the handle of a torch into his hand and fumbled into the darkness for something else. He spotted what she was searching for and pulled the box of matches from a small hole tucked into a crevice of the cave. They huddled together as she fumbled with the matches and finally struck a spark. A small flicker of light played over the contours of her face before she pressed the flame to the end of the torch.

Fire blazed forth as she grinned at him. "Lead on."

The torch lit the dusty cobwebs of the tunnel and the solid rock floor beneath them. The air became mustier and colder the deeper they moved into the cave system. The faint drip drop of water could be heard in the distance, condensation coated the rocks around them. Aria's grip on him increased. Aria pointed out gates hidden secretly into the walls, heavy iron gates that could be swung shut in order to keep out invaders.

"No wonder the king couldn't squash the rebellion! You live like rats beneath the earth," said Ashby.

Braith halted as Aria stopped abruptly and turned to face Ashby. "We did what was necessary, what we were *forced* to do," she grated. "And we don't always live within the caves; most of the time we live within the woods and only resort to the caves when it becomes necessary."

Ashby chuckled quietly. He reached for her shoulder, glancing quickly at Braith he thought better of it and dropped his hand back to his side. "Easy tiger, I was just making a comment. Don't forget I was forced out too."

Aria stared at him for a long moment before Braith tugged gently on her arm, pulling her forward as even Xavier began to smirk with amusement. Braith had to admit that though Ashby had gone about saying it the wrong way, he completely agreed with him. The hidden nooks and security systems they had set into place down here were amazing. Though most of the tunnels were natural, there were manmade ones running throughout the cave system also. She'd said there was only one other exit, and he believed her. She wouldn't put them all at risk by lying about that, but there was far more to this cave system than she was revealing. Especially when she shut some of the iron doors while leaving others open.

"Do you know all of the cave systems?" Xavier inquired in his deep timbered voice.

"Not all of them, there are far too many for that, but a fair amount of them. We're almost to the center of the cave now."

Braith could sense an opening ahead even before he stepped into the massive cavern. "Bats," Ashby griped with a shudder as Braith's eyes landed upon the rodents lining the ceiling. He'd started to smell them awhile back, but the smell was worse within the large cavern. He didn't bother to look down; he knew the floor was coated with guano.

The thought of staying here repulsed him, the fact that she had grown up among these caves disturbed him immensely.

No wonder she preferred the trees.

# CHAPTER 11

"You know, for an immortal vampire you're a bit of a wimp," Aria informed Ashby.

He flashed his dashing smile as he grinned. "I never said I wasn't."

As quietly as possible, so as not to wake the sleeping creature's, she closed three of the five gates. "They'll go out tonight." She pointed to the fourth gate. "That's the way out, when they leave to feed we'll lock it down and they won't be able to get back in."

"We're not staying here, are we?" Ashby inquired worriedly.

Aria shook her head. "No, we are not savages; we don't like the smell of guano any more than you do."

Braith squeezed her shoulder soothingly. "No one is saying that," he assured her.

Aria took a deep breath, trying to keep her control. It wasn't only their scrutiny and blatant revulsion that had her so wound up, but also the confining walls surrounding her. "I know," she said. "We always leave one of the larger caverns blocked off so the bats can't get inside. This way."

Her nose wrinkled in disgust at the pungent aroma of the bat droppings as she picked her way over it, moving steadily toward the fourth gate. It had already been closed off. "I'll go," Braith was moving toward her but she held up her hand and shook her head.

"No Braith, I have to go through this time. Its booby trapped and I know where the triggers are." A low grumble of displeasure escaped him as he moved to intercept her. She'd already prepared herself for this argument. "I helped Daniel design a good portion of them, believe me it is far safer for me in there than you."

"Aria…"

"Stop being so stubborn," she interrupted. "Besides, at this point in time, your life is far more valuable than mine."

She realized immediately that had been the completely wrong thing to say. He seized hold of her, lifting her as he thrust his face into hers. The gentle man from outside was gone, before her was the vampire prince that was used to being obeyed and expected it from everyone, except for maybe her. "Don't you ever say that again!" he snapped so loudly that Ashby's gaze darted nervously to the top of the cave. "Your life is every bit as important as mine, if not more so…"

"Braith," she whispered. "You must lower your voice."

"Do you think I care about a bunch of flying rodents?"

"If they leave their perch they'll leave this cave. They'll attract attention Braith, you must calm down." She touched his arm lightly, looking to soothe him. "I know these caves Braith, I'll be fine."

His jaw clenched, his head bowed as he pressed his forehead against hers. "Your life is just as important. Without you, I'm nothing."

Her gaze darted nervously toward Xavier; Braith had just revealed too much, she knew it. A surge of protectiveness shot through her, her hands squeezed around Braith's arms as she stared fiercely at the dark vampire, daring him to say something, to do anything that would hurt Braith. She would be nearly useless against the powerful older vamp, but she would do everything she could to keep Braith safe.

"It's ok," he whispered against her ear. "It's too late anyway."

Aria shuddered, it was too late, their secret had been revealed to Xavier, and if they continued on it wouldn't be long before it was obvious to everyone. Terror coiled through her belly, it spread out to her limbs, leaving a trail of cold across her skin and within her muscles.

She pressed closer to him as her hands grasped at his flesh. She needed the physical contact like a drowning man needed air. A low sigh of relief escaped as her fingers encircled the thick steel of his arms. Beneath the wiry hair of his forearms his skin was smooth to the touch. It eased the tension within her.

She forced herself to release him as she took a small step away. "I can do this, I know the traps well. I'll be fine."

His eyes closed, she sensed his inner struggle, she braced herself for more of a battle but then his shoulders slumped and she knew she'd won. "I'm going to be right by your side."

She went to turn away but he pulled her back to him. He tenderly clasped hold of her face, cradling it with an ease that belied the power that radiated from him. He could crush her in an instant, yet he held her with the gentleness of someone who had just been handed the most fragile flower in the world. His lips were a light caress against hers, so faint that she barely felt the brush of them.

"Just as important, and don't you ever forget that, don't you *ever* say something like that again."

She swallowed heavily and managed a small nod. "I won't," she promised.

He continued to hold her, seemingly torn and unwilling to let her go. Finally he stepped back and released her. She felt a sense of loss that she couldn't shake. She didn't look at Xavier as she turned away from Braith and moved toward the closed fourth gate.

"How do you get it open?" Ashby's voice was hushed. She turned toward him, startled by the paleness of his skin that she didn't think was entirely due to the bats. His lips were pinched; his eyes shadowed and haunted as his gaze darted nervously away from hers.

"I have my secrets, and talents," she answered with a small wave of her fingers, hoping to coax his cocky smile back. He remained uncharacteristically solemn.

"That's for sure."

She frowned at Xavier as she studied him. She thought he had spoken those words, but she couldn't be certain. She took the torch from Braith as she ran her fingers over the wall. She found the tiny switch set back into the wall and pressed against it.

The thick metal door popped open with a hiss of stale air. It smelled even danker and mustier in there, but it didn't stop her as she pressed her hand against the solid iron door and pushed it the rest of the way open. "Ingenious," Ashby muttered.

Aria gulped as she stepped into the dark tunnel. It was ten steps to the first trap, a set of four stones set into the floor that when stepped on would fire a rapid release of stakes from the cave walls. "Should we shut this?" Xavier inquired.

"Yes. William knows how to open it and we all know Ashby won't appreciate it if a bat gets in."

"You got that right."

"There are four stones here." She pointed them out. "Don't step on them."

"What happens if we do?" Xavier inquired.

"Nothing good. I'll be right back." She had to set the traps off, she knew that. William was well aware of their location, but there was no way that all of those troops weren't going to hit at least one of them. "Stay here."

She could feel the apprehension radiating from Braith. "These traps are old…"

"Not that old, and Daniel is a genius, believe me they're still safe to maneuver through."

She could tell that he didn't want her to go but he fisted his hands at his sides, locked his jaw and managed to give her a brief nod to continue. Aria placed the torch into a socket in the wall; she would not need it on the other side. She moved through the tunnel, avoiding the stones with ease. Reaching the safety of the solid rock, she knelt as her fingers sought out the small switch carved into the bottom of the cave and set about six inches back from the bottom.

"Move back," she told them.

Braith hesitated for a moment before pushing Xavier and Ashby back. When she was certain they were well out of the way she flipped the switch. Stakes exploded from the wall in a puff of dust and air that made it impossible to see the three of them on the other side. Ashby and Xavier cursed loudly.

"Aria!" Braith shouted.

"I'm fine," she assured him. He was gradually coming back into view as the dust began to settle. Though most of the stakes littered the ground, some had embedded themselves into the crevices of the rock wall. Ashby was gawking as he searched the scattered stakes; even Xavier's normally calm exterior seemed ruffled. "It's safe now."

Though Xavier and Ashby hesitated, Braith strode rapidly forward. His displeasure was evident, his tension high as his arm wrapped around her waist. "How many more of these traps are there?" Xavier inquired as he and Ashby picked their way carefully through the stakes.

"Ten."

"Crap," Ashby muttered.

"I can dismantle them all, don't worry."

Xavier's dark eyes were intense as he studied her. "You helped the man that designed these?"

"I had a hand in some of it, but for the most part he created them."

"Is this Daniel someone in your family?"

Aria wasn't surprised by Xavier's acute insight but she still didn't like it. "Yes, my brother."

He nodded for a brief moment; his eyes darted over the cave walls. "That little talent will come in handy."

"It will," Braith agreed. "How far until the next one?"

"Thirty feet."

"Lead the way."

Aria sighed in relief as he remained resigned to let her do what was necessary.

# CHAPTER 12

It took almost two painstaking hours but eventually Aria was able to dismantle all of the traps. She was exhausted and on edge by the time they finally made their way into another large cavern that was entirely bat free; a fact that Ashby commented happily upon. The torchlight played over the dark recesses as Aria made her way around, gathering other torches from their sconces in the wall.

"This tunnel will lead back into the main exit." She took hold of Braith's hand, running it over the wall until she found the switch. "This will open the gate when pressed."

Xavier and Ashby pressed closer, they murmured between each other as Ashby held the torch high to inspect the area she had just shown Braith. Aria left the three of them to marvel over the intricacies within the caves.

Her throat was dry and her clothes stuck to her as she made her way to the supply room at the end of another tunnel. There was another gate here but the key for it hung beside the door. There was no need to keep humans from taking what they might require. Grasping the key she lifted the light, frowning as she realized that the gate was unlocked. They never left the supply rooms open just in case an animal managed to get this far.

She grasped hold of the iron bars and pulled the gate open as she lifted the torch high. A set of wild and crazed pale blue eyes blazed out at her. A startled gasp escaped as she took a hasty step back. It was a man, of that much she was certain, but she wasn't sure exactly what kind of a man it was anymore. His skin was abnormally pale; he seemed unaccustomed to light as he blinked rapidly against the flame of the torch.

Revulsion filled her as his lips skimmed back to reveal a mouth riddled by missing gaps and rotten teeth. The torch slipped from her suddenly numbed fingers as the man leapt from the bags of stored grain. He seemed more animal than human as he rushed at her. Stunned, it took Aria a moment to realize that she was in jeopardy, that this person, this *thing* had every intention of attacking her.

A startled cry escaped her, she grasped hold of the gate and heaved it with every ounce of strength she had. It was too late though. The man slammed into the gate, ripping it from her grasp as he shoved it back open. Aria swung her fist up, connecting forcefully with his jaw, snapping his head to the side as he launched at her. Hands skimmed down her body, grasping and pulling as he tried to secure his hold on her.

She realized her mistake too late. So attuned to having to defend her throat, her blood, her life, Aria had not been prepared for a different sort of hunger. It wasn't until the frenzied man ripped her shirt open that she realized she was in a situation unlike any she'd ever been in before.

Taken aback by the ferocity of the attack, and his intentions, Aria was momentarily unable to defend herself. Then his hands were on her, over her, pushing and pulling at the skin exposed by her torn shirt. Reason returned as adrenaline doused her terror. She shoved at the man, turning her face away from the putrid smell of his breath. A scream built in her chest, rose up her throat, and erupted in a squeak that was cut off as the man succeeded in pressing his mouth to hers.

She almost vomited as his thick tongue shoved against her compressed lips. With a fresh surge of strength, she lifted her knee and drove it into his balls. The man squealed, his grip on her momentarily relaxed enough that she was able to throw herself to the side, nearly succeeding in ripping free of his grasp. It was the sharp right hook she delivered to his cheek that finally knocked his hold upon her loose. She staggered back, trying to keep her balance as she spun around and started to run.

She was almost to the end of the tunnel when his arms encircled her waist. The air rushed out of her as they fell to the ground in a tumbled heap that knocked the wind from her and skinned her knees and elbows. He was clawing his way up her back when the air rushed back into her lungs. Flipping beneath him, she swung at him again, shattering his nose.

He squealed, falling back as blood spurted forth. Aria crab crawled backward, trying to regain her feet as the man leveled her with a glare that was not only lustful but also murderous. A roar of fury suddenly reverberated throughout the massive cavern.

The man's head snapped up, his eyes widened. Aria hadn't been sure there was much reason left to him, but apparently his survival instinct was still intact as he reeled backward. She was well aware of just how terrifying Braith could be, just how deadly and inhuman, and all of that was being honed in on the man before her. The man leapt up, a wild cry escaping him as he raced down the tunnel.

Aria scooted away, clinging to her shredded shirt as she tried uselessly to cover herself up. Braith raced past her, barely a blur as the loud clang of metal echoed through the cave. The man had succeeded in retreating into the storage room and slamming the door shut. "Are you ok?" Ashby demanded as he fell beside her.

She wasn't frightened of Ashby, but when he reached for her, she shied away from him. "I wouldn't," Xavier cautioned.

Ashby looked torn and horrified as his eyes skimmed over her. "Fine," she managed to breathe as she clung to her shirt. "I'm fine, really."

Aria's attention was distracted from Ashby as a loud wrenching sound filled the cave. Xavier stepped forward as Braith ripped the gate from the walls of the cave. The gate was solid steel, without bars to prevent rodents from entering the storage room. The only hole in it had been a slit near the top to allow some air to flow through the room. Aria didn't know how Braith had managed to wrench the heavy door free. The door flew down the tunnel, causing Xavier to dart out of the way as it bounced rapidly off the rock walls, nearly taking him out in the process.

Xavier's mouth dropped, his gaze darted wildly to the door now lying at the opening of the tunnel. Aria knew it weighed a good five hundred pounds and it had taken seven men to get it in place. Xavier stared at Aria for a moment before turning to Ashby.

"I told you he could take the king," Ashby murmured so faintly that Aria wasn't even certain she'd heard him right.

Xavier's gaze came back to her as she tried to lurch to her feet. Inhuman squeals echoed from the storage room as Braith disappeared inside. "Wait no!" she cried, falling back against the tunnel wall as a wave of dizziness rocked her.

Ashby grasped her shoulders to steady her but she shrugged him off as silence suddenly enshrouded the tunnel. Horror pooled in Aria, her hand fell against the wall helping to keep her up as Braith emerged from the storage room. She knew the sudden silence had not been because he was injured, but relief still filled her.

The man was dead. She didn't have to ask, she knew Braith would not leave him alive. She thought she should be more upset, she wasn't. What had been in that room had no longer been a man, there had been no saving him.

Braith was before her suddenly. She did not shrink from him, did not shy away from his frantic, yet tender touch. "Are you ok?" he demanded, his voice hoarse and raw.

"Yes."

His hands moved steadily lower, stopping at the tattered remains of her shirt. "Get out of here!" he snarled at Ashby and Xavier.

They stood for a brief moment before slipping out of the tunnel. His hands trembled as he tugged the pieces from her hand and pulled them apart. He was stiff before her, barely moving as he gazed upon her. While in the palace she had been forced to wear some of the silliest and most uncomfortable undergarments she had ever seen in her life. Once free of the palace she had resumed her habit of wearing an undershirt, sometimes a slip.

The slip she wore now had also been torn, but unlike the ruined shirt it was still intact enough to cover her breasts. It was nearly see through, even in the dim light of the tunnel, and especially to the acute vision of a vampire but she wasn't embarrassed. Her breath froze, her heart hammered as he remained still as stone before her.

"You're bleeding."

The words were grated through his teeth. And then, before she knew what was happening, he lowered his head to the scratch marks on her chest. His warm mouth made her heart lurch and his tongue against her skin caused her entire body to simmer with pleasure. Her fingers curled into his hair, holding him close as he licked the cuts on her chest.

He pulled reluctantly away, embracing her as he kissed her neck, her ear, and finally her lips. The brush of his lips against hers made her forget the hideous assault of the pitiful man. The touch of his lips made everything that was so arduous and wrong in their lives, worth it.

"They'll heal faster now," he whispered against her mouth.

"What will?" she inquired, still dazed and adrift in the feelings he aroused in her.

His fingers were subtle, a mere butterfly caress against her raw flesh. "Your wounds."

Aria shuddered at the reminder. Braith could make her forget almost anything but now that she wasn't overwhelmed by his touch, the events of the past five minutes crashed back over her. His fingers wrapped around the back of her head as he pulled her to him. "Are you sure that you're ok?" he asked worriedly. She nodded, unable to form words as her fingers dug into his back.

"I'm fine Braith, I swear; a little shaken, but fine."

He rocked her soothingly, his cheek resting against her head as he swayed her back and forth. "Braith." A low growl of displeasure escaped Braith as Ashby appeared at the end of the tunnel. Ashby was undeterred by it though. "They're here Braith."

A regretful sound escaped him. "Ok."

"I brought a shirt." Ashby didn't come into the tunnel though; instead he threw it to Braith before turning away.

Braith grasped hold of her ruined shirt, his fingers quivered as he slid it from her shoulders. He tossed it aside and helped her shrug on the new one. Braith slid the buttons into place; his hands hesitated upon the last one as he lifted his head to hers.

"You're beautiful."

It wasn't true, but he made her feel every inch as beautiful as he thought she was. She managed a wan smile as her fingers encircled his. "I love you."

It was his time to smile now, it lit his face like a beacon and made her heart melt. It was magnificent, his smile, breathtaking even. "I love you too."

And even though the troops had invaded the cave, he gave her one last, lingering kiss.

***

"Did you ever, in a million years think that we would be sitting in one of *our* cave systems surrounded by vampires?"

Aria cocked her head as she turned to look at her brother. The firelight played over his features, harder and more masculine than hers, but similar all the same. "No," she admitted with a low laugh.

"Do you think they'll eat us?"

"It's a possibility," she joked.

William chuckled, but she sensed the tension beneath the laughter. He still wasn't entirely certain about this situation, or the vampires and humans surrounding them. "We've come a long way sis."

"We have," she agreed. William's hand was suddenly holding hers. She looked at him in surprise. They were closer than most siblings, always had been, but it had been years since they had held hands. It appeared he was as troubled as she was. She squeezed his hand with both of hers and relaxed against his shoulder.

They stood at the edge of the circle that had been formed around the fire within the center of the cave. It was still summer above, but down here it was cool and damp.

She watched as Braith stood with his head bowed while he conferred with the other faction leaders. The firelight played off of his hair, highlighting his handsome features and broad shoulders. He was nodding as Gideon spoke in quick, hushed whispers that were accentuated by the constant flutter of his hands. Braith's arms folded over his chest, he leaned briefly back on his heels and though she couldn't see it, she felt it when his eyes landed on her.

Her hand constricted around William's. "I'm afraid." It was the first time she had said the words out loud, the first time she had admitted it, even to herself.

"I know. So am I."

Tears bloomed in her eyes as she turned to her twin. She'd never expected such an admission from him. "Not of dying," she whispered.

"No shit," he retorted.

She couldn't help but laugh as their hands began to swing back and forth like they had as children. "You're not either."

"Never have been."

"Then what is it we're so afraid of?" She was asking because she didn't know. She knew she was scared of losing Braith, of losing this war, of losing any member of her family, but those were worries she'd always had, or that she'd learned to deal with since meeting Braith. This was something different, it was in the pit of her stomach, it was buried in the back of her mind at all times, festering like an infected lesion.

William was thoughtful before he answered. "The unknown…"

The hesitation in his words made it clear he wasn't entirely certain about his answer, but the minute she heard it Aria knew he was right. They had struggled with death and loss; starvation and thirst; dirt and homelessness their entire lives, but they had always had some sense of knowing. They'd had their father, Daniel, the other rebels, the caves, the woods, and the knowledge that vampires were the enemy to be fought and destroyed. Now they were on their own, surrounded by what had once been the enemy, in a cave system Aria had grown to hate, and filled with nothing but uncertainty.

"Yes," she agreed. "The unknown."

"It's not the same now."

"And it never will be again."

"Do you want it to be?" he asked.

"Sometimes."

"And other times?"

"I wouldn't change a thing," she admitted. "Not one thing."

"Because of him?"

"Yes, but also because of the hope that the unknown brings us now, because of the promise of something better for everyone. No matter how much we knew before, the outcome was always the same. If we were lucky we would grow older, if we weren't then we died young."

"Or became blood slaves."

"Yes." She did not shy away from it anymore. "You're not still angry at him because of that, are you?"

William hesitated for a moment before he shook his head. "No. If it hadn't happened then we wouldn't be here."

"Afraid?"

His smile was small and fleeting. "Afraid, and full of hope," he responded with a twinkle in his bright blue eyes.

Aria's gaze locked on Braith as she recalled their encounter in the hallway of that dilapidated house. She had one more thing to fear, what would become of them? Of her?

She knew Braith planned to leave when this was over, knew that the vampires would not accept her if she stayed. But he couldn't leave. They had voted him in for a reason, and even if he didn't see it, or *refused* to see it, it was obvious to everyone else that he was a born leader. He'd done some things he was not proud of, he'd hurt innocents, and he'd been a monster for a brief time, but at heart he was good, and he would do right by as many people and vampires as he could.

He may not intend to be the leader, but he already was, even if he didn't see that, *she* did and so did everyone else in this room.

Their hands stopped swinging as Braith beckoned them forward. William squeezed her hand before releasing her. "How long do you think it will be before you can find your father?" Braith inquired.

"Aria can usually track him within a few days," William answered.

"I don't know how far into the forest he has gone though and if there are a bunch of us..."

"There will not be," Braith inserted briskly.

She was beginning to realize that there was more to his clipped tones than trying to appear distanced from her. Something had aggravated him. "That will make things easier. Even if he's gone into regions that we've never explored, I can find him in a week."

"Are you certain of this?" he asked.

"Two, tops."

"Which is it?" Barnaby inquired sharply.

Aria's gaze darted nervously to him. "I think she's already answered that question," Ashby told him. "The longest it will take her is two weeks."

"So that means it could be almost a month before you return. And if there is a large group of them, even longer," Calista replied coldly.

"We were raised in these woods, we know them well. A group of us is far easier to move than you think. It will *not* be a month," Aria said firmly.

"Even if it is a month Calista, you will survive. It's not the most ideal situation but we knew it wasn't going to be easy," Braith informed her.

Calista shifted, her dark eyes narrowed for a brief moment before she gave a quick nod. "We can make do and the human knows the caves." Aria's head snapped around, a small gasp escaped her. There were only two humans here who knew this cave, and she didn't want either one of them staying here. Braith shifted slightly and she suddenly understood the tension in him, the terseness of his words. William didn't know how to track their father as well as she did, he wasn't a big fan of the trees, and he wouldn't be as quick as she would. William glanced anxiously at her; she seized hold of his hand again. "He'll come in handy for getting us out of here if it becomes necessary."

Aria was finding it difficult to breathe. She could feel Braith's gaze boring into her, pleading with her to understand, to do this, to not fight over being separated from her brother, *again*. She tried to be strong but she was terrified of leaving William with a bunch of vampires.

Everything in her body screamed against it. The other humans were used to the vampires surrounding them, she and William were not. The rigidity in her brother made it clear that he wasn't too pleased by the idea either, though she didn't know if it was because he was staying, or because she was going.

She swallowed the heavy lump in her throat. "Who will be going with me?" she inquired with far more strength than she felt.

"Ashby, Gideon, and I." Braith's voice was still cold but some of the strain had eased from it.

"I plan to go also," Xavier informed him.

Braith showed no surprise at his statement, but Aria felt a flicker of it deep in her belly. "Fine," Braith grated. "William will be staying behind with the others to help keep order, and to help find food if it becomes necessary. If they're forced to abandon these caves will you be able to find each other again?"

"Yes," Aria answered.

"Then we leave at nightfall."

Aria knew he didn't mean to be harsh, but that knowledge did little to ease the knot of sorrow in her chest. She craved his comfort more than anything but she reluctantly accepted that he couldn't give it to her right now, maybe not ever.

"Are you ok with this?" she asked William when the others turned away from them, shutting them out again.

"I'd be more ok if I was going with you, but it doesn't seem we have a choice."

"No, it doesn't."

# CHAPTER 13

After eight days Aria was exhausted, aching and feeling a little disheartened. She was also in desperate need of a blessed shower, or at the very least a bath. Her hair was a matted mess she wasn't certain she'd ever be able to untangle, and she had more mosquito bites than hairs on her head. She loved her woods but despised this area of hell they had wandered into.

She'd never ventured into the swamplands before, and she couldn't believe her father had chosen this part of the forest to take refuge in. She would like nothing more than to find him and escape as quickly as possible from this land of muck and filth. Her feet were blistered and her shoes hadn't been dry in three days. Yet they trudged endlessly onward through acres of dirty water. Ashby had given up complaining, but Gideon had taken to muttering about how he wished he killed humans. Xavier remained blessedly silent, though he grimaced often.

She could handle the mud and dirt, it wouldn't last forever, and she'd been filthy plenty of times in her life, but the smell… The *smell* was enough to make her want to vomit, and it had definitely induced more than her fair share of gagging. She couldn't get away from it and it twisted her stomach in ways that she had never thought possible. But then again, that could also be the incessant hunger that was tearing at her. She'd only planned on seven days of supplies; she had realized three days ago she should probably start rationing her food. She was growing increasingly hungry and she was beginning to agree with Gideon's craving to kill something.

Braith was becoming steadily agitated. Then again, they were all becoming short tempered and frustrated. He'd carried her more than a few times but she didn't want to seem weak in front of the other three, so she insisted upon walking most of the time.

The suction from the thick mud caused her feet to make a loud popping sound as she stepped onto solid ground. A dying pine lifted its branches to the fading light and she tilted her head back to peer into it. Light refracted off of something within the branches. Heaving a tired breath, Aria's shoulders slumped wearily.

Braith grabbed hold of her arm as she grasped the scratchy bottom limb. "Are you ok to do this?" he demanded gruffly. She managed a small nod and a smile. "I'll go…"

"It won't hold your weight and you don't know what to look for once you're up there."

"Something shiny."

"Yeah, something shiny," she agreed tiredly. "Which none of us will see if the tree collapses beneath your weight."

Thankfully, despite his foul mood, reason prevailed as he released her arm. She was slower getting up the tree, the blisters on her feet along with her weighted clothing and shoes made it difficult to move as freely as she normally did. Her hand curled around the piece of tin hanging from a thin line. She lifted herself further up, bracing herself as she stared over the treetops. Relief shot through her as she spotted the next marker only a mile away.

Pulling the piece of tin free, she made her way sluggishly back down the tree. "About another mile."

"How long is this going to continue?" Gideon demanded.

Aria shrugged as she wiped the matted hair from her forehead. "I don't know. Hopefully we'll get there soon."

Her head was beginning to pound, her stomach rumbled. Braith cursed as he pulled her pack from his back and tugged it open. Rummaging inside he pulled out her meager assortment of supplies. He shoved some dried meat, a canister of water, and a bag of nuts into her hands.

"Eat."

Saliva rushed into her mouth, the rumbling in her stomach increased. Her hands were shaking. "I have to ration the supplies, I can't eat…"

"I'll find you more food."

The swamp was vast and imposing but so far they hadn't encountered much wildlife, and there were few plants she was certain she could eat as she was unfamiliar with this area. She'd seen what could happen to a person when they ate something they shouldn't, and though they had survived it, they'd been sick for a week. Besides, she wasn't the only one going hungry right now.

"Braith…"

His hands enfolded hers, holding her tight. "Eat." She strived to stick to what she knew was right.

In the end, hunger won out. Shaking a little she broke off a piece of meat and lifted it to her mouth. Braith's shoulders fell in relief. "We'll make camp here for the night."

Aria watched as the four of them moved around, establishing a small camp. She wiped the salt from her fingers and took a sip of lukewarm water. They conferred with each other, but Aria wasn't paying much attention as she chewed on the nuts, savoring each bite as she tried to make them last.

"I'll be back."

Aria blinked up at Braith in surprise. "Back?"

"I'm going to search for some food. Ashby and Gideon will stay with you. You'll be safe."

"I know."

Kissing her tenderly, his fingers lingered briefly on her cheek before he reluctantly released her. She munched on the rest of her nuts as she watched Xavier and Braith head back into the swamp. There weren't as many places here to hide and find shelter, but they soon disappeared from view behind some high grass and rotten trees.

Finishing off her nuts Aria wiped her hands on her filthy pants and turned her attention to the pack Braith had left behind. She didn't speak with Ashby or Gideon as she pulled out a pair of lightweight pants that were dirty, but nowhere near as dirty as the ones she wore now. "I'll be back."

They didn't try to stop her as she slipped away in search of a place that would offer her at least a little privacy. She found a spot behind a drooping willow with its branches dangling into the water of the swamp. She cleaned the muck from her filthy pants before slipping her other pants back on. Remaining blessedly barefoot she made her way back to the camp with water to boil.

Gideon and Ashby were sitting by the pine; Gideon was leaning tiredly against it as he watched her from under hooded eyes. Ashby looked haggard, even when he had been exiled to a life of solitude and deprivation he'd never had to endure this kind of hardship. He was not prepared for it, and it was more than apparent that he didn't like it. Making a small fire, she heated the water and retreated back to the willow to wash her body the best she could before returning.

Aria settled onto the blanket. She didn't think she'd ever been this bone weary and exhausted. She meant to stay awake until Braith returned but when she laid down on the blanket, exhaustion won out. It was dark when she woke again. Braith's arms tensed around her as she attempted to sit up.

A sigh of relief escaped her as she rolled onto her back. She didn't know when he'd returned but he was nestled against her, his broad chest pressed against her side, his arms wrapped around her. The numerous stars were bright in the vast night sky. She'd never seen anything like it before. The trees blocked the stars in the forest, the light reflected them in the palace, and she hadn't bothered to take the time to look while in the desert.

Now she stared up at them, awed and fascinated by the seemingly endless sky. "Shouldn't you be asleep?"

"It's beautiful," she breathed.

He remained unmoving for a long moment before turning onto his back also. His fingers found hers, entwining firmly as he pulled her against him. "It is."

She rested her head on his chest, unable to take her eyes from the sky as the moon began to poke its head over the horizon. It was nearly full and the color of blood. Aria shuddered; it seemed a bad omen to her. Braith ran his hand nimbly up and down her spine, causing goose bumps to appear on her skin as he pushed the edge of her shirt up and his fingers found bare skin.

Her eyes drifted closed as pleasure swamped her. She pushed at the edge of his shirt, eager to feel his own bare skin beneath her touch as she melded against him. Her hand splayed against his firm stomach and she was suddenly consumed with the need to feel more as she stroked over the solid flesh of his chest.

His mouth was soft, tender against her cheek, then her ear, and finally her lips. Heat spread through her, she couldn't hear anything over the rush of blood in her ears. He pushed her back, leveling himself unhurriedly over her as he pressed her into the spongy ground. He clasped hold of her face as he kissed her with a reverence that left her breathless.

She couldn't think straight. He encompassed all of her senses as his hand enclosed her breast. A gasp escaped, something inside of her seemed to snap as her fingers dug into his firm back and she pressed closer to him. She was lost in a sea of need. He was so strong and powerful and yet he touched her with a tenderness that was humbling and shook her to her very core.

His arm wrapped around her waist, he lifted her as he pulled her against him, and leveled himself more firmly between her legs. The buttons of her shirt had come undone; he bent to press tender kisses against her chest. His dark hair blended in with the night surrounding them, but the light of the moon highlighted the planes of his face. She couldn't get enough of watching him as he moved over her. She dimly thought that perhaps she should stop this, they'd never gone this far, but then she realized she didn't want to. She wanted this; she wanted *him*, more than she had ever wanted anything in her life.

He was back over her, his mouth claiming hers as she shook and trembled, and clung to him as pleasure swamped her. Heat flooded her; she was unfamiliar with the sensations coursing through her body as she grasped his solid biceps and tried to keep from completely falling apart. Everything was right in his arms. Right now, in this moment, there was no fear but only the love they shared.

And then Gideon released a snort. Braith froze above her, his mouth stilled upon hers as his head slowly came up. His bright gray eyes latched onto hers, burning with excitement and frustration. She was torn between longing to continue, and the reality that they were not alone.

In the end, it was Braith that made the decision. His hands trembled as he buttoned her pants and shirt back into place. A sense of loss filled her as he moved off of her. A muscle ticked in his cheek as he pulled her against his side, pressing a gentle kiss to her temple as he lay next to her.

"I lost my head; I shouldn't have let it go so far. I tend to lose myself in you."

She thrilled at the admission. "I wish it had gone farther," she confessed.

He chuckled as he nuzzled her hair. "Do you know the constellations?" She shook her head as she turned her attention to the brilliant sky above them. She struggled to ignore the yearning that still thrummed through her body, but a deep ache remained. "That one, with the three stars at the end, and the four grouped together like a cup is the Big Dipper." Aria settled against him, comforted by the deep timbre of his voice as he pointed out the different constellations.

*\*\**

"Dad!" Aria squealed in delight as she raced across the clearing to the man standing in the middle of it. David's face came alive with pleasure; his smile lit his features as he braced himself for the impact of her body. He grasped hold of his daughter, laughing happily as he enfolded her in a big hug and spun her around.

Braith warily eyed the people surrounding them as he made his way forward. He wanted to grab Aria from her father, pull her back, nestle her at his side where she belonged, but he fought the urge as her father placed her down and cradled her cheeks with the palm of his hands. The humans studied him, shifting uncomfortably as they whispered among themselves. These were not the humans of The Barrens. These humans had been abused and terrorized by vampires. They knew only fear toward his kind.

"Are you ok?" Aria's father demanded.

"I'm fine," she replied with a brilliant grin that eased the knot in Braith's chest. He wanted her back, but her happiness was far more important at the moment.

"Where's William?" David asked worriedly when he realized his youngest son was not present.

"It was too tricky to move everyone through the forest, immortal or no, they're unbelievably loud," she informed him with a mischievous smile. "William stayed in the caves with them." David's hands tensed briefly on her face. "He'll be fine dad, I promise. We've been with them for awhile now."

Her father's gaze flickered toward him. Braith knew David disapproved of their relationship but he didn't care. The man was not going to tear them apart. "I see."

"Hellion!"

She released her father as her brother Daniel broke free of the crowd. "Daniel!"

She was laughing as she threw herself into his arms. Braith bristled, his fingers twitched as his jaw clenched. It was her *brother*, he reminded himself fiercely. Even so, it took everything he had not to pull her away from the slender man hugging her. Unlike his siblings, Daniel's hair was wheat colored but while he didn't share their coloring, he did have the same bright blue eyes that William and Aria possessed.

"Dear Lord you stink!" Daniel blurted.

Aria laughed loudly as she took a step back from him. "We've been wandering through swampland for the past three days."

"That would do it," Daniel agreed.

"I'm sure you're eager to clean up." Though her father said the words to her, his gaze was intent upon Braith.

"Very much so," Ashby agreed.

There was a shifting among the humans, and then Max stepped forward. Anger swelled through Braith. Hope spread over Aria's face and lit her eyes as she took a small step toward him. Max held her gaze for a weighted moment before he turned and disappeared into the crowd.

Aria's shoulders slumped as despair settled over her. No matter how much he didn't want her near Max, he hated to see her upset in any way. He would like to shake some sense into the selfish bastard, wanted to kill Max for making that crestfallen look appear on her face. Daniel watched him warily as Braith stepped forward, his arm brushing against hers as he offered as much comfort as he could right now. Aria turned to him; tears burned briefly in her eyes before she blinked them back and forced a smile.

"Perhaps we can go somewhere a little more private," Braith suggested.

"Yes, of course," Daniel said. "This is one of the few areas in the swamps that aren't just water and mud. It's not very hospitable but there are some homes here and we've erected temporary shelters."

The crowd parted as Aria's father led them down the street of the small town they had taken residence in. David led them into the ramshackle remains of a small house. Braith watched Aria carefully as she picked her way over some broken boards. He was braced to grab her if they happened to give out. David stopped to speak with a few younger men before leading them into what remained of the living room.

"Is there a lake around here?" Aria asked.

"Yes, but I've instructed them to heat water for a bath." Her face lit, joy spread over her as she looked eagerly at Braith. "For all of you." Braith felt almost as excited as she looked. "I thought you would prefer to talk after you were clean."

"I sure would," Ashby agreed eagerly as Jack entered the room. "Look at what the cat drug in!"

Jack's nose wrinkled. "I'd say the cat mauled you and hauled you through sewage from the smell and look of the five of you."

"And feel."

Jack grinned; he grasped Braith's hand firmly as he clapped him on the arm. "Good to see you brother."

"You also." Jack released him; his smile grew as his gaze raked Gideon's miserable, filthy form. "Well now, this is a pleasant treat."

"Wish I could say the same," Gideon retorted.

Jack laughed loudly as he shook Gideon's hand and then Xavier's. "Long time no see."

Xavier simply bowed his head briefly in response. Braith stood stiffly, immobile as he watched three young men carry in five separate wooden tubs. It took almost a half an hour before enough water was brought in to fill them. Aria remained by her brother and father, the brilliant smile never left her face as they talked.

"Go on," David urged her when the last of the water was brought in.

Braith was aware of the fact that four of the tubs had been taken into one room, while the other had been kept separate. Aria looked at him as he took a step toward her. "Wait," David said sharply.

Braith's hands fisted at his side. He could control his need to pull her away from them but he wasn't going to leave her alone and vulnerable while she bathed. He didn't trust most of these people, and he definitely didn't trust Max. The boy was lurking around here somewhere and he'd almost killed her once.

"Not alone," Braith growled.

David looked as if the top of his head was going to blow off. Braith stepped closer to her, pressing against her arm. "Its fine dad," Aria assured him. "It's not what you think. He won't even be in the room."

"She's not going in there alone."

"Aria is perfectly capable of taking care of herself!" David snapped.

"I know she is, and she's also perfectly capable of getting herself into trouble." Aria shot Daniel a dark look as he guffawed loudly. "I don't trust these people. I don't trust *Max*. Whether you like it or not, she is not going in there without me to stand guard."

"Braith!" Aria hissed as her father's eyes narrowed in rage.

"Who the hell do you think you are!?" David demanded.

"Hers." The simple, startling answer knocked some of the anger from David. Daniel's mouth dropped as Ashby shook his head. Xavier watched intently and Gideon simply strolled out of the room toward the other tubs. Jack dropped his head into his hands and began to massage his temples. "And she is mine." He touched her arm gently, nudging her toward the backroom. She hesitated, seemingly torn as she gazed from him to her father and back again.

David didn't protest anymore, but his jaw was clenched in displeasure as his gaze bored into Braith's back. The room they had brought the tub into was small with a single window in the back. Braith closed the shutters, locking them into place before turning back to her. Steam rose from the tub, a small sliver of soap had been set on the floor on top of some towels and clean clothes.

"A little diplomacy goes a long way," she murmured.

"They have to understand…"

"He's my father Braith. I know you don't understand what that means, not in the same way that I do, but he loves me. I'm his little girl. This is hard for him, it's hard for Daniel and William, but it's especially hard for my father." She was right, he didn't understand that. "You need to be nicer, and more patient." She tilted her head, peering up at him as she smiled faintly. "Do you think you can do that?"

He grasped hold of the collar of her shirt and pulled her closer. "I can try, for you."

"Just for me?"

He grinned. "I sure wouldn't do it for anyone else."

She laughed as he began to slide the buttons of her shirt free. He slipped it from her shoulders and tugged it from her arms. He touched her shoulders briefly and turned away before he couldn't. He listened as the rest of her clothes fell away before she slid into the tub with a groan of pleasure. It was excruciating torture. His teeth grated, he stepped into the doorway, leaning against it as he fought the urge to turn around and go back in there.

His body was so taught with strain from not looking that he didn't know she had approached until he felt her fingers slip between his own. He relished the supple feel of her skin against his as he pulled her against his chest and held her close.

# CHAPTER 14

She was sound asleep in his lap, her hand curled against his chest, her head resting in the hollow of his shoulder as she breathed in and out. As she slept, the tension of the day faded from her features making her appear even younger, more vulnerable, which only made him worry for her more. Max hadn't appeared again since he'd rebuked her earlier and Braith hoped that he never did.

Daniel was talking quietly, pointing at some of the designs and drawings he had created. "These are all of your cave systems?" Gideon inquired.

"Not all of them," David answered. "These are the ones closest to the palace. We had others, but some have been lost to cave-ins, and others are too far from the palace to be of any use."

"Are there often people within them?" Ashby inquired, glancing nervously at Braith.

"What do you mean?"

"The cave system where the troops are hiding had a man inside of it."

"That's not unusual, many know about the caves and the food supply," David told him.

"It looked like he'd been there for awhile."

"I suppose some may stay below hoping to avoid the king's troops. It's why we retreated into the swamplands. The king's raids have become more frequent and aggressive since you left the palace." Braith held David's steady gaze. "The man in the cave, what did he do?"

"He attacked Aria," Braith growled.

David's eyes widened, he leaned forward on the table. Braith lowered his head and inhaled her sweet scent. The soap she'd been given smelled of honey. Beneath it he could smell the faint hint of his blood as it flowed through her veins. She was the most enticing thing he'd ever smelled, and he needed her soothing effect right now.

"Why would he do that?" David inquired.

Ashby glanced nervously at Braith, but seemed satisfied that he would remain calm while holding Aria. "Apparently he hadn't seen a woman in awhile."

"Did he harm her?" Daniel demanded.

"He tried, but she's fine."

"And what of the man?" David inquired.

"Dead," Braith said unremorsefully. "Anyone that injures her will meet the same fate."

David sat back as he studied them. "What exactly is it that you intend for my daughter? What do you think you can give her?"

"Anything she desires."

Gideon and Ashby shifted nervously, well aware that this conversation was drifting into treacherous waters. Xavier leaned forward, his dark eyes eager as he absorbed the discussion. "I can see that she loves you, and though it's baffling and astonishing to me, I think you love her too. But I don't see how any of this can work. Will your people accept her? Do you have plans to make her a vampire?" David nearly choked on the word vampire but somehow managed to get it out. It was apparent the man found the thought abhorrent.

"Most do not survive the change; I have no intention of inflicting that upon her." Gideon, Jack and Ashby winced, Xavier quirked an eyebrow as he gazed at Aria.

David's frustration was nearly palpable. "Then what do you intend? To watch her grow old and die? To have her be an outcast among your people? Tell me Braith, what will you do when she dies?"

"I'll find a way to die also," he said simply.

Gideon groaned as he shook his head, dropping it into his hands. Ashby closed his eyes as Jack folded his arms over his chest and sat back in his chair. Xavier remained unmoving, he'd known there was a bond between them but he hadn't known the extent of that bond until now.

"But you have been voted the leader; your people will follow you…"

"Or Jack," he interrupted sharply. Despite his every intention not to, he found himself leaning forward as he met David's incredulous gaze, and Jack's completely aghast one. "I will lead them into battle, I will lead you *all* into battle, but I have not hidden the fact that I do not intend to lead afterward. Not unless Aria is at my side. I will stay long enough for whatever leader you elect to settle in, and then she and I will leave. I will not expose her to a life of unhappiness."

"I don't want it," Jack blurted.

"Neither do I," Braith snarled in frustration. "I never have, but I accepted it, and I *did* it. I've done my duty for the past nine hundred years, I've done everything expected of me and I will continue to do it until this is over, but someone else can step up afterward."

"It will be difficult on her, to grow old while you don't," David told him.

"I know that."

"You could let her go." Braith stiffened as fury ripped through him. Aria's fingers slipped beneath the buttons of his shirt to press against his flesh in an attempt to soothe him. They had woken her. "It would be best, for both of you, for everyone involved if you let her go."

"It's too late for that." He had managed to regain enough control to answer without smashing the table before him.

"I don't understand why. I know it will be tough, the last thing I want is to see my daughter unhappy, but she'll be hurt no matter what. There's no way to stop that now."

Her heartbeat had increased; the scent of her fear assailed him. "Ashby can explain it to you," he said bluntly. Aria gasped as he rose abruptly from his chair. Staying here was only going to annoy him further and he had promised her that he would try to be nicer. "Does it matter what room we take?"

David's jaw dropped. Aria's lashes flickered against his neck as she opened her eyes, he could feel the heat of her skin against his neck. He bit back a groan, he didn't understand these human customs, or perhaps they were simply *family* customs, but he was becoming increasingly frustrated with them.

"I'll sleep on the floor," he grated, hoping that would help to ease some of the tension that filled the room. He swore that once this whole mess was over he was going to build her a house that no one else would ever be invited to.

"Third room on the right, there's a small cot in there," David responded in a choked voice.

"I'll get you some blankets," Daniel volunteered.

"You can put me down Braith."

He held her for a moment longer before lowering her feet to the floor. She hurried to her father, pecked him on the cheek and gave him a hug. Braith was fascinated by the look of love on David's face as she spoke with him. He'd certainly never seen it on his own father's face. David patted her arm reassuringly as she kissed him again and rejoined Braith.

"I would like to retire also." Xavier rose to his feet, his fingers rested briefly on the table as he surveyed the room. "I am aware of the baffling vampire bond referred to as a bloodlink. I assume that is what Ashby will speak of as I am well aware of his relationship with Braith's sister, and not the one he married."

Apprehension flashed briefly across Aria's face, but she remained immobile at Braith's side. She didn't trust Xavier, not yet. Braith wasn't even certain he completely trusted him yet. "How do you know about that?" Ashby demanded, his carefree demeanor vanishing at the mention of Melinda.

Xavier moved away from the table. "My job in the palace was to pay attention, to record the histories, to take note of things and see the things that no one else saw. I'm not blind Ashby, the two of you tried to hide it and you succeeded with most." His gaze was pointed on Braith. "But not me."

Ashby looked wary. His eyes were hooded as he studied Xavier with annoyance and distrust. "Ease up Ashby, I never told anyone that you were having an affair with the youngest daughter while still married to the oldest."

"Watch what you say Xavier," Ashby's tone was low, deadly.

Xavier didn't look the least bit phased by Ashby. Braith pulled Aria back a step as Xavier stopped beside her. "But a human." He shook his head, something flickered in his eyes as he studied her. "That is unheard of." Aria's eyes narrowed, her chin tilted defiantly. Xavier smiled at her in amusement. "Quite a conundrum."

"I'm not Ashby. War or no war, followers or no followers, I will kill you if you touch her. Remember that Xavier, I am a *real* threat to you."

"I am well aware of that fact Braith. I have no ill intentions toward her."

Braith was not appeased by the words. He pulled Aria further back as Xavier stepped closer to her. "Don't," he snarled thrusting himself in between them.

Xavier held his hands up as he took a step back. "Easy Braith, I said that I would not hurt her, and I meant it. I've seen what you are capable of when it comes to her, and I have a feeling that cave was only the tip of the iceberg. We need her if we are to win this war."

"And after?"

"After will be up to you, and her. Now, where are those blankets, I'm exhausted."

Aria pressed closer to Braith's side, he stood for a moment, trembling with suppressed anger and uncertainty. Xavier had always been a little odd, or at least he had always seemed that way as he stood in the shadows calmly watching everything. He suspected Xavier knew more than he was letting on as he stared curiously at Aria, but exactly what his secrets were, Braith couldn't even begin to guess at.

"Uh, this way," Daniel awkwardly interrupted.

He stepped back as Xavier moved past him to the stairwell. "Are these things going to hold me?" Xavier pondered as he eyed the stairs.

"Yes."

Daniel led them upstairs, handed out blankets and hugged his sister goodnight. Braith wasn't pleased to see that the room really did hold just a tiny cot shoved against the wall. He wasn't even certain Aria would fit on it as he spread the blanket out.

"Xavier is strange."

Braith sat on the edge of the cot and pulled her into his lap. She wrapped her arms around his waist as she rested her head against his chest. "He is," Braith agreed, lightly rubbing her back.

"He's baffling but I don't think he would harm me. I think he's just as confused by me as I am by him."

He was glad she thought so, but Braith wasn't convinced that Xavier wouldn't do something. Xavier had never been power hungry before, but there was no way to know what was going on inside of his head, or any of the others they had aligned with.

"I'm glad you're not scared of him."

He felt her smile against his neck. "I'm not scared of anyone," she said laughingly.

He would have laughed too if it wasn't so true. For someone so frighteningly mortal, she was strangely unafraid of anyone or anything. It was terrifying. "I know."

"Don't get all bristly." She sought to calm him as she caressed him. "You must be hungry."

"I'm fine."

"You're stubborn."

"As are you."

She was grinning as she tilted her head back to look at him. "Yes, but it's been awhile, I'll be fine Braith."

He dropped his head to hers. "I know, I just…"

Her fingers were against his lips, and then her mouth replaced her fingers. "There is no, "I just", not now. I crave the connection Braith, just as much as you crave my blood. I want to feel you inside me." He shuddered at her choice of words, his arms constricted around her. A low groan escaped him. He would never get over how swiftly and easily she could unravel his composure. "I would love to satisfy you in every way, but with everyone in this house, especially my father…"

"I understand," he grated through clenched teeth. "Not here, not on this cot, and not with your family surrounding us. Not for you Arianna. I want better for you, it *will* be better."

When he opened his eyes to look at her, he was surprised to find her watching him with a look of absolute love that nearly shattered him. She unwrapped her arms from his waist and deliberately pulled the hair back from her neck. Marks from his other feeding were still visible upon her porcelain skin. He pulled her shirt down to reveal the nearly invisible marks from the first time he'd fed from her. His fingers brushed over it as she pressed against him, her breasts firm against his chest.

"Do you remember this?" His voice was tense.

"How could I forget?"

"I almost killed you that night."

"Braith…"

"Yet you continue to give yourself to me."

"I love you."

"Is it so simple then?"

"Yes. This is not an easy life."

It wasn't, but he hadn't once wished that he was back in that hideous palace with its vast supply of blood and every imaginable luxury. He would wade through a thousand swamps before he ever let her go again. "And I wouldn't change a thing," he whispered against her cheek.

"Why?"

"Because I love you."

"Is it so simple then?"

He smiled back at her. "Yes."

"Good."

She silently guided his head to her neck. His fingers slid up the back of her shirt to press flat against the slender curve of her back. A faint whimper escaped her, goose bumps broke out across her skin. He bypassed the marks on her neck to rest his lips gently against the first bite he had placed upon her; the first time he had marked her as his.

She moaned when he bit into her, reopening the wounds that had bound them irrevocably to each other. She slumped against him as the rest of the world faded away.

# CHAPTER 15

Aria looked up from the shirt she had been sewing as Jack stepped into the room. She hated sewing, she'd stabbed herself numerous times already, but she needed the shirt. She swore as she jabbed herself again and stuck her wounded finger in her mouth.

Jack quirked an eyebrow at her. "You're not very good at that."

"I know," she mumbled. He rocked back on his heels as he folded his hands behind him. She frowned as she dropped the shirt down. "What's wrong?"

"I need to speak with you."

"Ok."

"Not here. Take a walk with me?"

She wasn't sure why he would want to take a walk, there was no one around. "Uh yeah, sure."

Placing the shirt on top of the table, she climbed to her feet and followed him as he led the way out of the house. Braith had gone with Gideon, Xavier, her father, and Daniel to meet with the rebels her father had gathered to fight, to look over the supplies they'd accrued, and to do some hunting. Aria had opted to stay behind, she was tired, and she thought that perhaps it would be a chance for Braith to bond with her family. He hadn't liked it in the beginning, but Jack and Ashby had agreed to stay behind.

Ashby was standing by the woods when they emerged from the house. Remorse radiated from his eyes as he fell into step beside them. She glanced between the two of them, suddenly feeling very small and vulnerable. Why hadn't she grabbed her bow? She shook off the crazy thought. This was Jack and Ashby, they wouldn't hurt her.

"What's going on?" Neither of them answered her. Aria became aware of the pounding of her pulse in her ears. "Jack?" She was ashamed of the tremor in her voice.

"Just going for a walk Aria, we have to talk."

"About what?" He didn't answer her. She stopped abruptly, refusing to take one more step until she received some answers. "About what?" she demanded.

"The lake is just ahead, ok?"

Aria bristled at his placating tone. She almost refused to move further, almost turned around and walked away. She was certain she didn't want to hear what they had to say. She knew she couldn't run away though. "Fine," she relented.

Aria fell back as Jack led the way to a pristine lake. She stood for a moment, taking in the scene before her as it spread out in a glimmering array of sunshine and blue. Something inside of her chest eased, she took a deep breath, inhaling the fresh scent of the crisp water. Forgetting all about Jack and Ashby, she took a step closer to the water. She itched to dive into it, to swim out as far as she could and simply *be*.

The clearing of Jack's throat alerted her to the fact that was not going to happen. Sighing impatiently, Aria turned to him. "What do you want to talk to me about?"

Jack and Ashby exchanged a look, but it was Jack that spoke. "Braith."

Aria folded her arms over her chest as she studied them both. Ashby could barely meet her gaze; his eyes darted continuously away from her as if he were ashamed. There was a hollow pit in her stomach; it felt as if a rock had settled in there. She could barely breathe anymore. No, she definitely was not going to like this. "Perhaps you should talk to *him* then."

"I've tried, and so have Ashby, and Gideon. He needs to lead Aria."

Her heart hammered, coldness was seeping into her bones, stealing into her soul. "He does," she agreed.

Jack shifted nervously. "You know I love you Aria, I think of you like a sister."

"Just say it Jack."

"You have to let him go." She felt as if she'd been punched in the gut. She had braced herself for those words, had even suspected they were coming, but they still knocked the air from her. She was unable to stay upright as she rested her hand on a tree and leaned against it. "Aria…"

She held up a hand to stall him. She needed a moment, just one moment to gather her thoughts and hold back her tears. She'd suspected all along, no she'd *known*, that this was a distinct possibility. That in the end, she would have to give him up, that she would have to leave him, *again*. She just wasn't ready to hear it confirmed by someone else.

Ashby, looking to soothe her reached for her shoulder. She pushed his hand away, unable to take his pity at the moment. "Braith feels that when this is over he can simply walk away. That he can take you, disappear, and never look back. He thinks that he can leave Gideon, Ashby, or even I in charge. We know that he can't, and I think you know it too."

Aria lifted her head. She had to blink away the tears burning her eyes to focus upon him. "Our family line is the strongest, it always has been. Our bloodline has been traced back to *the* first vampire, it is the only line that can claim such a feat, and actually prove that it's true. It wasn't often that our line wasn't ruling, and as you've witnessed, even the most powerful vampires on our side have turned to Braith as a leader."

She stared silently at the lake, felt the rough bark of the tree beneath her hand. She needed these things to connect her, to join her to the earth. She felt completely disconnected right now, disjointed and broken. "Since the moment he was born it was expected that Braith would rise to power if our father died. He's been groomed for such an endeavor, trained for it; he *is* the one that can control the chaos that will follow the dethroning of our father. Even those within the palace, the non-aristocrats will follow him, because that's what they expected to do for the past nine hundred years. *Nine hundred years* Aria, that is how long it has been accepted that Braith would eventually rule.

"They won't follow me in the same way, and to be honest I can't control them the way that Braith will be able to. It's not in me, it never has been. They will look to destroy me in a way that they will not look to destroy Braith. Nor will they follow Ashby. He's not a part of our line and even if he marries Melinda, they will not accept him, and Melinda isn't strong enough to rule. Gideon is Braith's other option. But Gideon has been gone for a hundred years, and he has no tie to our line. He's not even a part of the second most powerful family, he is simply older than the rest of us, only a mere fifty years younger than Braith."

They spoke of fifty years as if it were nothing; to her it was a lifetime. "Xavier? Saul?" she managed to choke out. "Calista or Barnaby?"

"Xavier is a record keeper; he prefers to loiter in the shadows. Most see Saul as weak due to his defect, and the others are mere children. The oldest is Barnaby and he's barely three hundred. They can't take control."

"The second most powerful…"

"My mother's line," Jack said flatly. "My father had all of them destroyed in order to ensure they would no longer be a threat. He also decimated the third, fourth, and sixth in line. He eradicated any one he deemed a possible threat."

"The fifth?"

"Gideon." The lump in her throat was threatening to choke her. "Ashby is part of the seventh, as is his cousin who has remained in the palace. He has stepped into what should have been Ashby's role, assuming power as my father's second in command."

Ashby scowled, showing some emotion other than pity for the first time. "Coward," he muttered.

"I'm sure Braith understands this," she whispered.

"He does understand it," Jack confirmed. "But to him, *you* are the only thing that matters. He's stubborn Aria, he thinks that the vampire lines will accept one of us in place of him, as will the people, but he's wrong."

She didn't realize she was crying until a drop landed upon her hand. She wiped the tears hastily away, hating herself for crying in front of them. "We can't convince him to let you go, and we can't convince him to try and change you. Our people might accept you then; it's a rare feat for a human to survive the change. They may not embrace you with open arms after, but they won't deny you either, and the ones that did would be few.

"He is unwilling to realize these facts, but you need to." A sob escaped her. She shoved her fist into her mouth, trying to stifle her cries as something inside of her began to break. "It's for the greater good Aria. Think of the people, *your* people that will be freed. The future generations that will never know the fear and oppression that you have known. Think of the fact that they will not know starvation, filth, and enslavement as you have known it; as Max has known it."

Max, oh Max. His time as a blood slave had destroyed him. It had taken a proud, vibrant man and turned him into someone filled with hate and bitterness. It had broken him, as it had broken so many others before they were mercifully destroyed. Then there were the ones that never made it to blood slave status. She recalled the boy she'd been captured with, so young and vulnerable. He'd been selected for death.

"Oh." Her legs gave out; she slid limply to the forest floor. "Oh."

"He believes that he can make everything alright in the end. It's not possible Aria." Jack's tone had become softer, she could hear the ragged pain in it, but it was nothing compared to the anguish savaging her soul. "We need for you to agree to leave him when this war is over."

She knew it was the right thing to do, she knew it was the best thing for everyone involved, even if it destroyed her and Braith. But even so, hope blazed hotly through her as she realized something. "But that's not possible!" she blurted. "He can track me anywhere, his blood is in me; we are bound in that way. Ashby said I'm his bloodlink, that we can't live without each other."

"You have started the bond, but it's not complete, is it?"

"No, but…"

"As long as you don't allow it to be completely forged there is a chance that the bloodlink will not destroy either of you. As for his blood in your system, we're hoping that if you don't accept it again his blood will thin out and eventually leave your system."

"I was gone from the palace for over a month and he still found me."

Jack and Ashby exchanged a look. "We think that if another vampire's blood is added to your system, most likely mine, it may dilute his enough so that he won't be able to track you for long, if at all."

She recoiled; revulsion filled her, nausea surged up her throat at the mere thought. She was shaking her head no when Jack bent and grabbed hold of her shoulders. "Aria…"

"He'll die without me," she groaned. She didn't add she would die without him, she was dying now, and though she would continue to move through her days, she knew she would never live again, not without him.

"Maybe not, if the bond isn't completely forged."

The noise that escaped her was guttural. "He went berserk when I left him last time."

"We hope that having so many lives in his hands will help to keep him in control. He didn't have that responsibility before. No matter how upset and furious he is, we're hoping that the good in him will win out because of that."

"That's a lot of hoping."

"It's all we have, and one day, you will die Aria. Your death may sever whatever bond remains between you at the time, freeing him."

Freeing her also, she realized as she bent over, her arms wrapping around her stomach. "He will be blind again."

"He will, but he was blind for a hundred years before you, it never slowed him down. The world was dark to him, but it was not a weakness for him. Ashby, Melinda, Gideon, and many others will be there to protect him."

She almost laughed at the mention of Ashby, the one who had blinded him to begin with, but there was no humor in her. It was all too awful to even remotely be funny. "I know this is a lot to ask of you Aria, I know that you are young and in love, but…"

"Stop," she whispered.

Ashby clasped hold of her hands as he knelt before her. She almost jerked away from him, but the tears in his bright green eyes held her immobile. He was actually crying, not for himself, but for *her*. "Jack doesn't understand what you're going through; I know that, *you* know that, but *I* understand. I couldn't do this; I couldn't let Melinda go if someone asked me to. She is everything to me. No matter what they did to me it didn't matter as long as she was safe, and alive. I am so unbelievably sorry, I cannot…" his words broke off as tears slid down his cheeks. "I cannot imagine and I do not *want* to imagine your pain or his. It's not fair, I know."

His tears were her undoing. She wept as she fell against him, finding no solace in his arms. There would never be any comfort again. She was unable to regain control as Ashby rocked her, his tears mingling with her own. Jack stood away from them with his shoulders set stiffly, and his jaw locked as he stared into the dense forest.

Gradually, her sobs started to subside simply because there was no water left inside her to shed. Ashby continued to hold her, but he didn't pretend that anything he offered would do her any good. Braith's sense of rightness would prevail, she was sure of it. He may become irrational and explosive when she left, but she had faith that his good would win out in the end.

"There's more Aria." She could barely lift her head to look at Jack, never mind hear more of what he had to say. "He can't know about this. You have to act normal around him."

Horror filled her. "You mean we're not leaving now?"

"No. He'll tear these woods apart looking for you rather than fight. You can't leave until the war is over and he's been established as the leader. He has to realize he has a duty to thousands upon thousands rather than just himself and you."

"My family?" she whispered.

"Your father will be informed of our intentions when the time is right, he will not be able to leave though." So she would never see him again either. She'd thought she didn't have any more tears left in her. She was wrong as agony clenched at her. "Daniel will also have to remain behind as your father's second in command and most likely successor, but I think William will go with you."

She nodded in agreement. Yes, William would come with her, even if she told him to stay and enjoy the life that he was going to fight for, he would come with her. "And I think he should, even if you don't. I will also be going with you."

Aria blinked at him in surprise. "You can't leave him, Jack."

"I can't leave you either, not unprotected…"

"William…"

"You will need more than just William. Braith *is* going to look for you and we will have to get far from him as fast as we can. I'm asking this of you, and I will follow it through with you."

"And return after I'm dead?"

Jack shook his head. "No, I will never return. Even if time and distance ease his suffering and rage, he will still kill me if I return."

Aria bit on her lip, her head bowed, she felt as if she were being crushed. She couldn't find the right words, not anymore. Ashby rubbed her hair in an awkward attempt to soothe her further.

"I know it's going to be difficult Aria but you have to act normal around him." She blinked up at Jack; her lashes were sticky from the tears coating them. "If he suspects anything he'll take you and he'll never look back."

"I don't know how I'm going to do that."

"I know this is a lot to ask of you, I understand that I can't fathom what you are going through, what you will have to endure, but you are one of the strongest people I know, human or vampire, and I *know* that you can do this. I have absolute faith in you."

She was glad someone did, because she sure didn't. Not about this. How on earth was she going to act normal around Braith? How was she going to hide her misery and pretend that everything was fine, when her heart was shattering and her body was already aching with loss? How was she going to look him in the eye knowing that she was going to break his heart by leaving him again?

He would never forgive her. Even if it was for the best, even if it was for the good of so many, he would never get over her abandonment of him again. He would hate her. That realization was even worse than their time together coming to an end.

"He'll never forgive me either," she whispered, giving voice to her thoughts. "What if you're wrong? What if he loses it completely?"

"Then we'll deal with the consequences of that when it happens. Whether we bring you back or he steps down…"

"People could be killed before then."

"I don't think he'll go that route again Aria. Last time he was confused. He didn't know what was going on inside himself and his pride wouldn't let him go after you. This time he'll know, and once he calms down he'll understand that this is for the best. You'll leave him a note..."

"A note," she laughed humorlessly, as if that would be enough. As if a simple piece of paper would be enough to convey her regret over leaving him. How could she put her sorrow into words? How could she possibly write down how much faith she has in him or how she knows that he will be the best leader for all those depending on him? She didn't think they had enough paper for that. Even worse, Jack would have to write it for her.

"And he'll come to realize that though it's not fair, it *is* for the best. For everyone."

"Maybe they would accept me," she whispered.

"I'm sorry Aria," Ashby squeezed her shoulders, pulling her against him. "But that will never happen. Saul and Barnaby have already inquired about your relationship. Braith believes he can keep the true nature of your relationship from them, but they will eventually figure it out. They're on our side for now, but human and vampire bloodlines are not to be mixed, the children are shunned if they are human, tormented if they're not..."

"Children?"

"It never ends well for them Aria," Jack told her.

"There have been *children*?" she demanded stunned by this revelation.

"Yes, though if it is a blood slave carrying the child, she is usually killed before she can give birth." Horror shuddered through her body, her hand instinctively rested on her stomach. "The vampire children that have been created are relegated to a life nearly as bad as the human servants within the palace. I wouldn't be surprised if there aren't a good number of half-breed vampire children amongst the troops in that cave; a lot of them left soon after my father took over."

"Children," Aria breathed awed by the possibility. She had never given much thought to children, she'd assumed she probably wouldn't live long enough to have them, and she certainly didn't want them exposed to the hardships of her life. She hadn't thought a child with Braith was even a possibility, but now...

Jack knelt before her. "You *cannot* allow your relationship to progress Aria."

Everything inside her shriveled up like a plant without water. Fresh tears fell. It had all been right there in front of her: happiness, security, a family. And now it was gone, all of it, just gone. She felt empty.

Jack took hold of her cheeks, cradling them. "I'm sorry. I know this is a lot to ask of you, and this *isn't* fair, you deserve a happy ending, you both do, but..."

She grasped hold of his hands, squeezing them firmly as she leaned toward him. "But so do many others... I know... I get it," she whispered.

Jack's steel gray eyes were intense. "That's not what I was going to say. You know well enough that the world isn't fair, that bad things happen to good people but you're the *only* one that can do this."

She released his hands and looked away. The lake shimmered in the light of the sun, it was beautiful, but she found no joy in it. She didn't think she'd find joy in anything for a long time if ever again. She didn't know how she was going to do this but she knew she had to. Jack was right, Braith had to lead. He was strong, he was powerful, he was bred for leadership and they would all follow him.

Jack leaned back as he studied her. "Aria?"

She turned toward Jack. "I've always done what's needed to be done, as has Braith. I'll do it now, and he will do it when I'm gone. I don't know how I'll do it, how I'll pretend everything is fine, but I'll figure it out."

Jack grimaced as he closed his eyes. For the first time Aria realized a part of him had hoped she wouldn't agree, that she would absolutely refuse to go along with it. That she would go back to Braith and not care about the consequences of her actions. Jack didn't want to be the one to inflict this pain on his brother, or her, but now that she had made her choice, his road had been mapped out for him too. For the first time since he'd brought her out here she didn't see him as her enemy, as the person who had just ruined her life, but more of an ally in her despair.

"I'm sorry," Ashby apologized.

Aria had no idea how she was going to deceive Braith in such a way, but hopefully their lives would continue to be as hectic as they had been and he wouldn't notice if she was a little distant.

"We should return," Jack said.

She hated the idea of going back, but she couldn't hide here forever, and as of now Braith could still track her anywhere. It was possible that he would always be able to do so. Jack hoped that there was a way to dilute Braith's blood but she wasn't so certain. She knew full well that Braith's blood was a part of her now. Perhaps someone else's blood could alter that, but she didn't see how.

She started to share her thoughts with Jack but stopped herself. She knew she had to leave Braith, but it may be impossible for her to ever truly separate from him. There was nothing that Jack could do about that, or at least nothing that he *would* do. Jack was willing to take this road with her, willing to give up his old life for good, but if it became necessary he would not do the one thing that may be required to truly separate her and Braith.

He was like a brother to her and he was almost as stubborn as Braith. If she told Jack what she was thinking, he would only insist that someone else's blood would be enough to dilute Braith's within her, enough to separate them, even if it wasn't.

Jack would not consider the fact that there may be only one way to truly sever her bond from Braith. But she knew someone that would.

# CHAPTER 16

The reassuring thud of the arrow hitting its mark was typically like music to her savaged spirit. She fired off another arrow. Usually target practice soothed her, but nothing could soothe her now.

"Bad mood?"

She started in surprise; she'd been so entrenched in her melancholy that she hadn't heard anyone approach. She was even more surprised to discover that it was Max. Her arm lowered, her lips parted as her heart leapt in anticipation. She hoped he had come to speak with her, to try and salvage their tattered friendship. She couldn't handle it if he had only come to reinforce his intense disapproval of her and her decisions.

"Max." Though she tried to sound as aloof as he was with her now, she heard the longing in her voice. He heard it too as he offered a small smile and ran his hand nervously through his shaggy blond hair. "I haven't seen you around."

He shrugged before stuffing his hands in his pockets. His eyes shifted nervously to the target as he started to rock on his heels. "Been busy. There's a war coming you know."

"So I've been told."

"Glad to see you're still deadly with that thing," he said glancing at her bow.

She didn't know what to say, didn't know what she expected from him. What had once been simple and easy, was horribly awkward and uncomfortable now. "Yeah."

"How have you been?"

"I've been better," she admitted unable to lie to him. "You?"

"Possible imminent death and destruction aside, I've actually been doing better."

Hope swelled within her. "Really?"

His smile widened. "Yeah, really. I'm not looking forward to going back into that palace, but I am looking forward to getting some revenge."

"You're not going to do anything crazy are you?" she inquired worriedly.

"Me? Nah, I'm not angry enough for something like that anymore, but it will be good to free some others."

"It will," Aria agreed. She wanted to ask if he would ever stop being so angry at *her*, but the words froze in her throat. She couldn't bring herself to utter them, mostly because she was frightened of the answer. "I'm glad you're doing better. I know it was awful for you in there."

His smile had fallen away; he was staring at the target again. "It's been an awful time for all of us recently. Hopefully that will change soon."

"Yes," she whispered, knowing it wasn't going to change for her.

"Are you happy Aria?"

If he had asked her that question four hours ago, she would have given him a resounding yes, that despite everything that was going on, she *was* happy. She was frightened of the future and the possibility of losing a loved one, but happy. "Yes." It was the first lie in the web she was now creating.

"That's good." He rocked back on his heels again. The awkward tension was enough to make her want to scream. "I'm sorry about what happened the last time we saw each other. I lost my temper, I never meant for that to happen."

"It's ok."

He shook his head, his forehead furrowed as his clear blue eyes turned turbulent. "It's not ok. I still feel this is a situation you shouldn't be in. That's he too old for you, too different, it's not natural…"

"Max," she whispered. Her heart ached and her body felt as if it were starting to shred into a thousand pieces. She knew they were all valid points, but to her they had never mattered before. They certainly didn't matter after the conversation she'd just had with Jack and Ashby. She couldn't stand here and listen to even more reasons why she shouldn't be with Braith, why she *couldn't* be with him.

He seemed to sense this as he nodded. "But even so, what I did never should have happened. I could have killed you. I feel awful about it, it really made me rethink everything, made me look at what I was becoming and I didn't like that person."

"You're a good person Max. You had some terrible things happen to you, any person would be different after."

"I suppose."

"It's my fault. You were in there because of me…"

"No. I could have escaped being caught; I chose to go in there with you. I chose to let myself be captured. That's not your fault."

"But it didn't go the way you expected."

He finally looked at her again, finally met her eyes head on; finally seemed to *see* her for the first time in awhile. "Does anything?"

She pondered that for a moment. "No."

"I thought I'd be the one that rescued you, but then neither of us knew what Jack was, and I honestly didn't know how awful it was going to be in there, how drained I would be." He shied away from her touch as she squeezed his arm. Feeling as if she had been slapped Aria went to pull away but he seized hold of her hand. "It's not you; it's been awhile since someone touched me. I don't like being touched much since being in there."

For the first time since she had spoken with Jack, she felt something else unraveling inside of her, something strong and determined. She realized then that no matter how devastated she was, no matter how much she was going to hurt Braith, it was the right course to take. No one should have to go through what Max and countless others had been forced to go through. "What happened to you in there, it will never happen again, to *anyone*, if we win."

Max's smile was tremulous. "That's the only thing keeping me going."

"Max…"

"It's ok Aria." His eyes had become distant again. His fingers tightened briefly around hers before he released her hand. "I've come to accept it. I can see that you love him, that he loves you. I'll move on, I didn't think I would, but there are things I never thought I would get over and I'm already starting to come to terms with them. I'll get over this too."

"You will," she assured him. "I never meant to hurt you."

"I know. You tried to tell me how you felt; I just didn't want to hear it. It's my fault too." He nodded toward the target. "How bout we forget some of this for a bit and I kick the crap out of you in some target practice."

"As if," she snorted, chuckling as she handed her bow over to him. For the first time a semblance of normalcy settled over them as he grabbed an arrow from her and stepped to the line she had created in the dirt.

***

Braith followed her laughter around the corner of the building. The sound of it caused his lips to twitch involuntarily upward. Stepping around the corner of the house, he froze at the sight of Aria standing in front of Max, smiling smugly as she handed the bow over to him. For a moment Braith was too stunned to move, and then rage tore through him. Beside him, Jack groaned.

"I thought you were watching her!" Braith snarled.

"Braith."

His brother went to grab his arm but he was already storming across the field toward them. Aria turned toward him, the smile on her mouth froze in place, apprehension flashed across her features but she remained otherwise immobile. Max dropped the bow to his side, but Braith was well aware that the boy would like nothing more than to fire one of those arrows into his heart.

Aria's paralysis broke. She grabbed hold of the bow as she stepped in front of Max. "What is going on?" he demanded, never breaking eye contact with Max. Even without the bow he was a threat.

"We're just taking target practice," she answered.

"You shouldn't be with him."

"He's my friend, Braith."

"He nearly killed you the last time you saw him."

"It was an accident. A mistake, we've talked about it."

"And that makes it better!?" he barked.

Her hands twisted on the bow. He became aware of the fact that she might also like to take a shot at him. "Yes," she grated through clenched teeth. "It does."

Max shifted nervously behind her. "I should probably go."

"Yes," Braith informed him at the same time that Aria snapped, "No."

Frustration filled him. As he reached for her, she smacked his hand away. "Aria…"

"He is my friend Braith and that's not going to change, no matter how much you disapprove." He didn't get a chance to argue further as she slammed her bow into his chest and stormed off. Jack stepped hastily out of her way as she stalked past him, shooting him a dark look as she went.

Max stood uncertainly, looking torn between wanting to bolt, and wanting to laugh out loud. Braith glared at him. "If you hurt her again, it will be the last time."

Max nodded, an infuriating smile played at the corners of his mouth. Braith fought the urge to punch him but the boy hadn't done anything wrong, at least not yet. He didn't trust him though, not for one minute. In fact he thought the best thing would be for Max to leave and never return, but unless Max made that choice himself, or unless he did something to Aria again, it looked like that wouldn't happen anytime soon. Max was important in the cause, and for some unfathomable reason, Aria cared for him.

Braith turned away from him and moved swiftly into the house. She was in the room they had shared last night. She looked exhausted and worn, far more so than the encounter outside should have made her. He was bewildered by the distressed look on her face, the dark circles that marred her beautiful blue eyes.

"Did he do or say something to upset you?"

"No," she answered tiredly. "He apologized, and then he tried to help mend our friendship. I miss him Braith, I know what happened before but we were once good friends. I wouldn't have survived after I left the palace if it wasn't for Max. I was heartbroken and he helped to ease some of that."

Braith didn't like to think about that time, it hadn't been easy for either of them. "He's in love with you."

Tears shimmered in her eyes. "Maybe then, but he's accepted that I don't feel the same way about him, and he's trying to move on. He may not approve but he knows that I love you."

"I don't approve of *him* either."

"I wish you would learn to get along. Max was an important part of my life, and I would like to have him back in it. I'm not foolish enough to believe it can ever be the same, but I'd like to at least see the two of you come to some sort of understanding with each other."

"And if he hurts you again?"

"He won't."

"But if he does?"

A single tear slid free. "I'll stay away from him then."

"He almost killed you last time."

"Braith stop! It was an accident, a mistake. I will never know what happened to him in that palace. I was lucky that you stepped forward to take me from that other vampire." Braith's hands fisted, his muscles locked as he recalled the bastard that had almost owned her. "I can only guess at what was done to Max. You especially should know it couldn't have been easy or pleasant."

"That's not fair."

"Nothing is fair!" She practically screamed the words at him. He was startled by the ferocity of her reaction, the devastation that radiated from her; the tears that suddenly burst free and streamed down her face. He'd seen her cry before but he'd never seen this level of emotion over something he hadn't even realized was bothering her so much. She was almost irrational, something that she never was.

"I didn't realize this was upsetting you so much." He told her as she dropped her head into her hands. Her shoulders shook as she sobbed quietly. Her cries only increased when he wrapped his arms around her, pulling her against him. Desperation radiated from her as her fingers dug into his back. "Arianna…"

"I'm sorry," she sobbed. "I'm so sorry."

He was unbelievably confused. He'd been around irrational women before, not for long because he usually left them behind if it happened, but this was Aria. His unbelievably proud and fierce Aria was sobbing uncontrollably for some reason that he couldn't even begin to fathom. Her exhaustion must be getting to her, a fact that was evident in her pale face and shadowed eyes.

"For what?" he demanded, frightened and uncertain of what her answer would be.

She shook her head, seemingly unable to speak through her tears. He grabbed hold of her cheeks, pulling her face from his chest. "What are you sorry for?"

"I just…" she broke off, swallowing heavily as she tried to suppress her tears. "I just know how much you don't trust him, and I know I frightened you today. I didn't mean to."

It was true, but it didn't warrant this. "Don't cry Arianna, it's ok."

Absurdly, she began to cry more. He pulled her back against him, rocking her as she buried her face in his chest again. A large sob escaped her; she bit on her lip hard enough to draw blood which he scented in the air almost immediately.

"Braith?" Jack's voice interrupted.

Closing his eyes, he suppressed a groan as he turned her, making sure she was hidden from the doorway, and Jack. "Go away."

"Braith, it's time to redo the vote."

"Can't it wait?" he demanded.

"It's fine." Aria pulled away from him, she wiped at her eyes as she took a step back. She wouldn't meet his gaze, or Jack's, as she focused on the far wall.

"Aria…"

"I'm fine Braith. I'm just worn out, it's been a grueling road to get here and it's catching up with me now. I'll be fine after a good night of sleep." He was torn. He didn't want to leave her, not while she seemed so overcome with emotion. "Go. Go on. Give me a minute to wash up and I'll be down."

"Are you sure you're ok?"

She smiled tremulously. "Fine."

Reluctantly, he left her behind as he joined his brother in the doorway. Jack's jaw was locked, his gaze worried as he looked to Aria. She didn't look at either of them as she turned to the pitcher on the old nightstand and poured some water into a bowl.

\*\*\*

Aria slipped one of the gray cloaks around her shoulders pulling the hood up before sneaking silently out of the house. She knew she wouldn't make it far before Braith realized she wasn't there, but luckily Gideon had taken up residence only two doors away. She was shaking, trembling with trepidation as she moved through the shadows.

This was the path she had always thought she would take, the path that would lead to an early death. She had not chosen this path but rather, it had chosen her. She hoped that Jack was right, that they could somehow dilute Braith's blood in her system. It would not be a happy life without him, but as miserable as she would be, and even if she wasn't with him, she was also excited to see how everything would turn out. She was eager to see what Braith would do as a leader, the changes he would make. She knew they would be good changes and it would be a good world for those under his leadership.

All she needed to do was focus on the people whose lives would be saved as a result of her choices. Lives that would be far better than anything she had experienced. Braith would be good, he would be kind, and he would be fair. She was willing to do everything she could to see this terrible situation through, including going to Gideon now. Hopefully Braith would eventually find a way to forgive her and move on. The possibility that he never would nearly broke her.

If Jack was wrong about being able to dilute Braith's blood with another vampire's, than there was only one solution, and she was certain Jack would never be willing to carry it out. Jack would not allow her to be harmed, and he most certainly would *not* be the one to do it.

Gideon would understand though, and though he wasn't a bad man, she felt he would have no qualms about being the one to end her life in order to ensure peace. Swallowing heavily, gathering her waning courage, Aria took a deep breath, twisted the knob and slid silently into Gideon's temporary house. He was in the study, the shadows and planes of his face were highlighted by the candle before him. He looked up at her as she entered.

He didn't seem surprised to see her as she slid the hood of her cloak back. "I spoke with Jack and Ashby."

Gideon froze for a moment, his hand curled around the pen he was holding. "I see."

She was silent as she gathered her courage to speak. Once she uttered these words she would never be able to take them back. "I understand what needs to be done."

Gideon placed his pen down. "You do?"

For a brief moment tears shimmered in her eyes before she blinked them back, thrust out her chin and nodded firmly. "I do."

"He cannot know about this."

"He never will."

Gideon appeared lost in thought for a moment. "Your relationship cannot progress."

She flinched; did everyone know their business? For a moment she thought her composure would crumble. "It won't" she whispered.

Aria remained silent, watchful as the flame flickered over Gideon's features. What was she doing here? The right thing or at least that's what she told herself. But was it really the right thing? She was betraying Braith; she was going behind his back and plotting something that would devastate him. This was right on so many levels, but it was wrong on so many others. Guilt tugged at her heart, perhaps if she went to Braith…

She broke the thought off. He would never agree to let her go. He would never listen to reason. Jack was right, if she went to Braith and told him everything, he would take her and leave here tonight. There were so many things she loved about him; his determination, his stubbornness, and his love for her were among the things she loved most.

Unfortunately, those three things completely worked against all of them right now. This was wrong, she would hate herself forever because of it, but she could live with that as long as this all worked out and Braith was able to establish the world she knew he could.

She turned away from Gideon, but her step was not so sure or as silent as she made her way to the door. "You know what this may mean for you?"

She stopped in the doorway, her head turned back as she studied him over her shoulder. "If we are unable to dilute his blood in me my death may be the only solution to separating us for good."

"And you accept this?"

"It's what I came to you for," she breathed half fearful he would tell her no; half fearful he would refuse to be the one to do it. She'd taken a risk coming to him for this; it could all backfire on her.

"No one else can know about this." There it was then, the deal had been struck. If another vampire's blood, and distance, did not break Braith's ability to track her they both understood what would have to happen.

She would die, and Gideon would be the one to do it.

"They won't," she vowed.

# CHAPTER 17

"Would you like to take a walk?"

Aria turned away from the window she had been staring out. She was doing everything she could to keep up a brave front, to keep smiling, and to act normal. But it was so hard, harder than anything she'd ever done in her life. They were leaving tomorrow; she was actually looking forward to plunging back into those hideous swamps. At least it would help keep her mind off of everything and it meant they would be getting closer to the war, a war she desperately wanted over.

Braith was standing in the doorway, leaning against the frame. His dark hair was disheveled and there was actually an amused gleam in his eyes as he lazily perused her. Heat flooded her body, her toes curled as that look seemed to sear right through her clothes and straight into her flesh. It took everything she had to focus her attention on his words again.

She frowned in confusion at the book clasped carelessly in his elegant fingers. Then she recalled that she'd been the one to take it from Gideon's home. She'd forgotten that she even had it, but he must have found it in her bag.

It was Ivanhoe; she knew that without having to see the title. It was the first book they had read together, the one that he had taught her how to read with. She had vowed that she wouldn't cry anymore, she'd chosen her path, but even so she battled against the tears that threatened to break free at the sight of that book and the memories it elicited.

"Jack tells me there's a lake close by."

"There is," she confirmed.

He smiled. "Then let's go explore it."

They had so little time left; she was not going to spend it moping. She was going to cherish every moment, not cry and ruin everything from here on out. "I'd love to."

Her legs trembled as she stood, she'd been sitting for awhile, but she recovered quickly and was smiling at him as she took his hand. "I never knew you were a thief."

She laughed as he waved the pilfered book in front of her face. "I forgot I even had it," she admitted.

"I'm sure."

They didn't talk as they moved through the woods, they didn't have to. Aria inhaled the scents of the forest, relishing in them. Beneath the leaves, dirt, and musty animals, she could also pick up the hint of fresh water and fish. It was wonderful.

The lake emerged from the woods, shimmering in the early morning sunlight. She wanted nothing more than to jump into it, swim to the middle and float there for hours. She longed to feel joy over something so simple. Joy she was frightened she would lose when all of this was over.

Braith sat with his back against a tree; the dark glasses remained blessedly removed from his magnificent face. His smile was one of the most breathtaking things she'd ever seen. It was indolent at the moment and focused solely upon her as he held his hand out. He pulled her smoothly into his lap, settling her securely against him as he rested his chin on her head and wrapped his arms loosely around her waist.

"I thought you could use a break."

"I could," she admitted. "But you could also."

"Yes," he agreed.

She rested her head against his chest, closing her eyes as she reveled in the solid, reassuring feel of his body. He was beautiful. This entire moment was beautiful. She wanted to pretend that it was one of many, that there were endless days before them to sit together, read together, and simply enjoy the company of each other. To pretend that there wasn't a clock ticking steadily away at their remaining time.

She kept her eyes closed as her fingers curled against him. He opened the book and began to read to her. She loved the sound of his voice, the deep timbre of it, the rich tones and subtle nuances he inflected into the story. She knew this story almost by heart but she still loved to hear him reading it. Listening to his voice had become her favorite pastime while in the palace.

His voice became tired after awhile, she opened her eyes, sitting up as she took the book from him and continued reading. She was about halfway through the book when she realized that he had worked the braid from her hair. His attention was riveted on it as he spread it across her shoulders and played idly with the ends.

Her throat went dry as she lifted her gaze to his. The book in her lap was forgotten as she focused upon those beautiful gray eyes with the bright blue band encircling the pupil. Though they were over a hundred years old, the faint white scars around his eyes were still visible.

Her fingers trembled as she traced the jagged edges of the marks that had left him blind until she had come along.

He took hold of her hand and pressed a tender kiss against her fingertips. Her body tingled with excitement. She was suddenly breathless, suddenly aching and vulnerable as his mouth moved steadily lower, across her palm to press gently against her wrist. She couldn't move. She was caught by the love he stirred in her. She watched in fascination while he pushed her sleeves back and continued further up her arm.

His eyes never left hers as his lips nestled in the crook of her elbow. Though she knew she should tell him to stop she couldn't break the eye contact, the intimacy of the moment. This was one of the things that she wasn't supposed to let happen but even as she thought that, her body screamed for more. They both deserved this time alone and she was going to enjoy it for just a few minutes more.

He lifted his head from her elbow, his hand wrapped around the back of her neck as he pulled her closer. He held her against him, his lips just barely brushing hers. She was frightened her heart might explode in her chest as it quickened in anticipation. And then, just when she thought she couldn't take anymore, when she thought she was going to scream in frustration, he kissed her.

Solace swept through her, her fingers entwined in the hair at the nape of his neck, she pressed closer to him as the suffering within her finally eased. Every nerve ending she had lit with fire, she was consumed by the flames he ignited in her. He moved her, shifting her in his lap so that she was straddling him, her legs wrapped around his waist. His hand moved steadily up her back, maneuvering under her shirt to press flat against her skin. She moaned at the glorious sensation of him.

She hadn't realized how much she needed this, how much she missed his touch. How starved her body had been until now. And now he was feeding her starved soul as his tongue became more demanding. Aria lost herself to his urgency. She recognized the fervent, almost desperate need within him. She desired him, but she realized now that her own craving was nowhere near as intense or acute as his. He would completely devour her and at the moment she didn't care if he did.

And then he was lifting her, pushing her back as she fell into the soft leaves. Her shirt was slipping away, gone beneath the expert movement of his hands. She loved the feel of him over her, the weight of his body against hers, the muscles that flexed and bunched beneath her touch. His hand was firm against the thin slip that was all that kept her covered. She pressed closer to him as he shifted, briefly leveling himself off of her.

Then his hand found the button of her pants. She froze, her breath trapped in anticipation as her eyes fluttered open. He was watching her, his eyes dark and hazy with passion.

He kissed her again, his mouth firm against hers, his tongue hot and heavy as he slid the button of her pants free.

Panic tore through her as reality crashed into place. She was nearly half naked, already swept up within him and more than willing to give herself to him. She yearned to ease the frustration and need that poured from him. The only thing he truly craved was her, and it was the one thing she couldn't give to him. If she didn't stop this now, she never would.

"Wait!" she gasped.

He froze against her, his hand pressed flat to her lower belly as he lifted his head to look at her. "Arianna?" The word was a low, anguished groan.

"I… I…" she couldn't get words out.

"Do you want me to stop?"

No, she didn't want him to stop. Her body was screaming for this! She needed this almost as badly as she needed air. She ached with every fiber of her being, she wanted this more than she had ever wanted anything and she couldn't have it. For a moment she almost broke and told him everything. She was ready to pour her heart and soul out to him, but she somehow managed to bite the words back.

She knew Braith would do everything he could for the people he would lead, but he wouldn't put them ahead of her. He believed in duty and honor but he'd made it abundantly clear to her, and those closest to them, that she was his priority. She loved him for it but it didn't help the people whose hope was placed in his ability to lead.

"I just… I don't know…" His hand slid away from her and she immediately felt a profound sense of loss. Her hands clenched around his neck unwilling to completely break their connection.

"You're not ready." She was ready, she was unbelievably ready. She was in love with a man that would die for her. There was nothing that she wanted more than to experience this moment with him. "It's ok." He kissed her nose, her cheek then her lips ever so lightly. "I'll be here waiting when you are."

Tears burned her eyes. She had never hated herself more than she did at that moment. "I love you. I'll always love you."

His fingers caressed her face. "I hope so, because you're stuck with me." Nope, now she hated herself more, especially as she forced a smile to her lips. She didn't ask him why he took this so well, why he didn't become impatient with her. She already knew the answer to that: he loved her. "How about a swim? I could use a dip in something cold."

His halfhearted smile melted her heart. She wanted to finish what they had started. She wanted to say to hell with Jack, and Gideon, and everyone else. She wanted to be selfish, she wanted this for them, and she wanted to finally ease the needs of her body and his, to possess him in every way possible. Finally know only the things that he could teach her. But then she thought of Max and knew that she would never do, or know, any of those things. There were others out there in need of help, others that had no one to rescue them as she and Max had been rescued.

She threaded her fingers through his and pressed them close against her chest, over the heart that would always belong to him. "That sounds good," she murmured.

He climbed to his feet; she hesitated for a moment, ashamed of herself, but determined to see this course through. "Aria?"

She rose and bent to roll the legs of her pants above her knees. Her eyes widened and her mouth watered as Braith's shirt fell on top of hers. She lifted her head slowly, marveling at the broad expanse of his shoulders, and the rigid muscles etched into his chest and abdomen. Her breath wheezed out, heat flashed up her cheeks, not from embarrassment but rather from her intense need for this man standing so close but at the same time so far away.

She had always desired him, there was never any doubt of that, but it had never been this relentless. She almost said "screw it all" to the world and launched herself at him but she managed to hold herself back. She'd never been quite as completely rattled and utterly undone as she was right at this moment.

Confusion flickered over his features, she was well aware her thoughts were written all over her face. She turned away from him, running hard, pumping her arms and legs as fast as she could in order to escape him. She had to put some distance between them before she completely caved. She didn't hesitate as she grabbed the bottom branch of a large oak, swung her leg onto it and pulled herself up. She leapt up to the next branch, then the one above it as she raced out to the end and launched herself heedlessly outward, not caring how deep the water was as she dove into it.

She kicked hard beneath the surface, pushing herself deeper and deeper into the lake. She swam into the cooler depths as the world under the water became darker and further removed from sunlight. Her lungs began to burn, her eyes were raw from straining to see, but she continued onward, heedless of the pain starting to seize hold of her body.

Strong hands grabbed hold of her, dragging her from the depths of the cool water, pulling her back toward a world that she didn't want to face. Bursting free of the surface, she wheezed in a deep breath as her lungs eagerly inhaled the precious air.

"What are you doing?" Braith demanded, shaking her a little. She shoved the mass of tangled wet hair from her eyes, forcing a smile as she met his annoyed gaze. "Just seeing if I could touch the bottom."

His scowl deepened. "You didn't even know if it was deep enough when you dove off that branch!"

"I've jumped into more than a few lakes in my lifetime."

He stared at her for a long moment. "Always so reckless," he muttered.

His hands on her were enough to make her toes curl and heat spread through her body despite the chill of the water. She squeezed his bare arms, savoring in the firm flesh and fine hairs that bristled over it before she reluctantly released him. She moved onto her back, floating lazily through the water as Braith's fingers slid into hers.

*\*\*\**

Frustration boiled through him, his fingers twitched as his irritation mounted. He couldn't stand to watch as Aria labored through the swamp with her brother and the rest of the humans. It wasn't like it was easy for him and the other vampires, but their greater power and strength made it less difficult to move through the water and mud that clasped at them like quicksand with each step. She looked exhausted but continued onward, her head bowed, her face scrunched in aggravation as she worked at pulling one foot out at a time.

He froze, fury tore through him as Max seized hold of her arm, helping to keep her upright as she stumbled. That was it. "Braith!" Jack hissed as he grabbed hold of his arm.

"Get your hand off of me!"

"They can't know."

"They already know Jack."

He jerked his arm away from his brother, ignoring Gideon, Ashby and Xavier as he waded through the muck and mire. Max released her instantly, he tried to move to the side but the swamp hindered his movements. "Braith wait." He didn't listen to her as he lifted her from the mud with a loud sucking noise. Her feet kicked for a moment before he slid her onto his back. She faltered, and then her knees locked against his sides and her arms wrapped around his neck.

"You shouldn't have done that," she whispered in his ear.

"They're humans Aria, they won't hurt us." Her displeasure was evident in the stiffness of her body. She didn't lean against him, didn't relax as she had on their first trip through the swamps, but he'd be damned if he'd allow her to struggle, and double damned before he allowed Max to be the one to help her. "It will be fine," he muttered as he kept walking.

Her head dropped against his back, her forehead rested against his neck for a brief moment before she pulled away. He ignored the questioning stares directed at them, Aria kept her head down as he rejoined Jack, Gideon, Ashby and Xavier. Jack and Gideon looked as if their heads were going to explode, Xavier turned silently away. It was Ashby that held his attention though. He had paled considerably; his lips were clamped and nearly bloodless as he studied them.

By mid afternoon most of the humans were starting to waiver, the heat of the day and the exertion to continue onward was wearing them down. Aria had managed to squiggle from his arms over an hour ago but he kept her close to his side, helping to lift her when she became mired by the mud. Her sweaty hair stuck to her skin, her face was florid from her effort, but it was her eyes that bothered him most.

He'd become acutely aware of the fact that there was a distance in them that hadn't been there just days ago. There was a resignation to them, wariness, and a sense of loss that he didn't understand. She smiled at him, she held his hand, but he felt a wall in her that had never existed before. He knew better than to believe it was due to her apprehension over the upcoming war. She may be afraid, but she had never allowed it to rule her before.

He was also aware of a difference in his brother. It was not as pronounced as Aria's, but Jack was colder and a little more distant. Even though they were brothers, Braith knew

Jack's main loyalty lay with the rebellion, a fact that he had already proven by taking Aria away from him once.

A pit began to form in his stomach. No, it couldn't be possible. When Jack had taken her before, he had been unaware of the fact that Braith had already shared his blood with her, that he had established the connection that would allow him to find Aria wherever she went. Jack was well aware of that fact now, he wouldn't be so foolish as to think he could try and take her again and get away with it.

But something was up, he was certain of it.

Aria halted so abruptly that he almost snapped at her, almost grabbed hold of her arm and dragged her forward in his irritation. One of them was going to talk to him and it was going to be *her* if he had anything to say about it.

But she was staring at the world around her, eyes turbulent and her face paler than it had been moments before. He started to speak, but she held up a finger to him, as she used her other hand to wave behind her at the trudging humans. He was impressed, and a little amazed, when as one unit they all stopped.

Her forehead furrowed, her head tilted back as she searched the sky, then the treetops in the distance. "Something's wrong," she muttered.

Braith followed the direction that her eyes had taken but he saw nothing to signal that something was amiss. "How do you know?"

"I just do. Something is off. I feel it."

"Trust her on this Braith…"

"I do." He cut Jack off, fighting the urge to smash his fist into his brother's face. He had no tangible reason to hit his brother, but Jack deserved it for some reason, even if Braith wasn't sure what the reason was yet.

Aria went to step closer to him; her face scrunched in frustration, aggravation filled her as she stared down at the swamp. She gazed helplessly at Braith and then at the people behind them. Her eyes snapped to the tree line as a bird took flight about two hundred yards away.

"Braith."

He lifted her up, pulling her free of the muck and mire that encased her. She winced at the small sucking sound, but it was far more subtle than any sound she could have made. He held her in front of him for a brief moment, before sliding her around to allow her to grasp hold of him piggyback style. Her heart beat loudly against his back as he made his way forward as silently as he could.

She slid free of his back when he stepped onto solid ground. Xavier, Gideon, Ashby and Jack pressed closer to him as she grasped hold of the limb on a frail looking pine. He almost pulled her back, wary of the decrepit looking tree, but she was already moving up it with grace and agility.

The tree barely moved as she slipped from one branch to another. Near the top she hesitated, her hands rested against two thin branches that swayed almost imperceptibly. He could almost feel her holding her breath as she waited for the branches to stabilize before lifting herself above them. She released them suddenly and though he thought she was going to plunge heedlessly out of the tree, she scrambled far enough down to leap safely down. He kept his feet firmly planted as he caught hold of her.

"What is it?" he asked.

"There are seven men that I can see, through the trees that way." She pointed into the woods. "They may be human but I don't think so, and they're wearing your father's colors."

"They're not human then," Jack said.

Braith's mind churned as he slid Aria silently to the ground. They were still standing in the swamp, cornered if there were more troops in the woods. The swamp was impossible to maneuver in these circumstances, not silently, and not with any speed.

"They're heading this way Braith," Aria said, seeming to read his train of thought.

His teeth clenched. "I need you to stay here."

Her eyes heated briefly, they narrowed slightly but her attention turned to the swamp. Her brother and father had managed to creep closer, but they still weren't free of the mud yet. She looked as if she was going to argue, but resignation settled over her features. She slid the bow from her back and grasped it in her hands. She would not leave her family unprotected.

"Be careful," she whispered. She closed her eyes, went to grab him, but then her hand fell limply back to her side.

"Stay here." His tone was not as brisk.

"I will." She slid an arrow into the bow.

Braith gestured to the others and slid silently into the woods. They were about a hundred feet in when he began to smell them. The others spread out around him, filtering through the trees like wraiths toward his father's men. He heard them before he saw them; someone commented on a woman, the others laughed as the guardsman regaled them with a story. Though he was relieved that the guardsmen didn't sense their approach, or even feel that there was any threat within the woods, another part of him, the part that had been honed to rule one day, was irritated. They should be on guard no matter what, even if they felt safe and were far from the palace, they should be prepared for any threat at all times. Their lack of awareness was about to get them killed.

Jack appeared in the woods, his head poked up from behind a large fallen tree. Braith nodded toward his right, Gideon and Ashby were somewhere over there, while Xavier was on the other side of Jack. The guardsmen came into view. None of them were paying attention to their surroundings as they continued to exchange stories. They may be outnumbered seven to five, but the guardsmen didn't have a shot of walking away from this alive.

Braith waited, watching for awhile to make sure there weren't others out there. They could not take the chance of one of them escaping and returning to the palace, if it wasn't for the swampland he wouldn't engage them at all. When he was certain that it was only these seven men, he nodded to Jack and waved his hand toward the last place he had seen Gideon and Ashby.

They simultaneously burst free of the woods. Braith seized hold of the first guardsman and took him down before he was able to make a sound. He had a brief glimpse of wide, terrified eyes before he smashed his fist into the guardsmen's chest. Bone gave way beneath the tremendous blow, crumpling as easily as paper beneath the force of his fist. His hand wrapped around the heart and he ripped it free.

Braith launched to his feet, Gideon and Jack were encircling one of the last two guards, but the other one had turned and bolted into the woods. He raced after him, pouring on the speed as the guard ran toward the area where he had left Aria. The vampire ran faster as he sensed his impending demise. Concern for Aria drove Braith to levels of speed he'd never achieved before.

They came around a turn in the woods; Braith was honing in on the guard as a path opened up before them. Aria was standing there, her bow raised. The guard was stunned; he hesitated for a brief moment. Aria didn't. She released the arrow with deadly accuracy. It was only the small sidestep of the guard at the last minute that saved him from a killing blow to the heart. It drove into his shoulder, knocking him back a step.

The guard lurched forward, his hands curved as he dove at her. Braith surged forward and seized hold of the back of his shirt. He ripped the guard back, all sense of reason vanished as he drove his fangs deep into the guard's neck. The man bucked, a gurgled sound of surprise escaped him as he clawed at Braith over the back of his head. Disgust filled him as the man's life pumped into him.

This was not the way he liked to kill. This was not the way *any* of them liked to kill, very few of them allowed another vampire to feed from them. It walked a fine line between remaining completely in control, and becoming something unspeakable. But his desperate need to protect her had driven him to this.

He pulled away from the vampire, grabbed hold of his head and snapped his neck with a sharp, jerking motion. The guard crumpled before him, weakened by loss of blood and the severe injury but not yet dead. Braith seized hold of the arrow, ripped it from his shoulder and drove it deep into his heart. He remained kneeling over for him for a moment, struggling with the influx of vampire blood in his system and what he had just done. His actions had been bad enough, but he had just carried them out in front of *her*.

Slowly, guardedly, he lifted his head to look at her. He knew what he was, knew what he was capable of, especially when it came to her. He had tried to keep the worst of it hidden from her but it was too late now. Now, she could see it all, *had* seen it all.

She stared at him, her bow hung limply at her side. He had expected censure and disgust in her eyes, instead there was simply shock. Seeming to sense his need for her to accept him, even like this, at his most evil, her expression changed and the bow slid from her fingers.

Falling to her knees before him, she attempted to remove his sins by wiping the blood from his mouth. "It's ok." Her hands clasped hold of his cheeks, her forehead pressed against his as she comforted him. "It's ok."

Then, to his utter amazement she was kissing him, softly, tenderly, and with a love that humbled him. She'd seen the worst of him, she'd seen him do something atrocious and she still loved him. A groan escaped him as he drew her closer. He buried his face in the hollow of her shoulder as his love for her swelled and grew within him. He rocked her as the delightfully sweet scent of her blood washed over him and soothed his mind and body in a way that only she could.

Her hands were in his hair as she maneuvered his mouth against her neck. He didn't know how but she knew that he needed something else, that he needed reassurance from her that he wasn't a monster. His lips skimmed back, his fangs lengthened as they fairly vibrated with anticipation. She jerked slightly as his teeth penetrated her supple skin but then she relaxed and melded against him. Her blood filled him, replacing the foul taste of the guard's blood on his tongue.

The taste of her was enough to help wash away his transgression. He released his bite and licked the remaining drops of blood from her neck. "Arianna," he groaned. She pressed her cheek against his, her lips just barely brushing against his skin. "So sweet…"

The sounds of approaching feet silenced his following words. He kissed her cheek far too briefly before rising swiftly, and lifting her smoothly up with him. Her eyes were questioning but she threw back her shoulders and thrust out her chin as she picked up her bow and turned to face the oncoming vampires. If things were different, she would have made a magnificent queen, a superb leader and champion for her people. He was proud to have her at his side and always would be.

Jack rounded the corner first, skidding to a halt as he spotted the two of them. Then his gaze locked on the ruined body of the guard, his eyes widened, his jaw dropped. "What did you do Braith?"

"What needed to be done."

Jack gaped at him, he turned to Aria who stared unwaveringly back at him as she took a step closer to Braith's side. She didn't fully understand what had just transpired, the true nature of the transgression he had just committed, but she looked about ready to shoot an arrow straight into his brother's heart if it became necessary. Her fingers twitched on her bow as Gideon, Ashby, and Xavier appeared.

"Help me get this out of the way." His voice was detached, he felt a small recoil from Aria when he referred to the dead guard as a *'this'*, but he had to keep himself disconnected from this mess.

Jack eyed him from head to toe and then back again. Gideon's eyebrows were in his hair as he looked back and forth between Braith and the dead guard. Interestingly, Xavier was watching Aria. His eyes were latched on the fresh bite marks on her neck and the single drop of blood that quivered on her skin. Braith brushed it away, fighting against a rising wave of anger as he glared at Xavier in warning. Xavier didn't back down from Braith as he continued to assess her from top to bottom.

One of these days, preferably today, Braith was going to find out exactly what it was that Xavier was trying to figure out about her, or what it was that he thought he already *knew*.

"Give me a hand Jack," he commanded gruffly.

Jack looked discomforted as he grasped hold of the guard's arms. He didn't offer any protest as he helped Braith carry him into the woods. "Are you ok?" Jack inquired.

"Fine," he replied brusquely.

"Braith this isn't good, this isn't the way things are done. You know that, it's a sign of loss of control."

Braith dropped the feet. "I am fine Jack."

Jack's gaze darted toward the path they had left behind. "Aria…"

"You'll leave her out of this."

Jack swallowed heavily. "What did she see?"

"All of it."

Braith didn't wait to hear what else his brother had to say, he turned and made his way back to the others. Aria stood with her shoulders back as she warily watched Xavier, Ashby and Gideon. Braith stepped between them. She looked up at him, seeming not to focus on him for a moment before a small smile curved her full lips.

"Let your father know it's safe."

She nodded before taking off down the path, the bow bouncing against her back as she ran.

# CHAPTER 18

Aria stood in the shadows, a lump in her throat as she slipped deeper into the hollows of the cave. Braith spoke with a commanding, self assured tone to the group that would soon become an army. The cave was unnervingly silent considering the amount of bodies it now housed as they listened raptly to him. He laid out his plans, speaking of his new government with such passion that it brought tears to her eyes.

Gideon had said that the king had a way of making people believe him, Braith seemed to have inherited that charismatic ability too as he roused the crowd, garnering cheers from them as well as devoted agreement for the cause. He encouraged and excited his army in preparation for the coming war.

She refused to look at Jack. She could feel his eyes from across the cave as she slid further into the tunnel behind her. She was proud of Braith, so proud in fact that she could barely breathe through the emotion rippling through her. That same pride was at war with the feeling of being trapped that she constantly felt now.

She turned away, needing some time to herself. She moved carefully through the dark cave, navigating the turns with ease. She started to run faster and faster, pounding through the dark tunnels as she was consumed with the need to be free.

Her lungs were burning and her legs were tired but she continued to run toward the promise of fresh air. She burst free, nearly falling to the ground as she inhaled heaping gulps of air. She made it to a tree, collapsing against its trunk as she slid silently to the ground.

She drew her knees against her chest and hugged them. Shadows from the tree limbs played over the ground, the crickets chirruped and the frogs called to each other. What were usually soothing sounds, now offered her nothing.

She saw the figures emerging from the cave before they stepped into the moonlight. Having spent her entire life with them she'd know Daniels's assured gate and William's slight swagger anywhere. She also recognized the sadness that rounded both their shoulders in much the same way. They sat on each side of her and leaned against the tree.

"They really admire him," Daniel said after a period of silence.

"They do," she agreed.

"Jack spoke with us," William told her.

"I figured he would."

William's hand wrapped around hers, he squeezed it briefly before releasing her. "I understand where Jack is coming from. The vampire race, even if we are finally all united, is far different from ours, but you're a strong person Aria, they may accept you."

"Do you honestly believe that?"

He started to respond and then shook his head. She knew he wanted to make her feel better, wanted to give her flowery promises, maybe even wanted to believe them himself, but he wouldn't lie to her. "No."

"I didn't think so."

"I was on board with this. I thought it was better if you were separated anyway." Daniel squeezed her shoulder as she glared at him. "You're seventeen years old Aria, you've never been a child, but you're young and he's... Well he's far more advanced than you, he's a vampire and your worlds are so completely different that I saw only grief in your future. I thought it would be best if you returned to a more normal life, with people your own age and your own kind. I thought it would be best for the two of you."

"And now?" William prodded before Aria could.

"And now I don't think there's any chance that what Jack proposes will work out. Even he is somehow unable to track you through your blood, Braith is not going to let you go, not unless you ask him to, and even then I don't think it will be a good situation. It was bad enough when you first escaped the palace, you were lost and heartbroken. The two of you are closer now, your bond has grown and strengthened. I've never seen anything like it. If Jack is right then you know the choice you have to make, the one that you've already made. But if Jack is wrong it's going to be bad Aria, very bad, and you know that."

"What would you do?" she whispered, shaken by his words.

He shook his head, his hand slipped inside his shirt as he pulled something free. "I don't know. That's the kicker of it all, I don't know. But I know you, and I know that in the end you'll make the right choice, but only *you* will be able to make it. I'll miss you if you choose to leave, and I'll stand by you if you choose to stay."

"Thank you."

He grinned at her, flashing a smile that was so endearingly similar to what she remembered of their mother's. "For saying aloud the same things you already knew?"

She laughed dryly as she rested her head against the trunk of the tree. "For standing by me no matter what. How did it all come to this?"

"You let yourself get caught and hauled into that palace," William informed her.

"Yeah that's exactly what I *let* happen," she retorted.

They sat together for a long time, silent as they listened to the familiar sounds of the forest. "No matter what happens Aria, something good will come of it."

"I hope so. He's coming."

"How do you..." William broke off the question. "Never mind."

"This is for you." She started as Daniel slid something into her hand. Her mouth parted as she gazed wonderingly at the beautiful drawing before her. Tears clogged her throat. She'd always known Daniel was a talented artist, a trait that he never had enough time for, but this was far beyond anything she could have imagined. She was curled within Braith's lap, her head on his chest as he rested his chin on her head to look at the book in his hand. The looks of love on their faces nearly caused her to sob aloud.

"I came across you by accident. I just saw you for a moment," Daniel added quickly when her face colored faintly. "It was then I realized that what's between you isn't something easily broken, it's not a passing fancy, it's not a rebellious moment, it's not even just love. It's something more, it's this." He pointed at their faces in the drawing. "It astounded me Aria; I can only hope that I find something like this one day."

"Daniel," she breathed, tears rolling down her face. "It's beautiful."

"No matter what you decide, I think you should have this."

She nodded as he ruffled her hair affectionately. William was staring at the sketch over her shoulder when Braith emerged from the cave. "Do you want me to take it?"

"Yes."

William took the drawing from her and slipped it into his shirt. "I'll keep it safe."

"I know."

They remained seated; their heads tilting back as Braith stopped before them. "It's not safe up here."

"We're fine. We know these woods better than most of the animals." He didn't seem at all appeased by her reassurance. He stared hard at each of her brother's obviously wanting them to leave, while she wanted them to stay right where they were. "How did it go?"

He locked his hands behind his back. "We're going to run a few scouting missions to the palace and back. I would like for you to go on one Daniel, so you can get a feel of the town and its dimensions in order to formulate a design."

"Of course," Daniel murmured in assent.

"When do you think we'll be ready to make a move on the palace?" William inquired.

"Hopefully within two weeks. I would prefer to move by the end of this week but I realize that's asking a lot. Jack, Saul, and Barnaby are going into the outer towns to gather the vampire's Jack recruited there. We'll need them here before we can make any solid plans."

"I'd like to go on one of the scouting missions," Aria informed him.

He frowned at her, his fingers curled and uncurled at his sides. "Aria…"

"I've gone on plenty with Daniel and William before." A muscle jumped in his cheek as his jaw clenched. "I'll be fine, and I'm tired of feeling useless and confined. I have to do something useful."

"We'll keep her safe, even from herself," William nudged her playfully.

She rolled her eyes at him and shook her head. He wasn't helping. "No one will recognize me. I *need* to do this Braith."

The last thing she wanted was to fight with him, but she simply couldn't sit here for the next couple of weeks, being torn apart by her decision and feeling useless. She had to find something to do or she would go crazy.

"Fine," he relented, his shoulders slumping.

She didn't feel even a little good about the fact that she had gotten her way; she simply felt the gulf between them growing. It took everything she had not to cry as she bowed her head. She couldn't look at him anymore, it was too difficult.

# CHAPTER 19

Aria's head was down, her bow discreetly tucked away on her back and covered by the gray cloak. It billowed around her ankles, blowing back to allow the rain to wet the bottom of her pants. As much as she hated the cloaks she was grateful for the cover it provided from the surprisingly chilly rain. She stood at the top of the hill, staring down at the town that rolled out from the hollows of the knoll.

It was beautiful, deadly, and far too close to the palace for her liking. A palace that she could see the gleaming top of as it rose out from behind another hill. Braith moved closer to her but now that they were amongst his people again, he had returned to trying to keep his distance from her. Saul and Calista came forward to speak with Braith before returning to the small group gathered within the tree line.

William and Daniel stood beside her, the hoods of their cloaks pulled up. Max was also wearing the cloak but the hood was tossed back. Rain trickled down his face and had plastered his fair hair down. He was still handsome, but she was acutely reminded of the fact that the boy she had grown up with was gone. He looked older, wiser than his young years. He was only a couple years older than her, but there were lines around his eyes and the corners of his pinched mouth. Seeming to sense her attention he turned to her and offered a small smile.

Braith stepped in front of her, drawing her attention away from Max. For a moment his hands fisted in impotence as he grappled with his urge to protest her decision. Her father wasn't happy about this either, but at least he was used to them going on such missions and more accustomed to watching his loved ones walk away.

"Make sure your hair stays covered." His frustration was obvious as his hand twitched toward her. Her hair was already tucked beneath the hood, but she adjusted it again to try and ease the tension she felt running high in him. It did little good. "If anything goes wrong…"

"I'll be fine. I'm fast, you know that."

"You're not faster than a vampire, and you have a habit of throwing yourself on the sword to protect others. You need to run if something goes wrong, and I mean it."

She bristled at his commanding tone, but he was frightened and arguing with him about it would get her nowhere. He would force her to stay with him if she pushed him; she was still a little surprised he had relented to begin with. Then, not seeming to care about the others, he pulled her hood tighter, his hands hesitating on the edges as he held it for a moment.

"Don't do anything stupid."

Frustration filled her; she ached to touch him, to reassure him that she would be fine and that she wasn't doing this to be reckless. She wouldn't do anything to damage their cause, but she would be helpful down there. That's why she was going. She wasn't the girl who had nothing to live for anymore. Even if she had to give him up there was still plenty to live for, and even after her deal with Gideon she still hoped she'd be around to see it all.

Her fingers clenched as she restrained herself from grasping his hands. "I promise I won't."

He pulled on the hood again and walked away. Aria watched him for a longing moment, before she turned back to her brothers and Max. "Let's go," Daniel said.

She chanced a glance over her shoulder at Braith. He was watching her intently, his arms folded over his chest as Jack stepped beside him. She didn't look back as they began to pick their way down the hill, moving at a diagonal angle to the town below. Aria struggled to keep her balance as wet leaves slipped and slid beneath her beaten shoes. She was relieved when they made it to the road even though she felt exposed and vulnerable.

They received a few questioning glances as they moved past but the gray cloaks they wore were common place here, as were random people moving through in search of food or employment within the palace.

Not all of the people here worked within the palace and served the royal family, but they were still traitors to her. They didn't fight or go against the grain. They simply lived in this hollowed existence and did whatever they were told or whatever was expected of them.

They passed a bar that had its doors thrown open to let in the fresh air. Bawdy laughter filtered out from within. Aria was surprised to realize that there were people already inside, drinking and laughing loudly. Life in the towns was far different than life in the woods. She couldn't recall a day that had been wasted on such things.

"Keep moving." She hadn't realized she'd stopped until William grated the words at her.

She turned away from the bar as a woman's laughter joined in with the men's. She shook her head, uncertain about this place. Max grasped her arm gently, urging her along when she fell behind. "It's so different here," she muttered.

"Yes. Don't stop."

Aria fell back into step beside him as they wound through the town, taking in as many details as they could. She had been in the town once as a child, but she hadn't paid much attention to it. Now she noticed details that made her sick. The homes were not as opulent or fancy as the ones within the palace walls but they gleamed with the rain beading off of them. Their paint was fresh and their porches were decorated with more furniture than she'd owned in her entire life. Flowers, like she had seen in the palace flowed over people's walkways, their petals shining from the drops of rain.

Though the rain had driven most inside, the few that did brave the weather were wearing the deep blue cloaks that marked them not as servants, but as free people that held higher positions within the palace. It was a coveted position, one that had been earned by the ultimate betrayal against their fellow man. Her fingers itched to put an arrow in the hearts of every one of them.

She hated those blue cloaks more than anything. And judging by the stiffness in Max's shoulders he was fighting the same urge she was. These people were the ultimate traitors, they had no allies here, and as far as Aria was concerned they could all be killed in the upcoming days and she wouldn't lose any sleep over it.

She kept her head down so they wouldn't see her revulsion. She was supposed to be in awe of the people wearing the blue cloaks, not plotting their demise as she shuffled down the dirt road that was slowly turning to muck They reached the end of the main road and began to move through the more narrow side roads. The homes were smaller here, but they were just as nicely maintained.

"Why haven't we seen any soldiers?" Aria wanted to know.

"It's so close to the palace they don't fear anything. I'm sure there are some posted here but the weather has probably driven them inside," Max answered.

Aria's heart began to hammer; she shrank deeper into her cloak as they moved even closer to the palace that had nearly destroyed her and Max. It was situated on a mountain, tucked behind the hills and valleys that rolled through this area. She knew they weren't going to get much closer, but she couldn't stop the foreboding that pulsed through her.

To her surprise, Max seized hold of her hand. Though they had been trying to repair their fractured friendship things had still been uncomfortably awkward between them more often than not. But now his hand wrapped around hers, squeezing tight as they stopped to stare at the place where they had been imprisoned.

The golden gates gleamed, even in the dim light of the murky day they shined from the hours spent polishing them. Though the top spires of the palace were visible above the homes and hills, the main bulk of the massive building was obscured. She knew it well though, she would never forget it and she would be back within its massive walls again soon if everything went well. In the meantime, she would need to reign in her abhorrence for the place if she was going to be of any use.

Max's hand was sweaty in hers, small tremors rocked through him. She wanted to tell him it was ok, but it wasn't and she wasn't going to lie to him. It would be a long time, if ever, before he got over what was done to him.

As they watched, guards appeared. They marched across the front of the gates before disappearing from view once more. Goosebumps broke out on her arms and it had nothing to do with the chill in the air. After a minute or so the guards moved back across the front of the gates. "We should get moving," Daniel said.

She fell in beside her brothers again as they moved further through the town. She could practically see the gears turning through Daniel's head as he mapped out the roads, and plotted the best ways to move through the buildings and streets with all of their troops. They were all here to take in as much of the details as possible, but Daniel would be the one that remembered the most, the one that would see things the rest of them didn't and recall it far more vividly.

They arrived at the edge of the town, the road continued onward, winding up another hill before dipping from sight and reappearing again near the palace gates. Aria had had enough. She didn't want to see anymore of that place than she had too. "Let's go back."

The road was becoming muddier as they wound their way back through the town. The rain was picking up to a steadier flow that was starting to creep its way through the cloak to wet her clothes and skin. Her hair was beginning to cling to the back of her neck, tickling her skin. She wanted out of here, for the first time she wanted back into the caves and away from this oppressive place that she could practically feel draining the life from her.

They passed more people as they hurried through the town, but no one paid them much attention. She heard the laughter from the bar before she saw it again. She kept her head down as they approached the raucous place.

People emerged from inside. Two of them ran in the opposite direction, squealing happily as their laughter trailed down the street. Don't look, she told herself. Bending her head lower, she kept her attention focused on her feet. She was so intent on getting free of this town that she wasn't expecting it when someone grabbed hold of her arm, halting her abruptly as she was pulled sharply around.

"It *is* you!" a voice accused.

Aria had only a moment to get her bearings before someone seized hold of her hood and ripped it back. A sharp gasp escaped her, she scrambled to pull it back up, feeling exposed and stunned by the sudden assault. And then she saw her attacker. The girl was still grasping her arm, holding her with a bruising intensity as she glared furiously at Aria. The venom that spit from the girls blue eyes would have seemed out of place if Aria hadn't already figured out who she was.

"Lauren," Aria breathed horrified and staggered by the sight of the servant girl who had taken such cruel pleasure in abusing her while she'd been in the palace. Lauren was far different than Aria recalled; her blond hair had always been neatly coiffed, with every hair in place. She'd been refined and elegant in a way that only the palace servants could be. She was not so poised now. Her dress was dirty, her fingernails were broken, and there was a strange odor wafting from her. Laughter burst from the bar behind Lauren. Aria suddenly understood where the girl had come from, what the smell was, and what Lauren had been doing since Braith had banished her from the palace.

"I knew it was you," Lauren sneered, her pretty face twisting with disgust as her hand squeezed even more on Aria's arm. Her heart was pounding, astonishment held her so riveted that she couldn't react, not even when Lauren thrust her face into Aria's, so close that their noses were almost touching. "I know someone looking for you, bitch."

"What the hell?" Max, seeming to have just noticed Lauren's appearance was coming back at them. Lauren's eyes darted to him; amusement filled them as recognition sprang forth.

"Both of you," she whispered excitedly.

"Who the fuck are you?" William demanded.

Aria's surprise was wearing off. She tried to pull her arm free of Lauren's grasp but the girl clung like a burr. Lauren was trying to haul her toward the bar, pulling sharply on her arm. "Let go of me!" Aria snapped, as anger completely replaced any shock she felt.

"Get your hands off of her!" William was beside her, Max had circled behind Lauren, blocking her pathway to the tavern. Daniel seemed confused as if it hadn't quite penetrated his artist induced haze that something wasn't right.

Lauren was brought up short as she bumped into Max, her fingers twisted painfully on Aria's arm as she pinched her skin. Panic flashed briefly across Lauren's pretty face as Max's hands fell onto her shoulders. Seeming to realize she was cornered, she began to yell. "Guards! Guards!"

Terror filled Aria, reacting on instinct alone she fisted her hand and drove it straight into Lauren's nose. It was something she'd itched to do since she'd been a prisoner, but she felt no satisfaction as blood spurted forth and the girl groaned in pain. She finally released Aria as her hands flew to her brutalized nose and she staggered back.

"Run!" Aria shouted as Lauren began to wail loudly for the guards.

She bolted down the road, shedding the cumbersome cloak as she ran. Shouts echoed behind them but she didn't dare look back as they rounded a curve in the road. Her eyes darted over the tops of the houses, the roofs were pitched, steep, and slippery from the rain. She thought she might be able to navigate a few of them, but none of them in succession, and there was a good possibility she would fall from the slippery tops. If she didn't kill herself, she would at the very least break something.

It was a mess, it was all a mess. The muddy road hindered their progress. It tired them out quickly and made it difficult to get any real speed up. There was still too far to go, they would never reach the safety of the woods if they didn't do something. She'd promised Braith she wouldn't do anything stupid, but she'd never expected that they would be discovered.

She broke away from the others, racing toward the porch of a small house that would be easy to scale. "Aria!" Daniel barked.

"Keep going!" she yelled at him.

She ignored him as she leapt onto the banister and seized hold of the porch roof. Her fingers scrambled for purchase on the slippery shingles but she was able to get enough of a hold to lift herself onto the roof. Without the added burden of her cloak she was able to pull her bow and arrows swiftly from her back. The guards were closer than she had realized and there were more of them than she had expected. Her heart sank.

Lifting the bow, she had no time to take aim as she began to rapidly fire arrows at the rushing group. Some of the arrows hit their marks, others missed completely, and still more were dodged. Some of the guards fell back from their injuries, but most kept on coming.

Aria grabbed her bow and quiver and tossed them onto her back as she leapt to her feet and ran. She didn't attempt to jump onto the next porch roof, she would never make it. Instead, she leapt from the roof. Her legs scissored in the air before her feet connected with solid ground again. She leapt back up and took off down the road. She rounded a corner to find that William and Daniel had taken up shooters stances on either side of the road. Max was further down, his bow lifted as he prepared for the guards.

She heard the twang of her brother's strings seconds before Max started to fire. "Run Aria!" he yelled at her. She bolted past him, racing another fifty feet down the road before taking up position behind a water barrel that was over flowing with fresh rain. She grabbed her bow and arrow, steadying herself as she set up to take aim at the creatures hunting them. If they could keep this up, if their arrows held up, they may be able to escape this town intact.

Daniel and William appeared from behind a row of houses. Aria ignored the blood dripping from William's head, she couldn't think about that now. Not if she planned to survive. She was about to release her first arrow when an arm wrapped around her waist and she was lifted against a hard, broad chest. For a disconcerting moment she thought it was Braith that had seized her, the dimensions were about the same size, but there was something cold, unfamiliar, and wrong about the man holding her now. A hand snaked around her throat and clasped over her mouth.

She began to struggle in earnest, kicking and screaming against the hand muffling her. A cold certainty crept through her as lips pressed against her cheek. "Well well well look at what I have here."

Her body turned into a block of ice at Caleb's words. She hadn't spent much time with him, as Braith had gone out of his way to keep her away from his brother, but she would recognize his voice and the cruelty that laced his words anywhere. This was so much worse than she had originally thought.

Every horrible nightmare she'd ever had seemed to be screaming into reality as his arm constricted cruelly around her waist. "We're going to have so much fun you and I."

A scream burned in her throat, it pushed relentlessly against the hand that was currently twisting ever tighter on her face. "So much fun. I'll get to see just what it was that my brother saw in you."

Aria struggled within his grasp, she couldn't breathe; she was wheezing from lack of oxygen. She met her brother's gazes, horrified by the tears of torment that burned her eyes. They had to know that they had to get free; they had to run, now. Aria jerked to the side, throwing her head back, and kicking wildly as she tried to loosen Caleb's grasp on her. She had no hope of getting free, she knew that, but she needed just a brief moment of reprieve from his firm grasp.

His hand slipped on her as she managed to dig an elbow into his ribs. "Bitch!" he snarled his hand entangling in her hair.

"Run!" The scream, born of terror, ripped violently and harshly from her throat moments before Caleb drove his fangs into her neck. Agony exploded through her, tears formed in her eyes and froze there as her whole body went rigid. Even when he had deprived himself, even when he was on the verge of losing all control, Braith had never hurt her like this. Caleb attacked her brutally; he pulled her blood from her in deep waves that caused her heart to stutter and her muscles to lock.

Her fingers curved into claws but she couldn't move, couldn't feel anything other than the torture consuming every cell within her. He meant to draw out her suffering, she was certain of it, but she was fearful that in his fury over her actions, he was going to kill her. He pulled away before biting deep again in another spot, and then another and another. Her skin was raw; blood trickled over her as blackness rose up, threatening to drown her within the dark depths of unconsciousness. She struggled against it, certain that if she succumbed she would never wake again.

Her fingers were going numb; her body was growing colder as she felt her life slipping away from her. She had only a glance of William as he launched at them. Daniel grasped hold of his arm, trying to pull her twin back as he struggled to break free. Max rounded the corner, horror spread over his face as he skidded to a halt in the muddy road.

The last thing she saw was the arrow William shot at Caleb before darkness finally claimed her.

***

It was dark when she woke. Cold. It took her a long moment to realize that she wasn't in the caves. That she was somewhere far worse. Memories engulfed her in a rapid, brutal wave. Her chest constricted, she could barely breathe through the panic trying to consume her. She was in the palace dungeons, she was certain of it, and she was now at the mercy of Caleb and the king.

A chill crept down her spine; she couldn't bring herself to think about the implications of that as she mentally took stock of the damage to her body. She was sore, tired and weak, but she was alive and whole. For now at least.

Slowly, past the terror of her current situation and her pain, she began to realize something else. She would now know what Braith would do, how he would react without her there, if he would keep control of himself, if he would put the greater good ahead of her, or if he would allow the bloodthirsty, vicious, and malevolent side of himself take control again. He would come for her, she knew that, but would it be the vampire that came for her, or the monster that vampire could become.

Another chill slid down her spine but this one had nothing to do with fear for herself, and everything to do with the fact that holy hell may have just been unleashed upon her family, her friends, and her woods. And that hell may very well be Braith.

## *Where to find the author*

https://www.facebook.com/#!/ericastevens679

http://ericasteven.blogspot.com/

goodreadscomerica_stevens

## *About the author*

Though my name is not really Erica Stevens, it is a pen name that I chose in memory of two amazing friends lost too soon, I do however live in Mass with my wonderful husband and our fish Sam, Woody, Hawk eye, Klinger, and Radar. I have a large and crazy family that I fit in well with. I am thankful every day for the love and laughter they have brought to my life. I have always loved to write and am an avid reader.